THE ROSE OF A SULTAN'S SON

THE HEIRS OF THE ARISTOCRACY
BOOK 8

LINDA RAE SANDE

Twisted Teacup
PUBLISHING

The Rose of a Sultan's Son

Cover photograph © Period Images.com

Background cover image © DepositPhotos.com

Cover art by Twisted Teacup Publishing

All rights reserved - used with permission.

Edited by Katrina Teele-Fair

http://www.lindaraesande.com

ISBN: 978-1-946271-65-5

Twisted Teacup Publishing, Cody, Wyoming

ALSO BY LINDA RAE SANDE

The Daughters of the Aristocracy

The Kiss of a Viscount

The Grace of a Duke

The Seduction of an Earl

The Sons of the Aristocracy

Tuesday Nights

The Widowed Countess

My Fair Groom

The Sisters of the Aristocracy

The Story of a Baron

The Passion of a Marquess

The Desire of a Lady

The Brothers of the Aristocracy

The Love of a Rake

The Caress of a Commander

The Epiphany of an Explorer

The Widows of the Aristocracy

The Gossip of an Earl

The Enigma of a Widow

The Secrets of a Viscount

The Widowers of the Aristocracy

The Dream of a Duchess

The Vision of a Viscountess

The Conundrum of a Clerk

The Charity of a Viscount

The Cousins of the Aristocracy

The Promise of a Gentleman

The Pride of a Gentleman

The Holidays of the Aristocracy

The Christmas of a Countess

The Knot of a Knight

The Heirs of the Aristocracy

The Angel of an Astronomer

The Puzzle of a Bastard

The Choice of a Cavalier

The Bargain of a Baroness

The Jewel of an Earl's Heir

The Vixen of a Viscount

The Honor of an Heir

The Rose of a Sultan's Son

The Ladies of the Aristocracy

The Lady of a Grump

The Lady of a Sultan

The Tulip of a Sultan's Son

The Wager of a Wallflower

Beyond the Aristocracy

The Pleasure of a Pirate

The Making of a Mistress

The Bride of a Baronet

The Caton of a Captain

The Lyon's Den (Dragonblade Publishing)

The Courage of a Lyon

The Lady of a Lyon

Stella of Akrotiri

Origins

Deminon

Diana

PROLOGUE

 arch 1844

Several wooden crates were in the process of being unloaded from the Greek merchant ship, *Son of Apollo*, when Ziyaeddin hurriedly made his way down to the dock on the western shore of the Aegean Sea. His guards had already made the short trip from the palace and were spread out above the water's edge, as if they expected some threat from the ship.

"I cannot decide if I am happy to see you or not," Ziyaeddin said as he grinned at the sight of the ship's captain. The gray-bearded gentleman had just descended the ramp and was making his way to the front of the dock.

"I cannot believe you talked me into this," Captain Popodopolis remarked, his gaze darting to the bundle the sultan held against one shoulder. "Although, I suppose I would be offended if you chose someone else to transport your favorite son to England."

"Ertuğrul wishes to spend a Season in London, and Mr. Bennett-Jones has agreed to be his guide," Ziyaeddin explained. "With the construction of the two universities and the palace complete, it is time my heir be allowed a return to what he thinks is a more civilized world." He didn't add that it was a ploy to keep his heir out of the wars the empire was currently engaged in fighting. It seemed as if the Albanians were revolting every decade and now the Kurds in Botan were staging an uprising.

Popodopolis stepped off the dock and onto the well-worn path that led up to the sandstone palace, one of many scattered about the Ottoman Empire. "Where will they stay?" he asked as the two made their way.

"In Mayfair. The Bennett-Joneses are going to host them. I am assured by my sultana that Ertuğrul will be treated like royalty, which has me the most concerned," Ziyaeddin remarked. "I do not want him spoiled."

Popodopolis paused in mid-step, as if the sultan's words had reminded him of something. "Hold on a moment," he said as he turned and shouted a command in Greek to one of his crew. The man waved in acknowledgement, and the captain shouted another command.

Assured his crew understood what to do, Popodopolis turned around and did a double-take. Sultan Ziyaeddin I, the current ruler of the Ottoman Empire, had just lifted his five-month-old son into the air and was moving him about as if the babe were a bird. Obviously enjoying the experience, the boy emitted a series of giggles and gurgles that had his father grinning ear to ear.

Ziyaeddin caught the ship captain's look of alarm and quickly sobered. "What is it?" He lowered the babe to his shoulder, one hand cradling the boy's bottom.

Popodopolis scoffed. "How old are you?"

Ziyaeddin frowned. "Fifty years," he replied carefully. "Why do you ask?"

Lifting a hand to cover his mouth, the Greek worked

to stifle a chuckle. "Are you quite sure? You look as if you've youthened since I last saw you," he accused. "And you're behaving like a..." He clamped his mouth shut.

"Like a what?" Ziyaeddin challenged. "A new father? A man in love?"

"I was going to say an idiot, but..." the captain shook his head. "Maybe I am merely jealous."

"Perhaps I am an idiot," the sultan replied with a grin, absently sniffing his son's dark hair. "But I am enjoying my life these days. Probably more so than ever."

Popodopolis regarded the sultan with a curious expression before he pointed to the baby. "How many does this make?" he asked.

Ziyaeddin chuckled. "Twenty-one. Number twelve as sons go," he replied proudly. "I have named him Ahmet."

Entrusted with the care of his newly-fed son only moments before Ziyaeddin had spotted the arrival of the Greek ship from the balcony of his private chambers, he made his way down the series of stairs to the palace's atrium and out the front doors without anyone taking notice. Anxious to greet the captain and to show off his latest progeny, the sultan had left the palace without telling anyone of his whereabouts.

"So... you don't regret taking an Englishwoman to wife?" Popodopolis asked, referring to Charlotte, Dowager Duchess of Chichester.

"I do not," Ziyaeddin stated, grinning when his newest son babbled incoherently. "Sultana Charlotte is the second love of my life. She has adapted rather well to our ways. Taken on the responsibilities of a sultana in a manner befitting her station," he explained. "Although, she is still struggling to learn the language. We mostly speak English," he added.

"You treat her well?" Popodopolis asked, his manner

more serious.

Having agreed to transport Charlotte from England to Greece for a holiday two years prior, the captain had worried about the fate of the duchess when the *Son of Apollo* was boarded by pirates. Taken to the sultan's palace on the edge of the Aegean Sea, Charlotte and her lady's maid, Parma, ended up under the protection of Ziyaeddin. Within a few days, the sultan had fallen in love with the duchess.

In the meantime, Popodopolis and his crew had been able to dispatch the pirates when the *Son of Apollo* sailed into the harbor of Rhodes, where they met Charlotte's son, Lord James Wainwright, and his fellow traveler, David Bennett-Jones, heir to the Bostwick viscountcy. Determined to save Charlotte, they had set off for the palace, arriving to discover the duchess was not of a mind to be saved.

She had fallen in love with the sultan.

The trip hadn't been a waste, though. James had met and married the sultan's favorite daughter, Sevinc, and they were now on an archaeological expedition on a Greek island.

Meanwhile, David had become fast friends with Sevinc's twin brother, Ertuğrul, the two sharing an interest in architecture. The Bostwick heir decided to remain in the Ottoman Empire, helping to oversee the construction of a new palace and the universities while studying the mosaics that decorated the sultan's various properties.

When Popodopolis and his crew departed, the captain promised to keep in touch. Given his daughter, Elena, was the head servant in Ziyaeddin's palaces, the captain was always welcome. As the Greek captain who had sunk Ziyaeddin's ship during the Greek's War for Independence, Popodopolis had earned the sultan's respect—and ultimately his friendship—by saving him and his crew from drowning.

"Of course I treat her well," Ziyaeddin claimed, annoyed the captain would think otherwise. "She is my sultana. I give her gifts almost every day—"

"But do you *love* her?" Popodopolis pressed.

Ziyaeddin gave a start at hearing the query. "More now than the day she was thrown down before me by those damned pirates," he replied. "She has given me another daughter and now a son..." He took a deep breath. "At my age, I am fortunate to experience another love in my life."

The captain seemed satisfied with the answer, although his attention had gone to something—or someone—behind the sultan. "I am relieved to hear it," he said. "I made a promise a long time ago to see to it she made it to Syros and then onto a ship bound for Athens, and I still haven't fulfilled that promise," he explained.

"Well, if you ever do, you'll be taking me, too," Ziyaeddin warned. "I will not allow her to travel alone."

"Understood," Popodopolis remarked. His brows furrowed. "Are you about to be in some sort of trouble?"

Ziyaeddin frowned before his eyes rounded. "Is my sultana behind me?" he asked, just then remembering he hadn't told anyone he was leaving the palace whilst in possession of the baby.

Popodopolis nodded. "And she has someone with her," he said.

"That would be Zehra," the sultan guessed, referring to his youngest daughter.

"You are in luck. Duchess Charlotte doesn't appear to be angry," he added as he allowed a huge grin.

"Poppy!" Charlotte Sultana shouted happily as she rushed down the path. Her progress was impeded, however. Clasped in one of her hands was the much smaller hand of a two-year-old girl who was moving as fast as she could.

The toddler, dressed in a European style gown of pale pink with white petticoats, white stockings, and black slippers, called out "Baba!" when her father turned around and knelt. She collided with him a moment later, nearly knocking him backwards in the process.

Chuckling as his newest daughter kissed his cheeks and wrapped her chubby arms around his neck, Ziyaeddin managed to return to standing whilst holding both children, one against each shoulder. He kissed his daughter on the forehead and was about to do the same to his son, but the boy's attention was captured by his mother. His legs bent and straightened over and over at the same time his hands fisted and pummeled Ziyaeddin in his excitement.

"Oh, I see who you favor," the sultan accused. As the babe continued his display of happy excitement, Ziyaeddin turned around to discover Popodopolis laughing at his expense.

"I see what you mean, old man," the captain said as his eyes crinkled in delight. He lifted Charlotte's hand to his lips. "Your Grace," he said as he bowed. "Or should I call you... Your Highness... or Your Majesty now?"

"Well, I did marry him," Charlotte acknowledged, lifting herself onto tiptoes so she could kiss the sultan on his cheek. "But I suppose I shall always be a duchess to you." Ahmet took the opportunity to launch himself into her arms, babbling happily as he rested his head on her shoulder.

"She is my only sultana," Ziyaeddin acknowledged.

"Do you have time to spend with your daughter?" Charlotte asked of the captain, grinning when he took Zehra's chubby fist to his lips. The toddler giggled. "I spoke to Elena only a moment ago to let her know you had arrived."

"I would like that, if she can afford the time." His attention was on Ziyaeddin as he replied. "We'll need to set out around sunset," he added. "The winds will favor us then."

"Spend as much time with her as you'd like," Ziyaeddin said. "Enjoy a meal together. Your crew is welcome to eat as well."

The captain dared a glance toward the dock. "I appreciate the offer, but please do not take offense when I tell you they would prefer staying aboard the ship."

Ziyaeddin shrugged, well aware Popodopolis' crew were mostly Greeks, and many had been sailors in the Greek War for Independence from the Ottoman Empire.

"The boys are all packed, and a servant is seeing to their trunks right now," Charlotte said. "Even though I've known this day was coming, I cannot help but be sad that they are leaving us," she said, referring to David and Ertuğrul. "Again," she added with an arched brow.

Only the year before, the two had set off intending to go to England for the Season when the weather in the Mediterranean forced Popodopolis to put the *Son of Apollo* into port in Sicily. By the time the weather had cleared a few days later, David had sent word of their intentions to remain on the island.

"Having seen what Catania has to offer and learning of the numerous mosaics that can be found in the churches and public buildings here, I wish to continue my Grand Tour, and Ertuğrul has fallen hard for Baroque architecture. There is no talking him into a trip to England this year."

"Am I to return them here after the Season is over?" the captain asked as they climbed the path toward the palace. Newly bloomed tulips lined the way, their red and yellow petals still closed at the top.

Ziyaeddin directed a glance toward his wife, but Charlotte had paused to lower Ahmet so his face was closer to a tulip. The boys arms shot out in an effort to capture one of the flowers, but she used a hand to cover his. "You can look, but don't touch," she said. When she straightened, she had tears pricking the corners of her eyes. "If it can be arranged with your schedule," she answered, sniffling. "Although we'll be back in Constantinople by then."

"What's wrong?" Ziyaeddin asked, his brows furrowing at seeing her bright eyes.

She blinked several times. "I'm just sorry to see the boys go is all," she replied. "They're like my own sons," she added. "Especially Ertuğrul."

Ziyaeddin exchanged a quick glance with Popodopolis, his look of concern fading after a moment. "Are you worried you'll never see them again?"

Charlotte inhaled softly, her eyes rounding. "What if they meet some young ladies? Fall in love? Wish to marry?" she asked in a rush.

Once again exchanging glances, the sultan and the captain both chuckled. "Isn't that the reason they are going to London, my sultana?" Ziyaeddin asked gently.

Charlotte blinked again as she absently bounced her son on her shoulder. "Oh," she replied softly. "I suppose it is," she added after another moment, a watery grin replacing her look of worry.

At least Ertuğrul would return. He had to. One day, he would be the sultan of the empire.

As for David, well she supposed it would depend on

his plans for his future. His father's plans for him. He was the heir to the Bostwick viscountcy, after all.

$\mathcal{M}$eanwhile, at White's men's club, St. James Street, London

Fog following him through the glossy black door of White's, James, Duke of Ariley, gave up his greatcoat to a footman before making his way to the back of the elegant men's club. Given the time of year, more members were in attendance on this evening than had been for the past few months. Aristocrats were returning to London in anticipation of Parliament's start in a fortnight.

Pausing to glance into one of the smaller, more private rooms, he nodded to several men who acknowledged him. He moved on to the next room and did a double-take upon seeing George Bennett-Jones, Viscount Bostwick, engaged in a conversation with Marcus Batey, Viscount Lancaster.

"Gentlemen," he said. "I hope I'm not interrupting," he added, knowing full well he was. As a duke, it was his right, of course, but he'd lived long enough not to abuse it.

"Not at all, Your Grace," George said as he stood. "Lancaster and I were just discussing our wives' charities," he added.

"And speaking of wives, I won't have one if I don't get home before midnight," Marcus said as he pulled his pocket watch from his waistcoat and noted the time. "It's already past eleven."

James chuckled. "Then you best get going. I was hoping to speak with Bostwick for a moment... although..."

Marcus' gaze darted to George before he turned it back on the duke. "Is something wrong, Your Grace?"

"No. But... you have daughters, do you not?"

Arching a dark brow, Marcus said, "My oldest, Analise, is Countess of Middleton, and Charity gave me my second daughter, Miss Hope. Uh... we named her Faith Hope, but we call her Hope since there are so many Faiths her age," he added.

"She must be the one," James stated.

"Sir?" Marcus once again dared a glance at George, but the other viscount merely continued to stare at the duke.

"She's not married, is she?" James asked.

Marcus shook his head. "She's been courted a few times, but..." He shrugged a shoulder again. "Daughters of viscounts aren't exactly top of the list. We're hoping she meets someone this Season who can appreciate her boldness, or my wife has threatened to employ her matchmaking skills and marry her off to some wealthy tradesman," he said on a huff.

"Boldness is not a trait to dismiss lightly," the duke remarked. "Especially in the wife of an aristocrat."

Blinking, Marcus regarded the Duke of Ariley with a questioning expression. "If only the young bucks agreed," he finally replied. He turned and nodded in George's direction. "I'll bring Charity to the office in the morning," he said, referring to his viscountess. "And I'll see you both in Parliament," he added before he turned to give the duke a deep nod. "Your Grace."

"Have a good evening, and if you are in need of a witness for this evening, I'll vouch for you with Lady Lancaster," James offered.

Grinning, Marcus said, "Much appreciated," before he took his leave.

James watched him go and then moved to take the chair Marcus had been using. A footman appeared with a glass of brandy, setting the drink on the table that separated the two aristocrats.

"We haven't spoken in a long time," George commented. He had half a mind to ask what the duke had in mind when it came to Lancaster's daughter, Hope, but decided he would learn soon enough. With the Season beginning soon, gossip would spread through Mayfair like wildfire. "What's happened?"

Helping himself to his brandy, James said, "Nothing, which is usually a good thing, but..." He sighed. "I find Ariley Place rather crowded these days."

George furrowed a brow. "Oh? Did your duchess give you another heir?" He knew Helen Harrington Burroughs, Duchess of Ariley, was probably too old to bear any more children—she had to be in her sixties— but given the number of women in their forties who had done so in the past few years had him wondering if his own viscountess might be *enceinte*. "Or have some long lost relatives shown up on your doorstep?"

James winced. "No additional heir, but also no son-in-law and no daughter-in-law. I had hoped Waverley and Rose would both be married by now," he complained, referring to his son William, Earl of Waverley, and his third but only legitimate daughter, Rose.

Giving a start, George regarded the older man with an incredulity. "Waverley isn't yet thirty," he remarked.

"True. But close enough."

"Forgive me for asking, but has Lady Rose recovered from her accident?" George asked. "I understand from my daughter that she was quite badly injured. A broken leg, was it not?"

Inhaling deeply, the duke seemed to think better of

what he was about to say and finally let out the breath he'd been holding. "Indeed, but she has recovered. She can walk without a crutch now. I barely see her limp except sometimes late at night. If she's been walking too much."

"Well, this is good news," George said. "She'll have suitors banging on your door any day now that the Season is about to start."

"Except she won't," James replied, his brows knit into a graying caterpillar.

George considered how to respond. "Sir?" he finally said. "She's a duke's daughter. She no doubt has a generous dowry. She's a rather pretty young lady. Why do you think she won't have suitors?"

James sighed. "I think she believes she must only consider men of a certain rank."

Well aware of what the duke meant by his comment, George said, "Aren't you of the same opinion, sir?"

The duke scoffed. "Mayhap thirty years ago," he replied. "Not any longer."

George considered the comment, rather surprised to hear Ariley didn't require a duke's son for his daughter. "Have you told her that?"

Wincing, James shook his head. "Not yet. Only because I had to first assemble the list to determine who her options might be."

George once again furrowed his brows. "The list?"

James nodded. "The eligible young men of the peerage born between 1813 and 1823 who have completed university and their Grand Tours, and who live in or around London, and who haven't yet wed."

Blinking, George considered the conditions. "That's rather specific," he remarked. "Are there any who made the list?"

"There are fewer than twenty."

Inhaling sharply, George stared at the duke. "Is my son on that list?" He shook his head. "I only ask because he's sent word he's on his way back from Constantinople."

"Is he coming back to stay?" the duke asked, apparently intrigued by the news.

"Indeed. In fact, he plans to find a wife. As does the young man who will be accompanying him."

James straightened in his chair. "And who might this other young man be?"

George dipped his head. "Emir Ertuğrul Effendi, heir to Ziyaeddin the First, Sultan of the Ottoman Empire. Oh, and stepson of Sultana Charlotte, Dowager Duchess of Chichester." He paused as the duke simply stared at him. "I'll be hosting Ertuğrul at Bostwick House."

Draining his brandy, James took a moment to consider the information before he said, "Well, Bostwick, you've done it again."

"What's that, sir?"

James chuckled. "Given me hope. When will they arrive?"

Shrugging one shoulder, George said, "They should be here in a few days, if their ship has remained on schedule."

"Capital," the duke said, his good humor increasing. He suddenly sobered. "The emir won't be bringing his harem with him, will he?"

George shook his head. "I don't believe he has one, sir. He's… he and David have been very involved in some construction projects in the empire and haven't exactly had time for other pursuits."

Disbelief showed on the duke's face. "How old is he?"

Furrowing a brow as he calculated Ertuğrul's age,

George said, "Two-and-twenty, I think. Maybe three-and-twenty?"

James blinked. "Is that all? He barely qualifies for the list."

"David is seven-and-twenty," George offered. "I believe Lady Rose and he are about the same age?"

"Indeed," James agreed, although he seemed to be studying something in his mind's eye. After a few seconds, he said, "I'm not sure if you're aware, but we're hosting a ball in Rose's honor next week. I do hope your family will be in attendance. And bring the emir, of course."

"We will all be there, sir," George said. "But in the meantime, if you could keep the news about the emir and my son quiet, I would appreciate it. I'd rather my viscountess not learn of it until I hear further word from David. I would hate for her to get her hopes up again," he added.

"Understood," the duke acknowledged with a knowing grin. "Now... I should be returning to my duchess before she thinks I've taken a mistress."

"Me as well, Your Grace," George replied with a grin, glad he had something he could share with Elizabeth when she asked if anything might have happened at the club.

He also had a thought to compile the same sort of list as the duke had mentioned, and there was one particular person at Bostwick House who could help in that regard.

His youngest daughter, Adeline.

Not yet, though. He didn't want to raise any suspicions.

CHAPTER 1
AN ITINERARY IS REVEALED

April 4, 1844, at the Bostwick townhouse in Mayfair

A blustery wind accompanied Elizabeth Bennett-Jones, Viscountess Bostwick, when she rushed into her house followed by her daughter, Adeline. The butler, Elkins, hurried to close the door once the women's skirts had cleared the threshold.

"Oh, my," Elizabeth breathed as she allowed Elkins to help her out of her redingote.

"Of all the days to have to be at the charity," Adeline murmured under her breath, shrugging out of her own coat. "At least it was a good day, was it not?"

"Very," her mother agreed. "Although I intend to have a word with your father about a particular bank manager," she groused as she shed her gloves into Elkins' waiting hands.

Elizabeth's charity, *Finding Work for the Wounded*, specialized in placing wounded soldiers—and as of late, any men who were disabled in some capacity—into honest employment. She'd had a young man perfectly suited to a teller position, but due to a missing leg, he would be required to lean or sit on a stool as he performed his duties. The bank manager refused to hire him, despite Elizabeth's attempted bribe.

Even before she made it into the hall of Bostwick House, George Bennett-Jones, Viscount Bostwick, was out of his study and had his wife pulled into his arms. Despite their daughter's presence and Elkins still in the vestibule, he kissed her thoroughly.

Adeline rolled her eyes and crossed her arms as she waited for her parents to finish the kiss. Having paid witness to such outrageous displays of affection nearly every day of her life, she was used to it. She also knew that her father had overheard her mother's complaint and was using the kiss as a means to deflect her mother's anger—for the time being.

"I'm glad you're home and out of that awful weather," George whispered, once he'd finally finished the kiss.

Elizabeth gazed up at him for a moment before she blinked. "Well, I'm certainly glad I am as well," she murmured. Her dazed expression cleared, and she allowed a sigh.

"What is it, my sweet?" George asked, his eyes darting briefly to their daughter.

"It's not my fault," Adeline stated, her hands going to her hips. The move was exactly the same as one Elizabeth frequently employed when she was upset about something. "That odious Mr. Turnbull at Barclays refused to hire Mr. Cromwell because he cannot stand on his wooden leg for long periods of time."

George furrowed his brows. "Barclays?" he repeated. Having been married to Elizabeth nearly as long as she'd been running her charity, he had learned over the years who among employers were good about taking on disabled workers and who were not—even when a bribe was involved. "New manager?" he guessed.

"Will you have a word with him?" Elizabeth asked in a small voice. Over the years, she had tried hard not to involve George in the negotiations over hirings, but sometimes a man was required to talk sense into another man. Given his position as a viscount and hers as the daughter of a marquess, the couple rarely had to use threats of their relationships with aristocrats to convince someone to hire a deserving man.

"Forget Barclays," George stated, stepping away from Elizabeth to hurry into his study.

Elizabeth followed. "But they have a position," she argued.

"I'm surprised you didn't start with the Bank of England," he murmured, taking a seat behind his desk. "Teddy will hire him if he's qualified."

"I have prevailed upon him twice in the past two years," Elizabeth argued, referring to Baron Theodore Streater. Back in 1815, he had been her very first client at *Finding Work for the Wounded,* and he had worked at the Bank of England ever since, moving up into higher positions of authority as older employees retired or resigned. When his mother died a few years later, he inherited Warwick's Grammar and Finishing School and then married Ariley's illegitimate daughter, Daisy. The baroness was the headmistress of the school and mother to two children.

Despite his wife's protest, George had already begun penning a note. "I fenced with him earlier today," he said. "He was complaining about an incompetent clerk. Someone hired because he was the son of someone important," he added as he signed his name. He sanded the sheet and carefully dumped the fine granules back into the silver container. "I told him I would mention his need to you."

Elizabeth inhaled softly. "I hope the two clerks I placed there last year are working out to his satisfaction," she murmured.

"Oh, they are," George assured her as he folded the note. "Elkins!" he called out.

The butler was at the door in only a moment. "See to it this note is delivered to Mr. Streater at the Bank of England," he said as he handed over the note.

"Yes, my lord," Elkins replied as he nodded and backed out of the study.

George turned his attention back on his wife. He was about to tell her his news when she ended up back in his arms. "Oh, George. I do love you," she whispered before her lips took his.

Enjoying the kiss, George decided to continue it far longer than usual, even considering the thought of escorting her up to their apartments so he might engage her in a quick tumble. If she discovered he had kept her in the dark regarding news from their oldest son, though, she would be furious with him. Better he wait until later that night to make love to her.

"I have news about David," he whispered when he finally pulled away.

Her eyes glazed over from their kiss, she stared at him in confusion. "David who?" she asked in a whisper.

George threw his head back and guffawed. "Now I wish I *had* taken you upstairs for a tumble," he said as he continued to chuckle.

Her expression of confusion finally clearing, Elizabeth gasped. "Are you speaking of *our* David?" she asked in alarm.

"The one and only," he affirmed. "He's coming home.

For certain, this time, or so he wrote," he added as he lifted a white envelope from the silver salver on his desk.

"Oh! When?" she asked, taking the note from him.

"They are expected to arrive on the *Sun of Apollo* in Southampton the day after tomorrow," he replied. "I've already arranged for them to take the train from the Southampton Docks, and I'll have the traveling coach collect them at the Nine Elms station here in London," he explained.

"Well, shouldn't we be there to meet him in Southampton?" she asked as she flitted about the office, her movements indicating her mind was racing with plans.

Prepared for her reaction, George grinned. "You and Adeline have a garden party to attend—"

"I can miss a garden party—"

"At your mother's."

Elizabeth clamped her mouth shut. *"Damnation,"* she muttered. Her eyes rounded. "What about you? Can you meet him?"

"I can," he replied. "If you insist—"

"I do."

"I'll head down on the train tomorrow and spend the night at The Star Hotel," he said, referring to the lodgings nearest the docks in Southampton. Having already made the plans, he was relieved that Elizabeth insisted he go. Although he knew David could manage on his own, he also knew there was another whose comfort would be a consideration. He was about to mention him when Elizabeth's eyes once again rounded.

"You said 'they'," she accused. "Has he gone and done what Lord James did?" she asked as her eyes rounded. Her best friend's son had married one of Sultan Ziyaeddin's daughters three year's prior, shortly before her best friend, Charlotte, Dowager Duchess of Chichester, had agreed to marry the sultan.

"He has not," George assured her. "That is, if you meant has he taken a wife," he added. "However, he is bringing one of the sultan's sons with him. The Emir Ertuğrul Effendi," he explained. "The one he befriended when he first arrived at that Aegean palace. When he and Lord James went off to rescue Charlotte from the pirates," he added, not bothering to suppress a grin when he remembered how the event was described in David's entertaining letter on the matter.

By the time David and James had arrived at the palace in pursuit of the kidnapped duchess, Ziyaeddin had already fallen in love with Charlotte. Although Charlotte claimed she didn't know how she felt about Ziyaeddin and the matter of remaining in the Ottoman Empire, the boys knew she wouldn't return to England. Given they were on their Grand Tour, they simply adapted to their new itinerary, remaining at the palace at the sultan's invitation.

David's interest in architecture and mosaics landed him a position of sorts with the sultan's son, Ertuğrul, who was in charge of the empire's government buildings, and James met and married the sultan's daughter before taking her on a wedding trip that was by all accounts still going on. The last George had heard, James was on an archaeological dig in Greece with Viscount Jasper Henley, his wife and toddler son at his side.

"This Ertuğrul... isn't he the same one David was going to bring with him last year?" Elizabeth asked.

"He is," George replied. "It seems the şehzade still wishes to spend a Season here in London. Attend all the entertainments, although..." He allowed the sentence to trail off.

"What is it?"

George winced. "It's my understanding that sultans of the Ottoman sort don't usually marry. They have harems filled with concubines," he said. He couldn't help but notice how Elizabeth's face took on a blush worthy of a new bride. Charlotte had apparently shared what she had learned of them in her letters to his wife. "Which has me wondering why the heir-apparent to Ziyaeddin the First wishes to spend a Season in London."

Elizabeth considered his comment a moment. "Do you suppose he's looking to add an English girl to his harem?" she asked in a quiet voice.

Arching his brows, George considered the query a moment before he said, "David would surely tell him how unlikely it would be for an English miss to agree to move to Constantinople and become a concubine," he reasoned. "So... he's probably coming on a diplomatic mission on behalf of the sultanate."

"Makes sense," Elizabeth agreed. "But surely Charlotte would have sent word..." She stopped when she noted George's attention was once again directed toward the door. He held up a finger.

"What is it, Elkins?" he asked, acknowledging the servant who had been hovering near the study's threshold for several seconds.

"A letter has arrived for Lady Bostwick," Elkins replied. "It's marked 'urgent'."

Elizabeth was at the door and collecting the well-worn envelope before the butler could finish.

"It's from Charlotte," she said, recognizing the handwriting even before she popped the seal from the back. The *tughra* embossed in the dark red wax would have been her other clue, the symbol unique to the sultan. The battered parchment looked as if it had been trampled on its way from the Ottoman Empire. Unfolding the letter, she held it out and began to read aloud.

My Dearest Elizabeth,

I hope this letter finds you and your family well. My new situation, no longer so new I suppose, has me incandescent with joy nearly every day. Daughter Zehra is learning Turkish faster than I am, and Ahmet is... well, he's still a baby and a boy. Having raised two with a doting father, I expect he will be no different. Zi treats both as if they are his only children, but then he is that way with the others that remain with us. Two more married this past year, and several are betrothed to marry in the next year or so. The rest remain in school or with tutors. Zi is very insistent they get the very best education possible.

Elizabeth glanced up from the letter to see that George had settled one hip on the edge of his desk, and his arms were crossed as he listened. "Ziyaeddin does sound like an attentive father," she remarked.

"Indeed," he agreed. "Which has me wondering which one of his sons he will choose as his heir."

Her brows arching, Elizabeth asked, "Can he do that?"

George nodded. "Sultans are chosen by their father. They don't follow the laws of primogeniture like we do," he explained.

"Does that mean Charlotte's son could become the sultan?" she asked, her eyes rounding.

Chuckling, George said, "He could, but I rather imagine one of the older sons will be chosen, if he hasn't already been." He pointed to the letter. "Go on," he encouraged.

Holding out the parchment, Elizabeth resumed her recitation.

Ertuğrul and David remain unattached, which brings me to the real reason for my letter.

By the time you receive this, you will no doubt be in preparations for another Season. After what happened last year (the unexpected squall that required the Son of Apollo to put into port in Catania), those two young men are determined to make it to London for the Season. They are due to arrive in Southampton on the Sun of Apollo on or around March the 27th. I know your son has sent a note to George to let him know, but in the event that letter goes astray, I wanted to be sure you knew of their impending arrival.

Although David has been invited to remain here, to live in our palaces and continue his work as an architect, I know he is eager to marry. Nothing but an English miss will do for him, though (he is nothing like James in that regard—my boy loves his Sevinc. He never would have been happy with an English girl.)

"Well, this is a relief," Elizabeth said. "I was beginning to think our boy was going to end up married to one of Sevinc's sisters," she added.

George chuckled. "She would be beautiful." When he noted Elizabeth's pointed glare in his direction, he quickly added, "But not as beautiful as you." He was afforded an appreciative nod and a grin before she continued to read.

As for Ertuğrul... he has been looking forward to another trip to England since he finished his studies at Cambridge. For the past two years, Zi has said many a time he is free to travel. I believe he wants him to act as a sort of diplomat for the empire.

Ertuğrul is happy to act in that capacity, but I cannot help but think he wishes to go to London for other reasons. Architec-

ture for one—he is fascinated by the works of the Adamses—and perhaps to find a wife.

Although he should have a harem by now (made up of daughters gifted to him from viceroys and such), he has avoided the issue by insisting his older and younger brothers be the beneficiaries of those gifts. I cannot help but wonder if—and feel a hint of pride— he has set his mind on taking a wife because he has seen what it has done for his father.

I cannot imagine I am a good example, though, since I was so reluctant to become a sultan's wife. I have attempted to be a mother for him, though, since his (and Sevinc's) mother died when they were born. He is too old for a mother now, of course, but I have made it clear I am available to offer advice should he require it.

Neither of my sons have spoken with me the way Ertuğrul does, and it does my heart good to know that I can still provide motherly advice to at least one poor young man on this earth.

On this note, I ask that you be open to any queries he might have whilst he avails you of your hospitality. Since you have two sons of your own, I expect you'll have no trouble offering advice when it's requested. (The fact that you have two daughters of your own will also bode well. Although I now have one of my own, she is far too young to cause the sort of issues I expect yours have caused you and George over the years.)

Oh, dear—I do hope David has informed you of the arrangements he has promised—a guest chamber for Ertuğrul's use during his stay in London. I would also ask that you use your influence to see to it he is invited to all the very best entertainments. You needn't be concerned about a language barrier as his English is excellent.

Ahmet has awakened from his nap, and although Zi can entertain him for a few minutes (he lives for that boy's giggles), Ahmet will require his midday feeding.

Please give George and Adeline my love.

Your best friend,
Charlotte

Elizabeth paused a moment before she refolded the letter. When she glanced up, she discovered George regarding her with an expression of bemusement. "What is it?" she asked.

He chuckled. "I am of the opinion you are going to enjoy the next few months," he remarked. "Overseeing the potential love lives of not just one young lady but two young men as well?" he added as he rolled his eyes.

"George," she scolded. After a pause, she added, "I do like a challenge."

"Oh, is that how you see it?" he countered with a grin.

About to reply in the affirmative, Elizabeth's eyes suddenly rounded. "David's letter," she stated. "Was there anything else in it about this... this Ertuğrul?" she asked as she furrowed a brow.

George held up the note from David. "It's pronounced 'Er-too-rule,' I believe," he commented, managing to correctly roll the second 'r'. "Charlotte's letter contained far more information, of course," he added. "However, our son wished to make it clear that we're not to treat the sultan's son any better than we would any other guest in Bostwick House."

"But... isn't he the equivalent of a prince?" Elizabeth argued.

George's head bobbed from side to side. "Probably. But I've come to learn from David's past letters that this Ertuğrul is rather humble. He's not the oldest son, nor is he the youngest. We're not to fuss, my sweet," he warned. "We're not going to move into a larger townhouse or buy a mansion in Richmond," he added with an arched brow.

Scoffing, Elizabeth inhaled and let out her breath in a huff. "Oh, all right," she finally said. "But I will see to it he's in the very best guest bedchamber," she said.

"And that will do," George replied, knowing there was really only one guest bedchamber in all of Bostwick House. That it was currently decorated for more feminine tastes meant he expected to begin receiving invoices from drapers and decorators within a week.

Elizabeth could accomplish much in a day.

CHAPTER 2
BACHELORS ON A BOAT

eanwhile, on the Sun of Apollo
Leaning over the railing of the merchant ship, David Bennett-Jones squinted in an attempt to make out the distant shoreline.

"What do you see?" Ertuğrul asked as he followed his friend's line of sight. He spoke in precise English, accented with the lilting melodies of his native language.

"France, I think," David replied, stepping back to aim his gaze up at the crewman who had climbed into the crow's nest earlier that morning. The young Greek had a spyglass aimed in the same direction, his relaxed stance indicating all was well. "Won't be long before we're up to Southampton," he added.

The *Son of Apollo* had passed through the Straight of Gibraltar sometime in the middle of the night, the event marked by two crewmen who probably woke the entire ship's contingent with whoops and shouts about sighting the Pillars of Heracles under a half-moon.

For David, who had still been awake, it had been a

moment of shared joy. For Ertuğrul, who had been sound asleep, it had been a startling and not so pleasant reminder that he was a passenger on a ship captained and crewed by Greeks. Despite the fact that Captain Popodopolis and his father had been friends since the Greek War for Independence, Ertuğrul knew the crew harbored resentment against him and the Ottoman Empire. Some of their fathers had died in that war.

"Today do you think?" Ertuğrul asked, hope in his voice.

"Tonight or early tomorrow," David replied. He gave his friend a slight punch on his shoulder. "They don't hate you," he said in a quiet voice. "Despite what you think."

Ertuğrul shrugged. "What must I say to prove I hold no ill will against them?" he asked.

David winced. "Actions speak louder than words," he replied. "Which I know doesn't help now. But when you are the sultan..." He shrugged and allowed the sentence to trail off.

When—and if—Ertuğrul became the sultan of the Ottoman Empire, it would mean Ziyaeddin I had either died or stepped aside to allow his choice of sultan to take over the position. Given how much his godmother, Charlotte, loved the sultan, and how much she was enjoying her second chance at being a mother of two young children, David rather hoped Ziyaeddin would live a very long life.

"...You'll do what you must to prove it," David finally added.

"By the time I inherit the empire, there might not be much left of it," Ertuğrul murmured.

"The less there is, the fewer problems you'll have to solve," David countered with an arched brow.

"The less there is, the fewer taxes there will be to collect to pay all the bills," the sultan's son reminded him.

"The less there is, the fewer bills there will be," David countered with a chuckle.

Ertuğrul gave him a quelling glance. "You say that now that the universities and the new palace are built," he chided.

David angled his head to one side. "True," he agreed. "Still... I should think you will appreciate even more what you've been able to accomplish in a few short years," he commented. He clapped a palm against the şehzade's back, which had the young man sighing in resignation.

"I will appreciate it only if I can share it with someone special," the sultan's son said on a sigh.

David furrowed a brow, understanding Ertuğrul's comment more than the young man could know.

It was time he begin courting. Time to find an English miss to take to wife. Time to populate a nursery and prepare for the eventuality of becoming Viscount Bostwick.

Prior to leaving on his Grand Tour, there had been three young ladies he was particularly interested in when it came to marriage. He had no idea if any of those three were still unwed, but even if the one for whom he felt the greatest affection was still available, would she even consider marrying him? A mere viscount's son? With no hope of being more than a viscount?

As for Ertuğrul, David wasn't sure if the man realized what he was in for when it came to a Season in London. There were plenty of young ladies in search of husbands, but would any of them wish to marry a sultan's son—

even if it meant eventually becoming a sultana—and move to Constantinople?

He rather doubted it.

CHAPTER 3
AN ARRIVAL AND A HOMECOMING

Two days later, Bostwick townhouse, Park Lane, Mayfair

Led by George Bennett-Jones, David and Ertuğrul entered the vestibule of Bostwick House to discover dinner was to be served at seven o'clock, giving the three train travelers a couple of hours to settle in and change clothes.

"I'll show you to your room," Elkins said to the new houseguest.

"Thank you," Ertuğrul replied, aiming a worried glance in David's direction.

"You'll be in a guest room very close to mine," the Bostwick heir assured him. "Can you see to it hot water is brought up?" he asked of the butler as he handed his top hat to the servant.

Elkins gave a start. "Your father has seen to it Bostwick House features modern plumbing," he replied drolly.

David blinked before he turned his attention to his father. "Oh?"

George arched a brow. "Do you really need to be reminded that you are the son of Elizabeth Carlington Bennett-Jones?" he asked with a smirk. He gave up his cape coat and top hat to Elkins. "There's a private bath attached to the guest bedchamber."

Giving a start, David aimed a grin in Ertuğrul's direction. "I suppose not," he replied in a whisper. "When—?"

"About a month after you left on your Grand Tour," George said. "Take a moment to enjoy the quiet before your mother discovers we have arrived," he instructed. "Then be prepared for—"

"David!" Elizabeth shouted as she descended the stairs. The viscountess, garbed in a teal dinner gown with her mahogany hair dressed into a riot of curls atop her head, beamed in delight at seeing her son.

"—Your mother," George finished with a grin. He watched as his wife rushed to embrace her oldest child. Chuckled when David had Elizabeth in his arms and was swinging her in a circle that forced both him and Ertuğrul to step away lest they be upended by her skirts.

"Oh, David," Elizabeth said as she stepped away and regarded her son from head to toe. "Well, you look as if you've been getting enough to eat," she said with a grin.

"I have, Mother. Thanks to Aunt Charlotte," he replied. He sobered. "Viscountess Bostwick, may I have the honor of introducing you to my friend, Emir Ertuğrul Effendi, heir to the Ottoman Empire?"

Elizabeth quickly sobered, extracted herself from her son's hold, and curtsied deeply. "Oh, of course. Your Eminence," she said before she rose.

Ertuğrul bowed deeply and reached for her hand. "It's an honor to meet you, Lady Bostwick," he replied. He kissed her knuckles.

Elizabeth beamed in delight. "Oh, and you," she

gushed. "Thank you for befriending my son. For seeing to it he's had an avocation for the past few years," she added as she angled her head to one side.

Exchanging quick glances with David, Ertuğrul said, "It was my pleasure, my lady, I assure you," he said.

"He was always interested in architecture," Elizabeth stated as she took his arm and placed hers on top of it. She led them to the stairs. "Your tutelage has meant the world to him," she added as they climbed the stairs. "Although the circumstances of your meeting were not the best, I assure you my very best friend in this world does not for one moment regret what occurred to lead to such an advantageous situation," she went on as they moved onto the second flight of stairs.

David glanced over at his father. "He's doomed," he murmured.

George chuckled. "In the very best way," he replied.

"I'll see to it the footmen deliver your trunks to your bedchambers," Elkins said as he lifted the viscount's valise from the floor where George had left it. "And your correspondence is in your study, sir."

"Very good," George replied. He turned his attention on his son. "You probably want a bit of time to yourself after your travels," he guessed.

David wondered at the comment. "Truth be told, I'm looking forward to being around English speakers again," he said, "and attending the entertainments London has to offer." Although he hadn't missed some of the aspects of living in the capital, there were others, like privacy and anonymity, which he had whilst he was living in the sultan's palaces.

George lifted a brow. "I'm glad to hear it, especially since there's a ball tomorrow night. Your mother made sure to secure an invitation for Ertuğrul. The Weatherstones are thrilled to be hosting him."

Chuckling, David felt relief. "Happy to hear it."

"Best you go on up and dress for dinner," George suggested.

"I don't suppose my bedchamber has the very newest in hot water plumbing?" David remarked.

Scoffing, George said, "Never underestimate your mother, young man," he admonished. "And I look forward to your thoughts on taking a shower bath that doesn't involve a footman," he challenged with an arched brow. With that, George disappeared into his study.

Left dumbfounded, David watched his father before he aimed a glance at Elkins. "Much has happened since I was last here," he said in a whisper.

"Indeed, sir," Elkins replied.

Before David made it to the stairs, he turned and discovered his sister, Adeline, regarding him from the front salon. "Well, hello," he said as she rushed into his arms.

"I feared I wouldn't recognize you," Adeline whispered once her head ended up on his shoulder.

"Oh, come now," he replied. "How much could I have changed in only a few years?" he countered. He stepped back and regarded her, his expression changing from delight to consternation.

"What?" she asked in alarm.

"Where is my sister Adeline?" he asked. "What have you done with her?"

Adeline gave him a quelling glance. "Very funny," she remarked.

But David's expression remained serious. "How is it you still live here?" he asked in all seriousness. She seemed at least two inches taller than when he had last seen her, and her features had matured so the soft lines of her face were closer to those of their mother. Their grandmother's Italian complexion wasn't the least bit evident in her coloring, but her hair color matched Elizabeth's perfectly. He was sure his contemporaries found her attractive.

Her brows furrowing in confusion, Adeline allowed a shrug. "Well, I am still unmarried," she replied. "A situation I do not believe will change anytime soon," she added on a sigh. "I've become a wallflower, you see. A constant companion to the potted palms of ballrooms up and down Park Lane."

David pulled away from his sister's hold. "How many marriage proposals have you turned down?" he asked, suspicious. For a moment, he worried his sister might have gained a reputation for courting without the intent to marry.

Adeline blinked. "None," she replied with a shrug.

Glancing to one side, David felt a combination of anger and shock on his sister's behalf. "Are you not considered a diamond of the first water?"

Giggling, Adeline stepped back. "Hardly," she replied. She continued to grin, though, her peaches-and-cream complexion enhanced by the light of the gas-lit sconces lining the great hall of Bostwick House. "But thank you for the compliment," she said before she quickly sobered. "So... tell me about this sultan's son you have brought with you," she said as she motioned for him to join her in the salon.

David frowned. "He's become my best friend," he warned. "He's a good man, Addy," he added. "Humble and hardworking, and a master at overseeing construction. I brought drawings to show the buildings that have been erected in the past two years."

"I've read your last few letters to Father," she said. "Which is why I'm surprised you came back to England."

David winced. "I've been away more than three years," he reminded her. "I think it's time I take a wife."

Adeline glanced around, as if she feared someone was eavesdropping. Once he was over the threshold, she shut the door. "I thought you might marry a Turkish girl," she said in a hushed voice. "Mayhap one of the sultan's daughters, like James did. Don't you find them... exotic?"

A grimace passed over David's face before he said, "There are some very beautiful women there, yes." He cleared his throat. "As for Charlotte's stepdaughters, I rather doubt Ziyaeddin would allow another one of them to marry an Englishman, even though he is happy with James," he explained. "And besides, I still favor English girls." His eyes darted sideways. "That speak English. My Turkish is rot," he added.

Adeline struggled not to snort as she indicated he should sit. "Well, do have a seat," she encouraged.

He winced. "I've been sitting on the train all day," he said. "I need to get my land legs back."

Shrugging, she decided to remain standing. "You may find English girls are not as you remember," she warned. "But they do still speak English. And French, of course."

Inhaling slowly, David regarded his sister for a moment before he dared a glance at the closed door, as if he feared someone might be eavesdropping on their conversation. "Will you... apprise me of who has married since I was last in town?" he asked. "Maybe before dinner? I understand many of my contemporaries have already been caught in the parson's mousetrap, and my choices may be limited."

Knowing her brother had favored several young women who had married since his departure on his

Grand Tour, Adeline understood his request. "I will, if you'll tell me why this... Ertu..." She paused, unsure of how to say the name of their guest.

"Ertuğrul," David murmured.

"Why did he come?"

David inhaled softly. "He... he wishes to attend a Season in London," he said with a shrug.

"How does he even *know* about Seasons in London?" she asked.

His eyes darting toward the door again, David leaned in and said, "He attended university at Cambridge. He... he is of a mind to find an English wife."

Adeline gasped. "But, why?"

David gave her a quelling glance. "His stepmother is Aunt Charlotte," he replied, as if that was reason enough.

The oddest sensation passed through Adeline just then. "To add to his harem?"

Wincing, David shook his head. "I don't know that he'll ever have a harem," he murmured. "Other than... his unmarried sisters or aunts and the female servants," he added on a sigh.

Adeline stared up at her brother with a look of uncertainty. "What about... *concubines*?" she asked in a whisper.

David allowed a huff. "He's not like that. At least... not that I'm aware," he whispered. Despite how closely the two had worked together while two universities and a palace were under construction—David overseeing the placement of mosaic designs and other interior decorations while Ertuğrul saw to the overall buildings—he had never known the şehzade to speak of the women he took to his bed.

"Do *you* have a harem in Constantinople?"

"Of course not," he replied, his face taking on a

reddish cast. "And they're not quite what you're imagining."

"Oh, I can imagine quite a lot," she countered. "I have read about them. There are even some color plates of paintings in one of father's books," she claimed.

Wincing, David considered how to respond. He was fairly sure a male painter had never been allowed in a Turkish harem. Other than eunuchs and the sultan, no men were. "Just... promise me you'll get to know our guest before you make any judgments, won't you?" he pleaded.

Adeline regarded her brother with a furrowed brow before she finally nodded. "All right," she agreed. "But don't expect me to be the one to initiate any conversations with him. I'm terribly shy, you know."

Scoffing as a huge grin split his face, David began laughing. "You? Shy?" he repeated.

Giving him a quelling glance, Adeline nearly stomped a slippered foot on the marble tiled floor. "Wallflower," she said by way of a reminder.

Wondering what might have happened to cause his sister to gain a reputation as a wallflower, David decided he could find out from his father after dinner. They would no doubt play a game of billiards. Teach Ertuğrul how to play, if the şehzade didn't already know. David would simply use the time to discover what had happened in the Bostwick household since he last lived in it.

"I'll be here in the front salon," Adeline said. "Or in the parlor with Mother."

David's gaze darted around the small room, which faced Park Lane. Besides a couple of floral upholstered chairs, a settee and a low table, there was an escritoire and a chair against one wall. For a moment, he couldn't remember ever having been in the salon before. "What is this room for?" he asked.

"Me," she replied. "It's where I host my friends when they come for tea."

Pulling his head back as his brows furrowed, David regarded her with a curious expression. "Your own parlor?"

A flush colored Adeline's face. "What of it?"

David glanced toward the door again. "Isn't there a parlor on the first floor?"

Rolling her eyes, Adeline leaned toward him and said, "Yes, but it's Mother's parlor. Where she hosts *her* guests," she replied. "And one of my friends has been in an accident and can't climb stairs very well."

Suspicious, David was about to respond when there was a quiet knock. His father poked his head around the door. "I hate to break up your reunion, but might I have a word with you?" the viscount asked, his attention on his daughter.

Adeline's eyes rounded, and a look of guilt crossed her face. "Yes, Father," she replied.

"I'm going up to change for dinner," David said, his suspicious gaze still on his sister. He turned, stepped around his father, and hurried up the stairs.

George and Adeline watched him until he had made the turn at the landing. "What is it, Father?"

"Come into my study," he replied, leading her as they took the twenty steps to the other room's door.

Hesitating before she entered the study, Adeline gave her father a beseeching glance.

Whatever had she done?

WELCOMING A GUEST

eanwhile, on the second floor

Ertuğrul stepped into the guest bedchamber and stopped short. Given everything David had told him about bedchambers in London townhouses, he had expected a room half the size and only a bed and a dresser.

"Oh, dear. I suppose you're used to something far more elegant than this," Elizabeth said from where she stood next to the door to the dressing room.

"Oh, no, my lady," he responded, his gaze darting about in wonder. "This is... is this the master suite, perhaps?" he asked in alarm, fearing his host had given up his room to him.

"This is the guest bedchamber," she assured him. "It is about the same size as my husband's," she acknowledged proudly. "I had this room and the bathing chamber constructed from two bedchambers a few years ago. When we added the plumbing for bathing water," she explained. She opened the dressing room door. "There are hooks in here for anything you wish to hang, and the bathing chamber is through that door there," she said as she waved a hand to the adjacent corner. "Elkins will see to it there's a fire at night for warmth, of course, and should you require a valet, we can see to hiring one."

Ertuğrul's attention had gone to the crown mouldings and the painting on the ceiling. "I didn't realize private rooms were so well decorated here," he murmured.

Grinning, Elizabeth relaxed. "Not all of them, I suppose. I do hope you'll be comfortable here," she said as she moved to the set of chairs that were set in front of the fireplace. She repositioned a small pillow and then nudged the mantel clock so it was centered beneath a painting.

Chuckling, Ertuğrul glanced out the window next to where he stood, attempting to determine which direction was east. Despite the white Austrian sheers framed by dark blue velvet drapes, he could make out the back garden below. "I shan't want to return to Constantinople," he replied.

A pair of footmen appeared, the şehzade's trunk held between them. They followed Elizabeth's direction, placing it along the only open wall next to the largest dresser. Another followed with a valise and then paused to ask if anything else was required.

"That will be all until dinner at seven," the viscountess replied. As the servants bowed and took their leave, Ertuğrul continued to examine the furnishings, his hands smoothing over the velvet counterpane and a marble-topped nightstand. A quick glance out the other window showed the telltale signs of sunset, the twilight sky not yet claiming the last of the sun's light. His gaze darted to the head of the bed and back to the window.

"The bed is set on the south wall," Elizabeth stated, realizing he was trying to determine directions. "My husband thought you would prefer sleeping east. Facing Mecca? Is that right?"

Ertuğrul's eyes widened. "Indeed," he said. "It is kind of him to have seen to the arrangement." Now that he knew which direction was east, he visibly relaxed and then remembered something he had promised Charlotte he would pass along. "My stepmother wished for me to convey her glad tidings and appreciation for you hosting me," he blurted.

Elizabeth inhaled softly. "I received a letter from her only a few days ago. How is she?"

The sultan's son contemplated how to respond. "I think for a time, she was... a duchess out of place," he replied, understanding her query for what it was. "But now that she has learned her way around the palaces and is familiar with the servants and has made friends with my father's *ikbals*.... she is a sultana. And a very doting mother," he added with a grin. "My youngest sister is now my favorite."

The viscountess regarded her guest for a moment before nodding. "Believe me when I tell you that I feared greatly for her. I felt somewhat responsible, you see," she said as she settled onto the front edge of one of the chairs, the skirts of her gown spreading out in a fan.

"Responsible?" he repeated as he joined her.

"Lady Gisborn and I are the ones who encouraged her to take a holiday to Greece and the Kingdom of the Two Sicilies," she said. "I have been to Italy twice. My mother was born in Rome, so I have family there, you see," she explained. "I thought she would be perfectly fine given the arrangements that had been made on her behalf."

Ertuğrul took the other chair, his brows furrowing. "You could not have known her ship would be taken by pirates," he said as he shook his head. "Or that her destiny was to be with my father."

Elizabeth gave a start. "Destiny?" she repeated, sounding surprised.

"Fate?" Ertuğrul offered, thinking he had used the wrong word. "Perhaps I do not know the correct English word."

Tittering, Elizabeth took a deep breath. "Whatever it was that had those two meeting was doing its job," she murmured. "Charlotte seems very happy."

"As is my father," Ertuğrul stated. "He has youthened as well. Although he sometimes complains of aches in his joints when it is damp or cold, the troubles that used to vex him are no longer so troublesome to him."

Elizabeth angled her head to one side. "So... Ziyaeddin feels affection for her?"

Ertuğrul blinked. "He loves her. He would not have divorced his first wife and given up his concubines if he did not."

Her eyes rounding at hearing the conviction in the şehzade's voice, Elizabeth's gaze darted to the fireplace and then to the clock. "Oh, dear. I planned to have dinner served at seven o'clock," she said. "Which doesn't give you but an hour to dress." She stood. "My apologies, Your Eminence."

"Please, call me Ertuğrul, and I do not heed an hour to dress, my lady," he assured her.

Elizabeth paused on her way to the door. "Then when you are ready, come to the parlor down on the first floor. We'll have coffee and some walnuts before we go into the dining room," she said.

"I look forward to it," he said as he bowed.

Curtsying, Elizabeth took her leave and shut the door behind her.

Deciding he had enough time—the sky was growing dark behind the two windows—Ertuğrul fished his prayer rug from his valise and rolled it out over the Turkish carpeting. Removing his shoes, he knelt and said his prayers.

CHAPTER 5
A DUKE AND DUCHESS ON
THE VERGE

eanwhile, in the ballroom at Ariley Place
William, Earl of Waverley and heir to the Ariley dukedom, winced when an off-note sounded from the *piano-forté* his mother was playing in the corner. His sister, Rose, stood in front of him, one hand on his shoulder while her left hand rested on his right hand.

"I do apologize," Helen Harrington Burroughs, Duchess of Ariley, called out. "I haven't played in an age."

"It's all right, Mother," Rose replied, attempting to keep her head up and her back straight all while most of her attention was on making her leg work properly. When the music resumed, she felt the slight nudge of her brother's hand at her waist, and she stutter-stepped into the waltz.

From near the ornate entrance to the large salon, James, Duke of Ariley, leaned against the wall and crossed his arms. At almost seventy-three, the duke was still tall and handsome, his salt-and-pepper hair white at the temples. Despite the age difference between him and his heir—there were forty-five years between them—it was apparent William was his son. The two shared the same dark blue eyes, dark slashes for eyebrows, aquiline noses and thin lips that could frown their displeasure just as easily as they displayed wide smiles when they were amused.

Of late, the duke hadn't smiled much. At twenty-eight, his son still hadn't taken a wife much less courted anyone, and his daughter, only a year younger, hadn't had a suitor in two years. Given the cur had been a fortune hunter, James had been glad when Rose refused the bounder's offer.

I'm not an idiot, Father, she had said when she paid witness to his obvious relief at hearing the news she hadn't accepted his proposal.

I never thought you were, he had replied. Despite his response, he was never sure if Rose believed him.

His two older daughters, both illegitimate, had been of the same mind as Rose. Neither Diana nor Daisy claimed a wish to marry when they were younger, and yet they were both wed to aristocrats and had children of their own.

Although he had wished to wed their mother—he had been much younger and not as well versed in the expectations of a duke back then—Lily Albright had refused his offer with the explanation that he needed to marry the daughter of a duke, a marquess, or an earl.

By the time he finally married Helen Harrington, one of the three surviving daughters of the fifth Earl of Mayfield, the betting book at White's was filled with wagers having to do with if or when his duchess would give him an heir.

Helen had done her duty a few years after their wedding, bless her heart, and he was a thousand pounds richer from the wagers he had placed. Eighteen months after William's arrival, Rose was born.

James could hardly believe twenty-seven years had passed since he held this third daughter in his hands. She had been so tiny, she hadn't been expected to live. Yet her lungs had defied the naysayers, her nightly wails loud enough to be heard all the way from the nursery down to his master suite on the second floor.

Chuckling at the reminder of how he and Helen would occasionally race up to the nursery to be sure the nurse was seeing to her charge, James discovered his vision had blurred. He blinked several times in an effort to clear away the tears that had formed, stunned to discover a particular memory still had the means to affect him so.

Rose had survived her infancy, grown up to become a beautiful, accomplished and entirely too spoiled young lady, only to have her life upended—literally—by a carriage accident.

Sniffling, he watched as his progeny whirled about the salon in a fairly error-free waltz. Surely this would be the year William and Rose married. If not, he would have to threaten to evict them from Ariley Place. Threaten to cut off their allowances. The thought had him grinning in delight. He would never actually do such a thing, of course, but the expressions they might display upon hearing the threats would be rather entertaining.

When the last strains of the music finished, Helen glanced up from the sheet music and gave him a beseeching look.

Not sure what to do, James applauded. "Bravo. Brava!" he called out as Rose dipped a curtsy and William bowed.

"Well, I didn't step on your toes," William stated proudly.

"I didn't fall down," Rose replied, relief sounding in her voice.

"Any decent partner would not let you," her brother stated. "So… don't allow just anyone to sign up for your two waltzes," he warned.

"Whom should I trust to catch me?" she asked as they joined their father by the door.

"Father, for one," William replied, one of his dark brows arching.

Rose gave him a quelling glance and turned her attention to the duke. "Who will keep me from falling to the floor during the waltz if my leg decides to go out from beneath me?" she asked.

James winced, momentarily reminded that his oldest daughter, Daisy, also limped on occasion. But her leg injury had been due to a bullet wound she suffered whilst employed as a spy of the Foreign Office. She had been in Belgium at the time, during England's wars with France.

"Well, I'm not sure if you can trust him, but I learned earlier today that the heir to the Ottoman Empire has come to London for the Season," James said, as if he was sharing a secret. "He's the Dowager Duchess of Chichester's stepson, and he's being hosted by the Bennett-Joneses over at Bostwick House. It seems he wishes to attend all the entertainments."

William furrowed his brows and was about to respond, but his sister beat him to it.

"To what end?" Rose asked at the same moment her mother joined them at the door.

"I've not yet learned the answer to that question," James stated.

"Come. Let's move this conversation to the

parlor," Helen stated. "Where I can fill you in on what *I've* learned on the matter." She waved to a footman who hurried over and nodded when she gave him instructions in a quiet voice. The servant headed down the corridor in front of them, his long legs covering the distance to the butler's pantry in only a few strides.

William's eyes widened. "Is Bostwick's heir back in town?" he asked.

"He is," James acknowledged, turning toward the stairs to lead the family to the first floor.

"Bennett-Jones has been gone for…"

"Three years," Rose stated as she walked alongside her brother, a *huff* sounding at the end of her comment. She had been about to add, "two months and ten days," but she didn't want her brother knowing she had been keeping track. Not that she had, really. But the anniversary of David's and Lord James' departure from England had marked a pivotal moment in not only their lives, but hers.

That was the day she realized Lord James wasn't interested in marrying an English girl—even a duke's daughter—and the first day she thought herself on the shelf.

It had also been the last day she felt hope for a possible future with someone she had known her entire life.

The first day she had given up her guise as a proper young English miss and begun behaving as a spoiled rotten lady. She was a duke's daughter, after all, entitled to do what she pleased.

That had been a year *before* her accident. A comeuppance of sorts, she had begun to believe. A means to remind her that even if she was a duke's daughter, she was still a woman in a man's world and subject to the same rules those of lesser birth had to follow.

Arching a brow, William aimed an expression of shock at his sister. "Tell me how you *really* feel about David Bennett-Jones," he said sarcastically.

Rose huffed again. "I didn't mean it like that," she claimed. "It's just that when he left with Lord James, they were going on their Grand Tour. They were only supposed to be gone for two years."

"Lord James couldn't help it if he fell in love with a sultan's daughter," Helen said, her gaze darting to her husband, as if she wanted him to provide assistance in thwarting their daughter's complaint.

"Bennett-Jones was given an excellent opportunity," James stated, immediately understanding his wife's unspoken plea. "To oversee the placement of decorative arts for several buildings in the Empire... it's not an assignment he could have turned down," he added, hoping his claim was convincing. "In doing so, he has helped keep England in good graces with the sultan."

In reality, he would have loved the opportunity to do something similar back when he was David's age. Instead, he had been hopelessly in love with a courtesan and already the father of two young girls. If he'd had to do it over again, he wasn't sure he would choose domesticity over adventure.

A sense of guilt swept through him at the thought of what life would have been like if he hadn't fallen in love with the illegitimate daughter of a baron. If Daisy and Diana hadn't been born.

Daisy was now the Baroness Streater, Diana the Countess of Aimsley. They were accomplished matrons, mothers to their husband's heirs.

Entirely the opposite of Rose in so many respects.

Had he been the reason Rose had developed thorns as she aged? Or had his wife been too lenient with her? Rose was Helen's only daughter, born to her far later than most aristocratic women's children.

Deciding he best leave the past in the past, James listened to the conversation taking place as they made it to the top of the stairs and the first floor.

"Well, I hope David won't be too shocked to learn his first choice for a wife didn't wait for him," Rose stated as they entered the parlor.

A maid was setting a plate of cakes and biscuits on the low table in front of the settee, and the butler followed them into the parlor with a tea set on a silver salver.

William immediately helped himself to a biscuit and moved to the fireplace mantel, casually leaning against it as he crossed one foot over the other. "Oh, I think David knew Lady Grace wasn't going to wait for him," he said before biting into the lemon confection. "Besides... marrying her would have been like he was marrying a... a first cousin, I suppose, given their mothers are such good friends."

Rose furrowed a brow, but she joined her mother to assist with the tea service.

"I can't imagine why a sultan's son would wish to attend a Season in London," James said as he settled into an upholstered chair near the fireplace. "They don't usually even take wives unless there's no chance they'll inherit the sultanate."

Helen's eyes widened, and she paused while pouring a cup of tea. "Why, of course they do, darling. The Duchess of Chichester is married to a sultan." Her gaze darted to her husband. "To the father of this young man, is she not?"

"Ziyaeddin the First, yes," James replied, surprised she had sorted the relationship on her own.

The duchess finished pouring the tea and set the cup aside for Rose to add the milk and sugar. "Besides, if sultans didn't take wives, then how do they expect to have any legitimate heirs?" she added.

The duke displayed a grimace, realizing his response might send Helen into a state of vapors. "Sultans have *harems*, my sweet. Their concubines are the mothers of their children." He didn't add that most children of a sultan were illegitimate.

He knew about Charlotte Wainwright, of course, but he also knew that the circumstance of her marriage to Sultan Ziyaeddin I of the Ottoman Empire was rather unique. Having enjoyed the company of several women in his younger years, and now having grown very fond of his duchess after nearly thirty years of marriage, James could appreciate a man's desire to choose just one woman with whom to spend the rest of his life.

He was pulled from his brief reverie when he noticed Rose's expression of consternation.

After so many years of watching her friends marry and have children, he knew she was becoming desperate, even if she didn't put voice to her frustration. "A sultan chooses his heir, and it's not always by the order of a son's birth," James added, hoping their conversation could move to the young men who might have waited until they were older to take a wife.

Surely there was a more mature young man who could overlook his daughter's limp and occasional tart remarks, and grow to love her. Why, Lady Victoria, the Duke of Somerset's daughter, had finally married even though she had a crushed foot. Although her husband, Thomas Grandby, didn't have a title, his investments had made him rich, and these days, a fortune was probably more important than a title when it came to marriage.

"If they don't take a wife, then why ever has his heir come to London?" Rose asked as she offered a cup of tea to her father.

"Lady Bostwick says he attended Cambridge University and wished to return to England for a time," Helen explained, happy to finally say what she knew about the matter. "He's apparently been involved in some sort of important construction projects for the empire and has earned some time off."

"He was... *working?*" Rose asked in confusion, the last word said with a good deal of derision.

James chuckled. "What is it you think your brother has been doing these past few years?"

Rose opened her mouth to respond but turned her gaze on William. "Not working, surely," she said with a grin. Her eyes rounded as a tufted pillow sailed past her head in a blur, the gold tassels surrounding the edges splaying out as the silk pillow spun in the air.

"Waverley!" their mother scolded, her eyes rounded in horror.

"Apologies, Mother," the heir said as he dipped his head. His immediate attention had gone to his father, curious as to how he would respond to seeing such an immature act on his part. He was twenty-eight and far too old to be starting pillow fights in the parlor, despite his annoyance with his younger sibling. But the duke's gaze was obviously on his mind's eye, for his father didn't react at all. "I should have known better than to take offense at hearing her opinion."

Handing a cup of tea to her son, Helen furrowed her brows. Once all blonde, they were now silver gray, as was most of her own hair. The wig she wore now was closer in color to what her hair had been when William was a young boy, the ornate style much the same. "Your sister is unaware of what it takes to run a dukedom," she stated. "An oversight in her education I shall be sure to correct on the morrow."

"It's all right, Mother," William said. "She had no reason to know."

"She does if she's ever to become a titled man's wife," she whispered.

Willam almost repeated his mother's last words. For years, it had been assumed Rose would marry a duke's son. The son of a marquess at the very least. Now it sounded as if any aristocrat would do. "Understood," he replied, not sure what else he could say.

"You needn't speak about me in whispers," Rose said. "I am well aware of my diminished appeal, and I have accepted my lot in life. If I'm to be a spinster, then so be it. But know this, *brother*," she added with a fierce expression. "You had better start your nursery in the next year, for I have every intention of being an exceptionally doting aunt. The longer you wait to start your nursery, the more spoiled I'll ensure your children are."

With that, Rose took her leave of the parlor, managing to do so without limping. The three sets of eyes following her departure widened before William and Helen turned theirs to the duke.

His expression was impassive for a moment before he said, "Oh, Waverley. Now you've gone and done it," he warned.

"Done what?" his son asked in alarm.

"Your babes are going to be the most spoiled rotten children in all of London. More so than your sister." His impassive expression changed to one of mirth, and he laughed heartily for several seconds.

He glanced up at the mantel clock and took note of the time. In fifteen minutes, he would make his excuses and pay a visit to his daughter's room. Having the experience of raising two older daughters gave him far more insight into the matter of dealing with Rose than his duchess possessed.

Something was wrong with Rose, and he wanted to discover what it was before dinner.

CHAPTER 6
MAKING A LIST

*M*eanwhile, in the study at Bostwick House

"Am I in some sort of trouble?" Adeline asked as she made her way into her father's study, pausing when she was far enough into the oak-paneled room so George could close the door. The Aubusson carpeting seemed to swallow the sounds of the household beyond the door.

"Of course not," her father replied as he made his way to stand behind his desk. He motioned for her to take the chair in front. "I merely wished to learn what happened yesterday."

Adeline blinked. "Yesterday?" she repeated as she sat down.

"At the garden party."

Relief settled over his daughter as George settled himself into his brown leather chair and leaned back. Adeline was about to chide him—he loved hearing the latest *on-dit*—but she knew if she accused him of being a gossip monger, he would merely pretend it was information that could benefit him in Parliament.

There were times she wondered if he secretly wished to be a matchmaker. He seemed most interested in learning who was courting whom before he would make mention of who he thought might be a better match. "The weather was fine, so it was well-attended," she said with a shrug. "Grandmother was most pleased."

George simply stared at her. When she didn't say more, he said, "Go on."

Adeline huffed. "No one announced any betrothals, if that's what you're asking," she said. "It's too soon."

Grimacing, George sat up straight. "Were your friends there?"

She shrugged. "Most of them. Rose, of course," she said, referring to the daughter of the Duke of Ariley. "Lily..." She paused for a moment after mentioning the oldest daughter of Baron Theodore Streater and his wife, Daisy. "Oh, and Lucy Turnbridge and Hope Batey." Lucy was the oldest daughter of the Earl of Fennington, and Hope was the youngest daughter of Viscount Lancaster.

When her father continued to stare at her, she sighed. "Helen and Eva haven't yet returned to the capitol," she said, deciding the cousins were the reason he asked. "They're due back sometime soon."

Helen Tennison, the only daughter of Harold and Stella, Earl and Countess of Everly, was a few years older than Adeline and had made her come-out in 1839. Despite having a half-Greek mother and a dark-haired father, her blonde hair, blue eyes, and facial features made her appear as if she could be her Aunt Evangeline's daughter.

Helen's cousin Eva, a proud bluestocking, was the daughter of Jeffrey and Evangeline Tennison Sommers, Baron and Baroness Sommers. Fair of skin, she took after her father with her dark brown hair, and although she was four years younger than her brother, Charles, she behaved as if she was far older.

Deciding they couldn't abide another Christmas in London, the cousins had spent the winter at the Tennison country estate in Shropshire with two trunks of novels they had managed to procure from the Temple of the Muses before the huge bookshop burned down in 1841.

"Is either one of them being courted by anyone?" George asked.

Adeline stiffened in her chair. "Not that I'm aware," she replied. Her eyes rounded when she realized why he was asking. "Oh, Father, what are you conjuring now?" she asked in alarm.

Although she was of an age to marry, anyone she might have hoped to wed had already married, leaving mostly older men who were delaying their marriages until they were closer to thirty years of age. With her unmarried brother home from the Ottoman Empire, she realized her father's queries had more to do with David than they did with her.

George gave a start. "Nothing," he claimed. "Nothing at all. I just... I hadn't seen them of late and wondered is all."

Not convinced, Adeline considered what to say of her other unmarried friends. Those she frequently hosted in her salon and with whom she shared the spaces next to the potted palms at balls. The areas in which could be found the wallflowers.

"If you must know, no one is courting Lady Rose," she stated. "Ever since the accident..." She left the comment hanging. Although Rose and her mother had survived when the duke's traveling coach was upended when a wheel broke, Rose's leg had suffered a break, and despite a doctor seeing to it later that day, it apparently hadn't healed correctly.

Straightening in his chair, George leaned his elbows on the edge of his desk. "She'll be on the shelf soon," he murmured. "How old is she?"

"She's... six-and-twenty, I think," Adeline remarked, "and I rather doubt her father is going to allow her to wed anyone less than an earl." Given the young lady was sometimes forced to walk with a wooden crutch or be pushed about in a wheeled chair, Adeline had the impression Rose had given up on the idea of ever being married. "Which means she'll be holding off until..." Adeline rolled her eyes and waited while her father furrowed his brows.

"What do you know?" he asked in alarm.

"You've obviously not seen the list," she said.

George's eyes darted sideways. "The list?" he repeated.

"Yes. The list of eligible sons of aristocrats who are known to us and who are still bachelors but of an age to marry."

George blinked, wondering if perhaps his wife had seen to compiling such a collection. If so, was it the same list the Duke of Ariley had alluded to when he'd come to the club the week before? "How... how many men are on this list?" he asked.

"Seventeen, I think," Adeline replied. "Young men born between eighteen-sixteen and eighteen-twenty who have returned from their Grand Tours and are still unmarried."

"That's rather specific," George murmured, thinking it sounded exactly like the list the Duke of Ariley mentioned.

"But it also includes Rose's brother, Waverley, so if we

take him out and include only those who have already inherited or who are due to inherit earldoms, marquessates, or dukedoms, we're down to..." She held out a hand and began counting with her fingers. "Eight. Maybe nine."

Appearing rather impressed, George settled back in his chair and crossed his arms. "Any of them of interest to you?" he hedged.

"Me?" she squeaked. "I thought we were talking about Lady Rose."

"Wouldn't you say you're after the same qualities in a potential husband?"

She inhaled softly, about to admit she didn't much care about titles. The time she spent at her mother's charity had opened her eyes to the plight of men whose lives had been upended by war or by accidents. Although her father was well aware of them—he'd been her mother's largest contributor to *Finding Work for the Wounded* since its inception—he didn't seem amenable to the idea of Adeline marrying one of them.

"You can speak freely," he said in a quiet voice.

Adeline allowed a shrug. "So many on the list are good friends, it would be like marrying my brother."

"Such as?" he prompted.

She scoffed. "I cannot imagine marrying William Wellingham," she said, referring to the heir to the Trenton earldom. "Or Robert Roderick." He was the spare heir to the Reading marquessate, and his older brother, Raymond, had married one of her best friends the year before. "Or Duncan or David Fitzwilliam." Duncan was the oldest of the twins and was due to inherit the Norwick earldom. "I cannot even tell those two apart," she added with a wince. "And then there is George Merriweather."

"Middleton's heir?" her father asked. At her nod, he said, "Good family. Who else?"

"The rest either don't live here in London, or I don't know them well enough to consider marriage to them."

Arching a brow, George leaned his elbows on the desk. "Who are the others on this list? The ones in town who are not future earls or marquesses or dukes?" He paused a moment. "And who have returned from their Grand Tours."

Sliding her hand into a pocket, Adeline pulled out a folded parchment that looked as if it had been crumpled and retrieved from a wastebasket. She peeled apart the edges and winced at hearing her father's chuckle.

"When you said there was a list, I didn't realize you carried it with you," he teased.

She huffed. "My fellow wallflowers helped compile it," she said as she felt her face flush with color.

"Go on," George encouraged. "I'd like to hear who made the cut."

She gave him a quelling glance. "This isn't in any sort of order," she said. "And just so we're clear, I haven't settled on any of them."

George sobered. "Understood," he said. "Go on."

Adeline inhaled and began reading. "Octavius Whitney—"

"Grandson of a duke," George murmured as he nodded his approval.

"Andrew Burroughs—"

"Grandson of a duke," George repeated again, continuing to nod.

"Mark Cunningham—"

"Future viscount," her father whispered. "And he'll be rich as Croesus, given his father's investments."

"Jasper Truscott—"

George furrowed his brows. "Sir Donald's son?" he whispered. "I wonder if he's taken up spy craft like his parents?"

Adeline shrugged, not sure what her father meant. "Jasper is always very pleasant when we dance, but I do get the impression he's hiding something," she said. She glanced back at the list. "Mark Fitzsimmons—"

"Ooh," her father said.

Adeline reacted with a start. "What is it?"

"He's a viscount now," George said, referring to Matthew Fitzsimmons' only son. The head of the Foreign Office, Matthew had died in 1841 leaving a bereft widow and a son who was known for his serious nature and sterling reputation.

"Chamberlain has absolutely no sense of humor," Adeline complained, referring to the young viscount.

"Perhaps he merely needs someone to help him develop one," George suggested. Realizing Adeline didn't wish to be that person, he quickly added, "Who else?"

"Theodore Streater, which would be like marrying my own brother," she complained. Her father's best friend was Baron Theodore Streater, and he had been her mother's first client.

"Understood," her father replied. "Who else?"

"Marcus Henley."

George winced. "Isn't he off digging in the dirt with his father?"he asked.

"He is an archaeologist, yes," Adeline replied. "Lord James has joined his dig," she added. "With his wife, the..." Her eyes rounded. "Our guest's sister," she finished, remembering what her mother had read to her from one of Charlotte's letters about the situation.

"Our guest's *twin* sister," George murmured. "Apparently Sevinc Sultana is very interested in archaeology and stays with Lord James on his expeditions."

"I think they've only been to London once since their wedding," Adeline remarked.

"If you wed Marcus Henley, you'd essentially be a widow," George said on a sigh. "Unless you joined him on his expeditions."

Adeline angled her head to one side. "When I travel, I think I would prefer not stopping all the time to discover what's beneath my feet," she admitted.

"Who else?" he asked when she didn't offer another name.

"A couple of sons of dukes who don't live in town. Then there is Thomas Grayson—"

"Marquess of Billingsley," George said with appreciation.

"—who I think has his eye on Rose, but I'm not sure, and Marcus Higgins."

"Greenley's heir," her father stated. "Who *doesn't* live here in town," he added with a wince.

"Exactly."

George's gaze went to the clock on the fireplace mantel. "I need to go up and dress for dinner. Do be sure to join us in the parlor before we go down. I want to introduce you to the sultan's son," he said.

Adeline pretended boredom. "Is he... a proud sort?" she asked, wincing at how prickly she sounded.

Her father shook his head. "Not a bit," he replied. "In fact, he's almost too humble," he added. "Do be nice. He'll be our guest for the entire Season."

Inhaling sharply, Adeline said, "I'm always nice," she replied on a huff.

"No pretending to be a wallflower."

"But I am," she countered, her hands going to her hips.

George moved around the desk and wrapped an arm around her shoulders. "I think it's admirable that you spend your time at balls with the less fortunate girls," he said, sure she did so because Lady Rose hadn't been able to dance given her leg, "but it may be time to allow yourself to shine at this Season's events," he gently chided. "Remember, you are Elizabeth Carlington's daughter."

Adeline's eyes widened at hearing her father's comment. "What's *that* supposed to mean?" she asked in alarm.

Chuckling softly, George said, "Ask your mother." He leaned over and kissed her forehead before taking his leave of the study.

Watching him go, Adeline crossed her arms and let out a huff. She had thought the way she spoke of the unmarried men would have her father understanding she had no desire to marry any of them—or at all—and now she wondered how she was going to convince him she would prefer to simply run her mother's charity and be a spinster.

Well, there was an entire Season in which to prove her point, she supposed. She trudged up the stairs to change for dinner.

CHAPTER 7
A DUKE PROVIDES A SHOULDER

*M*eanwhile, *at Ariley Place*

When the knock came at her bedchamber door, Rose was sure it was her mother. She glanced at the clock, realizing exactly fifteen minutes had passed since her abrupt departure from the parlor.

Fifteen minutes of tears was to be her limit, it seemed. She hadn't cried like this since the accident. Hadn't dampened this many hankies since seeing the ugly scar on her leg when the physician removed the bandages. Even now, she winced every time she removed her stockings at night.

It will fade over time, she remembered the doctor saying the following week, as if it was no worse than a scratch.

If she'd been a giant, maybe.

What man would want a wife with such a hideous scar? At least she could hide it beneath stockings.

The knock came again, and before she could muster the energy to call out, "Go away," the door opened to reveal the duke.

"Father," she whispered in surprise.

"Last I checked I still was," James said with a grimace. "Seems you took exception to something your brother said?"

From the manner of his query, Rose wondered if he hadn't seen the decorative pillow fly through the air in all its golden glory. If he hadn't heard what was said between William and their mother. He'd been sitting far closer to them than she had been, but she had also noticed that James Burroughs, Duke of Ariley, had been noticeably preoccupied during their time in the parlor. More interested in something in his mind's eye.

"Something *Mother* said, actually," she replied as she waved him into the room. She hiccuped as he settled a hip on the edge of her bed. "At least, what I think she said."

"The pillow didn't hit you," James stated.

She winced. So he *had* seen the flying pillow. "No, but... it wasn't like Waverley to do such a thing."

"It wasn't like you to tease him about his duties."

Rose inhaled softly. "Duties?" she repeated after a sob briefly robbed her of breath.

"Duties, yes," her father said. "Since you seem to not have noticed, probably because your nose is too far up in the air—"

"Father!" she started to say in protest. The duke's raised hand had her clamping her mouth shut.

"—please allow me to inform you that I have essentially relinquished my ducal responsibilities to your brother. Several years ago now. He's even accepted a writ of acceleration and will take a seat in Parliament starting tomorrow," he explained.

"You're giving up your title?" she asked in surprise.

"Not giving it up. I couldn't if I wanted to. Just turning over the *work*," he said. "Despite what you think, it is work to run a dukedom with as much land and as many buildings as the Ariley dukedom owns." When he realized he had her attention, he continued. "There are reports that must be read and acted upon, invoices to pay, letters to write, ledgers to keep, and—"

"But you have a man of business to do all that," she argued.

"Ah. So you *have* been paying attention," James remarked. "Well, my man of business sees to the *properties* here in town," he explained. "I have several foremen who oversee the farms, too, but they, like the man of business, must be managed. Investments must be tracked. The stables, the animals, the equipment... yes, I own it all. But that means I am responsible for it, and it is work to be sure it's all sorted," he went on. "Just as it is your mother's responsibility to see to all the houses and the staffs of servants, to manage the menus and the entertainments. To be my hostess..." He allowed the sentence to trail off, unsure of what else his wife had been managing in the name of the Ariley dukedom. Unless she preceded him in death, he would probably never know the rest of what she did.

Rose sucked in a breath as another sob caused her to hiccup. "I suppose I owe him an apology."

"Mmmm, probably not," James said with a grin. At her look of shock, he said, "There was the flying golden pillow. I think you're even."

Displaying a wan grin, Rose sighed. "If I don't marry—"

"You *will* marry," James stated.

Rose's eyes widened. "Have you heard something?" she asked, not meaning to sound so desperate.

Caught off-guard, James dipped his head. "No. Not directly," he admitted. "However, there are a number of young men who haven't yet succumbed to marrying before their twenty-eighth birthdays," he reminded her. "Most will be at the ball tomorrow night."

Twenty-eight.

The number reminded Rose that most young men in the aristocracy waited until sometime between their twenty-eighth and thirtieth birthdays to take a wife. That gave them time to sow their wild oats, drive coach-and-fours at break-neck speeds on the road to Richmond, and drink and gamble until the wee hours at their clubs. The age also allowed those who returned from their Grand Tours to have some time to carouse and become reacquainted with their fellow heirs.

A few years ago, there had been a spate of marriages among her friends. The men weren't anywhere close to twenty-eight. Once the first one married, it was as if a game of marriage dominos had been set in motion, and before she knew it, seven of her male friends had fallen and said their vows, many of them to friends of hers.

That had been in the spring of 1839.

Five years ago.

There were babies now, their mothers young matrons who were now part of a completely different social group. Although she desperately wished to feel welcome when she was invited, Rose never felt comfortable among those who spent the time discussing their children and husbands.

What could she contribute to such a discussion?

"Do you have someone in mind you'd like as a husband?" her father asked in a quiet voice.

Rose gave a start. "The three I had in mind have all married," she replied before she sniffled.

James winced. "Do you have someone *else* in mind? I could… make some inquiries—"

"Don't you dare!" she replied, shocked he would use his title to influence a potential suitor.

"I am a duke. I have some clout. I should hope I could use it for something as simple as finding you a suitable suitor," he reasoned. "Not that it's… *simple*," he quickly added, once again wincing at how his comment must have sounded. "You have the reputation of a rose."

Rose crossed her arms and stared at him in annoyance, the effect momentarily ruined when she hiccuped. "What's *that* supposed to mean?"

Unable to hide his sudden mirth, James was too late in lifting a hand to cover his mouth. "Apologies, but you looked exactly like your mother just then," he said, his eyes crinkling in delight. "The night I first met her."

Curious, Rose uncrossed her arms and regarded her father with furrowed brows. "When was that?"

James inhaled to answer and raised a finger to scratch his brow. "Let's see. Lily was still alive, but not many knew we were essentially living together. I kept her in the townhouse in Green Street, you see. Daisy was a toddler, and Lily was already expecting Diana."

Rose sat very still as he spoke, fascinated he could remember details from what had to be fifty years ago. She made sure to keep very quiet as he continued with his recollection. "I was introduced to Helen at a ball, as I recall. She was betrothed to some nincompoop, and I might have said something to that effect—"

"Father!" Rose scolded, even as her face lit up in delight.

He chuckled. "I think I must have known back then we would eventually end up together. I teased her mercilessly. And then she challenged me to do better."

Rose blinked. "Better?" she repeated. "Do better at what?"

James lifted his gaze to hers and made an odd sound. "Just... better." He cleared his throat. "It was the first time in my life someone called me out for my poor behavior," he said quietly. He paused a long time before he added, "My assessment was correct, though. Helen's first betrothed was a nincompoop—"

"Father," Rose whispered, but she dared not say more. She had never heard her father speak of the time before he had married Lady Helen Harrington.

"A second son who was an officer in the British Army. He was on the Continent... probably for two decades," he murmured.

"Did he ever marry Mother?" Rose asked in wonder.

James made a rude sound in his throat. "Never. He was shot and died of his injuries at Quatre Bas." He allowed a huff. "I proposed a month later."

"Father!"

"Oh, don't 'father' me," he said as he waggled a crooked finger. "By then, I had her convinced *I* was the better choice. Even if I was old."

"You couldn't have been *that* old," Rose countered.

"I was over forty, but I had a good role model for a late marriage."

"What do you mean?"

"More like *who*. Milton Grandby, Earl of Torrington," he replied with a huge grin. "He didn't marry until he was six-and-forty. Waited for the woman he had loved since he was a young boy to become a widow, and he still managed to sire twins."

It was Rose's turn to wince. William Grandby, heir to the Torrington earldom, was one of the young men she had hoped might one day propose to her. Instead, he had fallen for the daughter of the Earl of Trenton.

To see them now, Rose wondered how she had ever

imagined herself married to William Grandby. He was so beholden to his Anne, Rose doubted she would have been held in such high regard.

As for William's twin sister, Angelica, she was enjoying her life with Sir Benjamin Fulton, an astronomer and the eventual Earl of Wadsworth. They spent their nights stargazing in his observatory, which meant they must have been doing their lovemaking during the days, because Angelica was expecting her third babe any day.

"I cannot imagine waiting to have babies until I'm well past thirty," Rose murmured.

James dipped his head. "I suppose not." He was quiet for a moment before he said. "Tomorrow night, at the Weatherstones'..." He paused, as if he was struggling to sort how to say what he wanted to say.

"Yes?"

"I know you like standing with the wallflowers—"

"Since I have become one," she interrupted.

"Yes, well, could you maybe mingle a bit more? Avoid spending so much time with the potted palms? I have this fear that one will take you off into the gardens, wrap his fronds around you, and have his way with you."

Rose stared at her father. "A potted palm?" she repeated in alarm.

"I wasn't being serious. At least, not that last part, but what I said before. About spending time with the wallflowers? You're far too beautiful to cast your lot with them."

"Father," she scolded. "Your words imply my friends are not. Their only fault is they are shy or their fathers are mere viscounts or barons."

The duke emitted a sound of disbelief. "Are you including Miss Adeline in your assessment?"

Rose opened her mouth to respond but instead sighed.

"Why *do* you two consort with those who prefer the company of potted palms?" he asked, his manner suspicious.

As if she knew she would be caught in a lie if she told him anything other than the truth, Rose said, "Since the accident, I have come to understand their lot in life. That men will only ask us to dance if they are shamed into it or if they can find no other partners. We are their last resort."

James grimaced. "Is that true for Miss Adeline as well?"

Rose shook her head. "She has been learning much about the unfortunate while she works at Lady Bostwick's charity. Besides the wounded in search of employment, there are those who are in search of wives."

"And why does that have her communing with the wallflowers?"

Blinking, Rose straightened on the bed. "You don't understand?"

He shook his head.

"Adeline understands she is fortunate. That she will never be in such dire straights as to require the help of a charity to make her living or to find her a willing husband."

"I hope you understand that, too," he said, his frown more apparent.

"I do, which is why I feel sympathy for them. As does Addy," Rose explained. "I suppose I was vain enough once to believe my presence among them would help draw more men to our side of the ballroom. To ensure they were asked to dance as often as I was."

"You're saying you're no longer vain?" he asked gently.

She huffed. "Certainly not since the accident. I no longer attract the young men as I once did," she murmured. "Adeline still does, but I don't think she cares if she marries or not."

This last had James giving a start. "Bostwick hasn't said she intends to be a spinster," he remarked.

"Would he tell you such a thing if he knew?"

Her father dipped his head. "Touché," he whispered, briefly reminded of how many fencing matches he had lost to Bostwick over the years. After a moment, he said, "I suppose she intends to run her mother's charities at some point." When Rose nodded, he said, "Well, Lady Bostwick has proven she can be a viscountess *and* run two charities. She's been doing so since before her oldest son was born."

At the mention of David Bennett-Jones, Rose hiccuped. When her father's gaze settled on her, he arched a brow. "The sudden color in your cheeks would suggest you're blushing," he said in a low voice.

Her eyes widening, she said, "I cannot imagine why I would be."

James regarded her for a moment before he sighed. "No, I don't suppose you can."

"What did you mean when you said I had the reputation of a rose?" she asked.

Dipping his head a moment, he seemed to struggle with how to respond. "Every rose has its thorns, and yours have become rather barbed these past few years."

"What?"

"You are your mother's only daughter, but you are my third and, unfortunately, you are the most spoiled." He watched as her eyes rounded and her mouth dropped open in shock. "There isn't a man in all of London who wishes to wed a spoiled rotten woman," he claimed. "They want someone they can spoil."

Rose looked as if she was about to burst into tears once again as he stood. He leaned over to kiss her on the top of her head. "I will see you at dinner, daughter. You'll want to get a good night's sleep tonight. Tomorrow will be a long day, with lots of dancing," he added. "And champagne." He gave a nod and then took his leave of her bedchamber.

Rose watched him go, all the while wondering how it was she could feel so heartened that he had spent so much time with her, be so shocked by his assessment of her, and then feel such relief upon his departure.

CHAPTER 8
AN INTRODUCTION IN THE PARLOR

A half-hour later, in the parlor of Bostwick House

Peeking into the parlor, David was surprised to discover only a footman occupied the room. He recognized the servant, only the second he had seen since his arrival that afternoon. "Watkins," he said as he made his way to the fireplace.

"Sir," the older footman replied with a grin. "It's good to see you back at Bostwick House. Coffee?"

"Thank you, and yes." David's gaze swept the rest of the parlor. "I see mother has redecorated," he commented, his attention on the carpet below his shoes. At one time, all the carpets in Bostwick House were from Aubusson's manufactory, but the pattern on this one suggested it had come from somewhere far away. "Turkish?" he guessed as he tapped his foot.

"Indeed, sir. She had it replaced last year, when she thought you and your guest would be here then."

Guilt had David sobering. "Better late than never, I suppose," he murmured, taking the cup of coffee from Watkins.

"If I might be so bold as to suggest you mention the fringe and tassels on the settee, sir? Her ladyship was quite fortunate to secure the very best craftsmanship for that item," the footman said in a hoarse whisper.

David's attention went to the piece of furniture. Having spent his last few years in plush Ottoman palaces featuring all manner of fringe and tassels, velvets and silks, he wouldn't have noticed the trimmings in the parlor. "I appreciate the heads-up," he said. "Anything else I should make mention of?" he asked, his gaze darting about as if he expected to find some exquisite antique or a decorative item crafted by an artist.

His perusal stopped at the painting over the mantel, and he furrowed his brows. "Was that done by Lady Plymouth?" he asked, referring to Samantha Fitzsimmons Range, Marchioness of Plymouth. "Lord Chamberlain's niece?" he added, remembering he had learned of the relationship at some point during his boyhood.

"Lord Chamberlain's cousin, I think you mean," Watkins replied. "The elder Chamberlain died shortly after you left on your Grand Tour," he explained.

"Ah, I'd quite forgotten," David said with a wince.

"Lord Bostwick commissioned the painting for Lady Bostwick so it was ready when the rest of the redecoration was complete," Watkins explained.

David studied the landscape for a time before a grin split his face. He recognized the scene from somewhere in the Lake District, sure his father had asked for it based on where he had taken Elizabeth for their wedding trip. "I can imagine how she showed her appreciation," he murmured as he rolled his eyes.

When Watkins didn't reply, David turned to find the man's face bright red. He chuckled, deciding the servant had no doubt paid witness to his mother kissing his father. No doubt every servant in the household had.

When he noticed the footman's attention had diverted to the door, David turned to see the subjects of their conversation entering the parlor. They were engaged in an animated discussion about something that had happened at the garden party the day before. His father let out a guffaw.

"That will teach him not to take liberties with the young ladies," George said, accepting the cup of coffee Watkins offered.

"Take note, son. Your grandmother's gardens are not to be the setting for your amorous liaisons," Elizabeth said with a titter.

"Do I dare ask who got caught?" David queried, helping himself to some walnuts.

George moved to stand next to the fireplace mantel and positioned himself so he could see both his wife and anyone else who might come into the parlor. "One of Norwick's twins. Your mother is not sure which one," he replied.

Although he was curious as to which twin might have been caught kissing someone in his grandmother's garden—he couldn't recall that either one of them were old enough to show much interest in young ladies when he was last in London—David wanted to be sure to comment on the redecorating before their guest arrived. "I like what you've done with the parlor, Mother."

Elizabeth's eyes widened. "Why, I'd quite forgot. You haven't been here since I had it redone," she replied happily. She helped herself to a plate of walnuts and moved to one of the chairs near the fireplace. "You don't think the apricot is too light with this olive green?"

About to reply, David caught his father's quick shake

of his head, immediately understanding he was on treacherous ground. "I like it better than the peach, and..." He paused when he saw his father point to a bouquet of daffodils on a side table. "Jonquil would have been too bright," he finished, hoping he understood his father's pantomime.

"My thoughts exactly."

"The tassels and fringe are exquisite, as is this Turkish carpeting. It must have cost Father a fortune." His gaze briefly darted to the viscount, who merely shrugged. Perhaps the carpet had been acquired with the help of Sultana Charlotte.

"Your sister was of an entirely different opinion, of course," his mother murmured. "Why isn't she here?"

George cleared his throat. "My fault. I kept her in the study far longer than I should have."

Elizabeth regarded him with worry. "Did she do something wrong?"

Shaking his head, George said, "I merely wished to be apprised of the eligible bachelors and, uh, young ladies of an age to marry this Season," he said, his gaze going to his son.

"Am I to understand the pickings are slim?" David asked before he popped a walnut into his mouth.

"For you... probably not," Elizabeth remarked proudly.

"What's that supposed to mean?" he countered as he straightened.

"Well, it's not as if there is a plethora of princesses and duke's daughters of an age to marry," she said at the very moment Ertuğrul appeared on the threshold. Next to him stood Adeline, looking as if she had already made the emir's acquaintance.

"Your Eminence," Elizabeth said as she stood. "Do

come join us," she said as she waved a gloved hand to the settee.

"Ertuğrul, please, my lady," he stated as he bowed.

"Have you two met?" George asked as he made his way to the şehzade and offered his hand. The sultan's son shook it as he nodded.

A blush colored Adeline's face. "Not formally, of course," she replied. "I found him when I was about to come down the stairs. He was admiring the statue, and I offered to show him the way here."

Realizing she referred to a marble statue of a nearly naked Aphrodite, George struggled to keep an impassive expression on his face. "Well, Ertuğrul, may I present my youngest daughter, Miss Adeline Bennett-Jones?"

Adeline turned and dipped a deep curtsy as Ertuğrul bowed. He reached for her gloved hand, and not expecting he knew of the courtesy, she nearly let out a gasp as he lifted it and brushed his lips over the back of it.

"It's very good to meet you, Miss Bennett-Jones," he said after he had straightened.

Blinking, Adeline said, "And you, of course, Your Eminence."

"Please, call me Ertuğrul," he insisted. "I shouldn't wish there to be formality," he added, struggling with the last word.

"All right," she replied at the same moment Elkins appeared behind them. "Perhaps you'd like a cup of—"

"Dinner is served," the butler stated before he stepped back.

"Thank you, but I will wait until after dinner for coffee," Ertuğrul murmured, his gaze going to his hosts.

Elizabeth and George immediately moved toward the door, but the viscountess slowed a moment. "Oh, dear.

He should go first," she whispered as she considered the order of how they would make their way into the dining room.

"He doesn't know the way, my sweet," George reminded her. In a louder voice, he said, "Ertuğrul, would you mind escorting Adeline? David, you can follow behind."

Ertuğrul regarded Adeline, noting how she had her arm half-lifted. "Will you show me what to do?" he asked as George and Elizabeth passed them, making their way toward the stairs.

About to answer, Adeline instead gripped his coat sleeve and pulled it up until it was level before straightening her hand to rest atop it. "Just follow them," she said.

Recognizing the manner in which his father escorted Charlotte about the palace and in town—at his side rather than her behind him as most couples did in public—Ertuğrul gave a quick glance behind them to discover David waiting for them to move.

"It's not quite like it is at Cambridge," David said by way of encouragement, once they were descending the stairs. "If you knew the way to the dining room, you'd be escorting my mother."

"I would be honored to do so," Ertuğrul replied, *sotto voce*. He couldn't help but notice how Adeline reacted, as if he had said something to offend her. "But I am just as honored to escort your sister," he quickly added.

Adeline glanced over her shoulder, prepared to provide a rebuke should David say something to tease their guest. When her brother gave her an innocent glance, she said, "Thank you, sir."

"It's my pleasure, Miss Bennett-Jones."

The way in which he said the word 'pleasure' nearly

had Adeline missing a step. "Oh, you can call me Adeline," she suggested.

Ertuğrul dared a glance in her direction before he said, "So... you are Sultana Charlotte's goddaughter?"

Adeline inhaled softly. "I am," she replied. "Do you... see her often? Speak with her?"

Grinning at her sudden interest in him, Ertuğrul said, "Nearly every day. My youngest brother and sister as well. I will miss them most while I am here in London," he added.

Her face beaming in delight, Adeline said, "Did you hear that, Mother?"

Elizabeth turned slightly when she had reached the ground floor and said, "Indeed. Ertuğrul has already been a dear and caught me up with news from Charlotte. Perhaps he will do so for you?"

Adeline blinked and dared a glance at their guest.

"I will, of course," he said, ignoring the chuckle that came from behind him.

She would have to add the sultan's son to the list. After only a few minutes in his company, Adeline was sure he would be perfect for Lady Rose.

CHAPTER 9
AN INTENTION IS MADE CLEAR

few minutes later, in the dining room
"So, besides the parlor and the updated plumbing, what have I missed these past few years?" David asked before tucking into his meal. He glanced in Ertuğrul's direction, relieved to see that the future sultan of the Ottoman Empire had opted to use a fork instead of a spoon to eat his dinner. Then he remembered the young man had attended Cambridge in his younger years.

"A couple of bad harvests for most," his father commented. "However, William Gibbs has managed to make a fortune importing guano from Peru."

"Guano?" David repeated, his brows furrowing as he struggled to remember if he'd heard of it before. His eyes suddenly rounded. "Isn't that...?"

"Sun-dried bird droppings, yes," Elizabeth said, directing a footman to see to the next course. "Seems it makes an excellent fertilizer."

"The man has made enough blunt to purchase Tyntesfield in Somerset and to take a wife," George said, referring to a gothic estate near the port of Bristol.

"And he has a magnificent house here in London," Elizabeth said, managing to say it without sounding too jealous.

David kept his attention on his mother as the conversation around the dinner table continued. Although he had only been gone from England a few years—he and James Wainwright had been on their Grand Tour when they took a detour to the sultan's palace on the Aegean and their lives changed overnight—David couldn't help but notice his mother's hair was shot with strands of gray. There were slight lines radiating from the corners of her eyes when she smiled, and he was reminded of how her mother, Adeline, Marchioness of Morganfield, appeared when she was amused.

When his gaze turned to his father, he discovered the viscount hadn't changed in appearance much at all. Although his temples were gray, his hair was still dark. His eyes, a sort of sapphire blue, were directed on Elizabeth.

No change there. The man was hopelessly in love with Elizabeth Carlington Bennett-Jones and had been since the moment he had spied her during a ball in 1815.

"Is it open for touring?" Ertuğrul asked, referring to the house his hostess had mentioned. "I would like it very much to see these houses you speak of."

Elizabeth straightened in her chair. "I rather doubt it, but I can find out for you," she offered. "And even if it's not, you'll see the interiors of plenty of houses during the Season," she promised. "The invitations have already started to arrive. Balls, *soirées, musicales*… and we have a box at the theatre," she added.

"In other words, we shan't have a night free for the next six months," David said dryly as he arched a dark brow in Ertuğrul's direction.

"I'll have to take you two to White's as my guests," George offered. "Your visit has a number of my fellow aristocrats rather curious," he said to the sultan's son.

"I would be honored to meet them," Ertuğrul replied. "But I suppose I should be honest as to the reason for my coming to England."

Elizabeth and George exchanged quick glances before turning their attentions back to their guest. "Oh?" George replied.

"Were you thinking to conquer Great Britain?" Elizabeth asked lightly. "To add it to your empire?"

Ertuğrul's eyes rounded. "Oh, no, my lady. Merely the heart of one of its young ladies," he replied. "You see, besides spending time in your most amazing museums and buildings, I am here to find a wife."

Knowing his friend had made a mistake in announcing his intentions—especially to his mother—David hid his smirk behind a hand. "You may regret having said that," he whispered so only Ertuğrul could hear.

The emir gave David a worried glance. "What have I said wrong?" he asked.

George was quick to respond. "Nothing at all. It's just... you'll find the matrons... the mothers of young ladies... rather overwhelming when it comes to their daughters." He winced, realizing their reactions to the sultan's son might be very different than what it would be for the son of a British aristocrat.

"Overwhelming?" Ertuğrul repeated.

"They'll either hide their daughters behind their skirts or they'll be shoving them in your direction at every turn," George warned.

"My father speaks the truth," David said. "Especially when they learn you're to inherit the Ottoman Empire."

Elizabeth and George exchanged quick glances from opposite ends of the table. "Perhaps we can assemble a list of eligible young ladies," George suggested, his gaze darting to Adeline. Beneath the table, he patted his waistcoat pocket to be sure the list he had hastily assembled was still there. He wasn't sure he remembered every one of the young ladies Adeline had mentioned whilst in his study, but he had a good start. "Help narrow down the choices a bit before you have to meet them all at a ball or two."

"That shouldn't be difficult," Adeline remarked. "Since there are no unwed princesses at this time, that really only leaves the daughters of dukes, I should think," she reasoned. "And the only one of an age to marry who isn't betrothed is Lady Rose." She said this last with a hint of triumph, as if her plan to see to a suitor for her friend was already set in motion.

"Ariley's daughter?" David guessed. From his expression, it was apparent he was confused.

"Yes," Adeline replied happily.

"How is she not already married?" he asked in disbelief. "She's almost as old as me."

About to explain what had happened to Rose, Adeline turned her attention to her plate when her mother provided the response, including all the gory details of the young lady's accident, subsequent limp, and occasional need to use a wheeled chair.

"She's still a duke's daughter," Adeline whispered to no one in particular. "And she's very beautiful," she added, directing her last words to Ertuğrul. His gaze was on his plate, though, his furrowed brows suggesting he was curious as to the food on it.

"Is there something wrong with your cod?" she asked.

The şehzade lifted his gaze to hers. "I merely

wondered what kind of fish it was, and now I have the answer. Thank you," he said.

Adeline blinked. "You're welcome. Do you have this sort of fish in the empire?"

He shook his head. "I don't think so," he replied as he glanced over at David, as if for confirmation.

"The fish out of the Bosphorus are rather excellent," David commented. "There is one, a sort of turbot—"

"Kalkan," Ertuğrul interrupted. "The word means shield in our language, and the fish looks like an iron shield."

"Studded with nails," David finished for him. "Comes down from the Black Sea in the spring. Sultana Charlotte orders it as often as she can, but I doubt she's actually seen one before the cook has cleaned it or we would probably never have it."

"Are there foods I should have my cook attempt to replicate for you, Ertuğrul?" Elizabeth asked as she motioned for the footman to bring the next course.

Ertuğrul glanced up from his plate, obviously not used to the attention, especially while he was eating. "Meatballs, perhaps?" he replied as his gaze darted to David.

"They call them *kofte*," David said, "and they are delicious. Although we have the beef and lamb, I'm not sure about the spices required."

"I'm sure our cook can sort it," George offered, intrigued by the thought of something different for dinner. The current menus seemed the same from week to week, and he didn't know if it was because Elizabeth had requested them that way or if she had simply left it to the cook to decide since she spent so much time at her charities.

When the meal concluded, Elizabeth and Adeline stood to leave for the parlor.

"Are you up for a game of billiards?" George asked, directing his query to the young men. "Adeline has helped keep me sharp in your absence," he added as he gave a nod in David's direction, "but it means my viscountess has been left to her own devices after dinner."

"I've been looking forward to it all day," David replied.

Elizabeth grinned as she moved to kiss her husband on the top of his head. "My own devices meaning responding to invitations and such," she said before she curtsied. "I'll see you all at breakfast in the morning."

The men all bowed as she and Adeline took their leave of the dining room. The footman appeared with a tray of port and small glasses.

"Gentlemen, we're off to the billiards room," George said with a huge smile. "Perhaps we can refine the list of available young ladies you might consider for matrimony."

Although David's expression showed a hint of fright, Ertuğrul appeared pleased with the plan. "Lead the way, sir," he said.

CHAPTER 10
A YOUNG LADY MAKES AN ANNOUNCEMENT

few minutes later
"He is certainly not what I expected," Elizabeth said as she settled into her chair at a small escritoire in the parlor. A salver piled with white notes was set off to one side.

"I wasn't sure what to expect," Adeline remarked. "I certainly didn't feel as if I was in the presence of royalty."

Elkins entered with a tea tray. "Your tea, my lady. Where would you like this?"

"Card table. Adeline can do the honors. It's been some time since she's done so," she said with a pointed glance in her daughter's direction.

"I did it for my friends the day before yesterday," Adeline said in her own defense, moving to prepare the cups and pour the tea. She added sugar to both and set Elizabeth's cup on the escritoire.

Elizabeth handed her one of the invitations from the salver. "If you help, we'll get through these much faster," she said. "I certainly don't want to have to do them in the morning. With you in the billiards room with your father these past few years, I've become used to doing my correspondence in the evenings, and I think I'd like to continue the practice."

Adeline opened the invitation. "The Marchioness of Reading is holding a *soirée* in a fortnight," she stated.

"Write it on this calendar and pen a note that we'll attend. Be sure to say there will be five of us," Elizabeth said as she handed her daughter a sheet of bright white parchment, a bottle of ink, and a quill. She opened another letter and glanced over it. "And you might mention our guest's title in the note," she added before taking a sip of tea.

Adeline frowned as she moved back to the card table. "What might that be?"

Elizabeth looked up and furrowed a brow. "Emir, I believe. George says 'şehzade' is the word for the son of a sultan, and a sultan is sort of a king, I suppose." Her eyes rounded as a look of delight appeared. "Which would make him a *prince*."

"I'll use 'emir' in my response," Adeline replied drolly as she dipped the quill and began to write. "Sounds more exotic," she added with a grin. "That long hair of his certainly qualifies."

Chuckling softly, Elizabeth paused her pen to say, "When I was young, most men wore their hair longer. They either wore wigs or they pulled their own hair back into a queue."

Adeline angled her head to one side. "I don't think his would look very good pulled back," she remarked, the fingers of one hand flicking when she considered what it might feel like to run them through his dark hair.

They worked in relative silence for a few minutes before Elizabeth set aside the letter she had been penning. "You mentioned you found our guest admiring a statue on your way to the parlor this evening," she murmured as she prepared to respond to another invitation.

"I did," Adeline admitted absently, concentrating on her writing.

"Pray tell, which statue was he admiring?"

Adeline lifted the quill and held it aloft as she glanced over at her mother. "The one by the stairs on the second floor," she replied, well aware of where her mother's thoughts were going.

"Aphrodite," Elizabeth murmured. "Did he look as if he was admiring the female form or—?"

"The art, Mother," Adeline said in a huff, not about to admit she had spied the emir well before she had made her presence known. Watched as he seemed to study the carving of the hair around the statue's face. Perhaps he was looking for evidence of the rasp or chisel marks in the marble. Or perhaps he was merely intrigued by the hairstyle. At no point had his gaze settled on Aphrodite's bare breasts or the curve of her hip or the bare ankles that showed beneath the hem of her chiton, although one of his hands had hovered over a shoulder, as if he intended to grip it. Instead, it smoothed through the air, an inch above the marble surface, down the side of the torso and finally to his side. Adeline was sure she overheard him sigh at the same moment an odd sensation coursed through her own torso.

She might have imagined a certain young man sliding his hand down her side, late at night when she was on the verge of sleep.

Maybe on more than one occasion.

That had been before he decided to marry someone else, though. Once he announced he was betrothed and then married shortly thereafter, Adeline gave up her erotic thoughts of the future Earl of Torrington.

Even so, thoughts of him touching her had never resulted in such a pleasant sensation as the one she experienced watching the şehzade almost caress Aphrodite.

Perhaps it had been her slight gasp that had him stiffening, his attention quickly returning to Aphrodite's face as his hands clasped together behind his back.

Pretending she had been making her way down the corridor, Adeline stutter-stopped, pretended surprise, and greeted him with a "how do?" before dipping a curtsy.

"I suppose he's seen hundreds of nude women," Elizabeth remarked, jerking Adeline from her reverie. "I wonder how many women he already has in his harem?"

"He doesn't have one, Mother," Adeline replied, attempting to concentrate on her note. She had almost written the word 'nude' instead of 'number,' and now 'harem' instead of 'five."

Elizabeth straightened as she turned and stared at her daughter. "How do *you* know?"

Adeline sighed as she set the quill in the ink pot. "David told me. Before we went up to change for dinner."

Delight once again crossed Elizabeth's face. "Why, that's wonderful," she said.

"From what Father had me read on the subject, it's really not, Mother." She took hold of the quill and finished the reply to the invitation before her shocked mother could form a coherent response.

"Perhaps the possession of a harem is not the show of power it used to be," Elizabeth remarked, which had Adeline impressed. Apparently her father had talked her mother into reading the same book she had. "Sultan Ziyaeddin gave up his harem so Charlotte would marry him," Elizabeth added.

"*After* his concubines had borne him all those children," Adeline countered, arching a brow. "Ertuğrul has eleven brothers. Any of them could be named the heir if Ziyaeddin changes his mind."

Elizabeth blinked, a moue of disappointment showing on her face. "That doesn't seem fair at all," she murmured, allowing a sigh as she opened another envelope. Her eyes widened. "Ariley's duchess is hosting a ball in honor of Lady Rose," she said happily.

Adeline winced. "Yes. I learned of it the day before yesterday when I hosted Rose for tea."

"Why didn't you tell me?" Elizabeth asked in surprise.

Shrugging, Adeline folded the note she had finished, addressed the outside with '*The Most Hon. The Marchioness of Reading,*' and handed it to her mother. "Do you really care what happens to Lady Rose?"

Elizabeth inhaled sharply. "But of course I do," she insisted. "I realize her accident has made it unlikely she'll land a husband of high quality, which is unfortunate—"

"Unfortunate?" Adeline repeated in alarm. "She deserves the very best. I would expect you of all people to know she needs to land the very best husband she can."

Reeling at hearing her daughter's scold, Elizabeth stared at Adeline for a full ten seconds before she dipped her head. "Which is why I know she won't end up with the man she should," she said in a hoarse whisper. "My time with *Finding Wives for the Wounded* has proven that a hundred times over," she added in frustration. "Her infirmity will limit her prospects."

It was Adeline's turn to react. Her mother was right, of course. A perfectly respectable man did not always land the woman he had set his heart on after he was wounded in war. Sometimes practicality ruled the decision. Sometimes it was something more visceral. More disturbing.

For Lady Rose, her wounded leg meant she would be overlooked by those who just two years earlier would have been lining up to dance with her. Lining up to ask her father for permission to court her.

Lining up to propose marriage.

"I am sorry, Addy," Elizabeth whispered. "It is not her fault, it is not your fault, it is nobody's fault, but... Lady Rose will be lucky to end up a viscountess or a baroness," she said quietly.

"Which is why I thought..." Adeline audibly sighed. "She might make a perfect sultana."

Elizabeth winced, her thoughts immediately going to Rose's mother. What would Helen Harrington Burroughs think if her daughter ended up married to a sultan's heir and living in Constantinople?

Would the Duke of Ariley even allow such an arrangement?

"There is an entire Season in front of us," Elizabeth said as she waved at the stack of invitations still on the salver. "Much can happen, and will."

Wishing she could be in the billiards room, playing as a partner with her father against David and Ertuğrul, Adeline thought she might have some sway over who the two young men might consider for courtship.

She'd been through three complete Seasons after all. She knew all the eligible young ladies. Knew all the eligible bachelors. Which is why she had decided that this Season would be her last. She would be free to work at the charity and see to it that those who deserved a better life would have it. Her father had already promised she could have her inheritance if she wasn't married.

Spinsterhood was looking rather promising.

CHAPTER 11
BILLIARDS LEADS TO A LIST

eanwhile, in the billiards room
When the tip of David's cue tapped a white billiard ball, the resulting collision with a red ball sent it toward a corner pocket. The ivory sphere dropped into the leather cage. "I thought I'd lost my touch," he murmured happily.

"I was hoping you had," George remarked as he retrieved the ball. He set it on the table and stepped back to allow Ertuğrul to take a turn.

"Well, it's certainly not archery," Ertuğrul remarked as his yellow cue ball careened off a side rail and sent the red ball toward a different corner pocket. He gave a start when the red ball fell into the leather lacings.

"And yet you play as if you've been doing this your whole life," David complained.

"I have not played since I was at Cambridge," Ertuğrul said as he fished the red ball from the pocket. "But from what I remember of the rules, it would seem this particular past-time has been around a long time."

"Billiards is based on a game we call croquet," George offered. "Which is why the felt is green. It represents a lawn," he explained.

Ertuğrul straightened, his attention on the cue and its tip. "What is this made of?" he asked.

"The cue—the wooden part—is a hard maple, and the tip is leather," George replied.

"And why is this long furnishing called a pool table?" His hand hovered over the smooth wooden rail that surrounded the table. Around each of the six pockets was an ornate carving into which the leather strips that made up the pocket were attached.

David chuckled. "Good question." He looked to his father, who was grinning as his latest shot resulted in a perfect set up to sink not one but two balls.

"Do you race horses in the Ottoman Empire?" George asked as he bent to line up his next shot.

Ertuğrul exchanged a quick glance with David. "Of course. We have some of the best racehorses in the world."

"Arabians," David said as he watched his father sink the two balls. "Damnation, Father, you've obviously been practicing," he said in awe.

"Every night with your sister," George replied. "If you challenge her, let me know. I'll want to get in on the betting action, which brings me to why these tables are called pool tables. Or can you sort why?"

David furrowed a brow before his eyes rounded. "Because the betting parlor for horse races is called a pool room," he murmured as he sorted the reason. "And we always play billiards in between races to pass the time." He puffed out his chest. "Did I get it right?"

George gave him an appreciative glance. "I'm glad to

know you've learned some logic these past few years," he replied. "Now that you've taken some practice shots, are you up for a game? You two can play first," he offered. "First to get to three-hundred points wins."

The young men nodded and gathered the three balls onto the twelve-foot table.

"Do you own racehorses?" Ertuğrul asked as he watched David set up the table.

"I have two," George admitted. "Both from the same dam and sire, a year apart in age."

"They've both won races," David said proudly. "Although age restrictions mean they no longer qualify for some of the races," he added.

"Actually..." George hedged before he moved to the fireplace. He casually leaned against the mantel. "Those two have been retired, although I may race one of them in the Cesarewitch Handicaps in October. The horses in that contest must be over three, and I think the two-mile, two-furlong course at Newmarket is better for the older nags."

"So... you acquired more horses while I was gone?" David asked, his manner suggesting he felt left out. "Did you find them at Tattersall's?"

George chuckled. "*Acquired* isn't exactly the correct term," his father replied with a grin. "Connie insisted the two we had would create perfect racers," he explained, referring to Constance Roderick, Marchioness of Reading, and a cousin to Daniel Fitzwilliam, Earl of Norwick. She had been breeding horses for nearly thirty years, at one point borrowing a Bostwick stallion to create a line of championship racers for the Norwick earldom. George had benefitted by receiving not only a stud fee some years later, but also several colts from the arrangement. "So I left them in a pasture together down in Sussex, and now

I have a two-year-old colt and a three-year-old mare," he explained.

"Are they bred for speed or for stamina?" Ertuğrul asked, obviously interested in the discussion.

"Both," George replied. "Our race courses are turf, and they vary considerably from location to location. When my racers are younger, I put them in all the races, and when they get older, I just put them in the longer ones."

"I've been to Newmarket," Ertuğrul said. "While I was at Cambridge." His gaze darted to David. "Don't tell my father," he quickly added. "I didn't have a horse to enter, of course, but I made some money on bets."

George and David exchanged quick glances.

"Do you remember whose horses you bet on?" David asked.

"It belonged to a marquess. I believe Reading was his title," Ertuğrul replied.

Letting out a guffaw, George said, "The Connie I spoke of is his marchioness. His wife," he added, not sure how familiar the sultan's son was with titles in England. "Although Reading knows his horses, she's the brains behind their breeding program."

"You say that as if it's their... their *business*," Ertuğrul murmured. "Their means of making their livings."

"Considering how much they make in winnings, it is to some extent," George agreed. "However, raising horses is expensive. Reading has stables here in London—behind his house as well as on the west end of town—but his main horse stables are in Reading. The seat of his marquessate. It's west of here about forty miles," he added.

"If they breed such excellent horses, they must have some heirs as well," Ertuğrul reasoned. "A young lady or two? I understand I must be sure to dance with as many of them as I'm able at all the balls I'm told we're to attend."

George chuckled. "Reading has two heirs about your age but his only daughter has been married for at least ten years."

"Will Gisborn bring his family to the capital this year?" David asked, referring to Henry, Earl of Gisborn. Henry had married Elizabeth's other best friend, Hannah, shortly after Elizabeth and George were married. "Grace is surely of an age to marry," he added before he took his first shot.

"Was," George replied. "Elizabeth sponsored her last year, and Christina and Richard joined us for the Season," he added, referring to David's oldest sister and her husband, Viscount Hartwell. "They thought you'd be coming home."

David straightened, his face momentarily betraying his disappointment. "I'm too late, aren't I?" he asked in a quiet voice. Although he didn't know Grace Foster well, he had always thought she was the most beautiful creature he had ever seen. Like her mother, Grace looked like a fairy princess from the pages of a book, her blonde tresses, cornflower blue eyes, and pale skin almost ethereal. "So... who did she marry?"

His brows furrowing, George said, "Reading's heir, Raymond. She'll be a marchioness one day. I thought you knew."

Feeling as if he'd been punched in the gut, David struggled to keep an impassive expression on his face. "I must not have received that particular letter," he managed to get out before he stepped aside so Ertuğrul could take his turn.

George dipped his head, understanding exactly how

his son felt. At one time, for about an hour, he had believed Elizabeth had accepted an offer of marriage from the Earl of Trenton. That had been the worst hour of his life, the sense of disappointment and loss so intense, he wished he were dead. The memory of the elation he had felt moments later, when Elizabeth proposed to him, sustained him whenever he experienced one of life's disappointments.

"I have a list," George offered, pulling the sheet he had quickly penned while Adeline had been in his study earlier that day. He had managed to put them into the order of their ages, at least as closely as he could remember.

"A list?" David repeated.

"Eligible young ladies, born between eighteen-seventeen and eighteen-twenty-three, and not yet courting anyone."

Ertuğrul blinked. "That's terribly specific," he remarked, moving to the other end of the table so David could take his turn.

George chuckled and said, "Yes, but helpful."

"So... who is on that list?" David asked lightly, pretending nonchalance.

George's eyes narrowed a moment, but he held up the bit of parchment and wished he had his reading spectacles. Holding it out farther from his chest, he grinned. "Well, the first one on the list is dear to my heart because I had a hand in her parent's marriage," he said proudly. "Faith Hope Batey. Viscount Lancaster's daughter with Charity, our matchmaker at *Finding Wives for the Wounded*."

Ertuğrul glanced over at David, as if to gauge his interest. "Marrying Hope would be like marrying my sister," David claimed as he shook his head, referring to Faith by her more common name.

George rolled his eyes but went to the next names on the list. "Barbara and Grace Whitney, daughters of Augustus Whitney, who is the Duke of Huntington's brother."

David furrowed his brows. "Grace is a friend of Adeline's, but I don't recall meeting Barbara," he replied, pretending interest. "Next?"

"Helen Tennison, the Earl of Everly's only daughter."

"How is she not already married?" David asked in surprise. "She had her come-out before I left on my Grand Tour." He turned to Ertuğrul. "Her mother is half Greek," he added, arching a brow.

George frowned. "As for Lady Helen... I really couldn't say why she hasn't married, other than she hasn't been courted by anyone. Her father is an explorer. A naturalist, I think they call them now," he said. "Everly always claims his wife is Aphrodite, although a more loyal version, of course. She gave him another son a few years ago." He winced. "I can't imagine being a father again at fifty."

Ertuğrul's eyes widened at hearing the reference to the Greek goddess, but then he grinned at George's last remark. "My father is past fifty now, and obviously enjoying his newest progeny," he remarked. "I think children keep him feeling young."

"Until he has to marry them off," George replied with a smirk. "Nothing ages a father more than his daughter's courtships."

Ertuğrul and David exchanged quick glances as they both winced. "Does that mean there is a suitor for Adeline?" David asked.

His father's brows lifted. "Not that I'm aware," he replied in alarm. "I was referring to your oldest sister." Christina had married a viscount a few years earlier, even though the man's true identity—a bastard son of the Marquess of Reading raised as the legitimate son of a viscount—had been a source of concern for the few who knew the truth.

"I thought you liked Hartwell," David said, referring to Christina's husband, Richard, Viscount Hartwell. His own brows furrowed in worry.

"Oh, I do. Very much," George replied. "It's the *courting* that had me aging prematurely. The sending them out to the park. All that angst. The tears." He paused before adding, "That's when you know she's in love, though."

Ertuğrul displayed an expression of worry, but didn't say anything. As for his own twin sister, he couldn't recall her shedding tears over Lord James, but she claimed to love him. Perhaps tears weren't always necessary.

"Who else is on that list?" David asked, the game forgotten.

"The Earl of Fennington's daughter, Lucy Turnbridge. Very proper. Very pretty. Very shy."

"Go on," David encouraged.

"Eva Sommers, Baron Sommer's daughter. And yes, she's a bluestocking, but I understand she can hold her own in a conversation with just about anyone," George remarked.

"Then she'd do best with a member of the Royal Society," David replied. "I don't know that I'd want a wife who is more clever than me."

The sound of a suppressed chuckle had George grinning at Ertuğrul. "He has become a bit high on his horse, hasn't he?" he asked rhetorically.

Ertuğrul's expression of confusion had David laughing. "I think you're imagining a blue sock, aren't you?" he teased.

The sultan's son winced. "What is a bluestocking?"

"A woman who reads a great deal and is educated," George explained. "Your sisters could probably all qualify."

"Sevinc Sultana, certainly," David said, referring to Ertuğrul's twin sister. "Who else?" he asked, lifting his head to indicate the list.

George held out the parchment again. "Oh, a couple of the Fulton girls. The Earl of Wadsworth's daughters, Patience and Faith."

Although they were both amiable, neither one elicited a bit of excitement in David "Next?"

Giving his son a scolding expression, George said, "Here's one you know well. Lily Streater." She was Theodore Streater's only daughter, and her mother was a duke's illegitimate but acknowledged daughter.

"Lily?" David repeated. "She's like a sister to me," he complained. He turned to Ertuğrul. "Beautiful, perfect young lady—"

"Because her parents own a finishing school and her father is a baron *and* my best friend," George put in with a grin.

"—Who I have known since she was *born*," David finished. He returned to the table and lifted his cue. "Who was born in eighteen-seventeen?" he asked. "She's on the shelf, is she not?" He bent to line up his shot.

Wincing, his father dipped his head. "Lady Rose."

His concentration shattered. David's aim was off enough that when the end of his cue hit the ball, it caused the ivory sphere to bounce at an odd angle, completely missing its intended target.

Despite having learned about the young lady's unfortunate accident during dinner, he couldn't help but feel a glimmer of... of something. She was a duke's daughter. Never would he have considered her a possibility when it came to courtship, but if others had passed her by—Raymond Roderick, the Marquess of Reading's heir, obviously had—then perhaps there was a chance she might consider his suit.

"Careful. You nearly tore the felt," Ertuğrul said in a hoarse whisper.

Jerked from his reverie, David glanced up. "Oh. Uh... the cue slipped," he said as he stepped back from the table. "I need to use the chalk." He turned to his father. "Is that everyone?"

Regarding his son with an odd expression, George shook his head. "I'm sure there are others we're not as familiar with," he hedged. "Some who don't live in London but will no doubt come for the Season. You'll meet them all at Weatherstone's ball tomorrow night."

David and Ertuğrul exchanged appreciative glances.

"Which means you'll want to practice your dancing."

The young men's expressions sobered.

Ertuğrul stepped forward. "Sir, might I ask if it would be possible for me to visit the British Museum on the morrow?"

George shrugged. "Of course. We can arrange for the town coach to take you." He turned to David. "It's not your favorite, I know, but Adeline might be available to tag along if you don't want to. She loves to go there, and I never let her go alone, of course."

"I need to see a tailor in New Bond Street," David said as he turned to address his friend. "I rather doubt any of my formal clothes are fashionable these days, so if you're all right with the idea of attending with my sister..." He allowed the sentence to trail off.

Ertuğrul gave a nod. "I look forward to it," he said, hoping he didn't appear too enthusiastic. "But on the day of a ball, will she still wish to go?"

Grinning, George nodded. "Wild horses wouldn't keep her away."

CHAPTER 12
A MUSEUM'S CONSTRUCTION EXCITES

A few minutes later, in the parlor

"The museum? *Tomorrow?*" Adeline asked in disbelief, her attention immediately going to her mother.

George held a finger up to his lips, as if to encourage her to keep her voice down. "I thought you'd be pleased."

Adeline inhaled to respond and then let out a huff. "I was going to work at the charity tomorrow—"

"But you're certainly excused," Elizabeth said with a grin of satisfaction. "What do you think, darling? Do we need to send a footman or a maid along to chaperone?" she asked as she turned her attention to her husband.

Crossing his arms over his chest, George regarded his viscountess with suspicion. "Normally, I would say yes, but it sounds as if you don't think it's necessary?" he hedged.

"Oh, I don't mind," Adeline said with a shrug. The last time a lady's maid had accompanied her, the poor woman got lost amongst the Egyptian statues. Adeline hadn't even missed her until she realized she wasn't on her heels a few hours later. A museum employee had to be dispatched to find the maid when the building was about to close.

"I told Ertuğrul he could use the town coach, of course," George said. "So I'll take you on the phaeton when you're ready to go to your office," he said to his wife.

She beamed in delight. Riding on her husband's high-perch phaeton was always a welcome adventure. "I won't stay all day," she promised.

"As for David..." George sighed. "I suppose this is the reason Reading asked if I might wish to acquire his extra phaeton," he groused. "Damn thing's yellow, though."

Elizabeth tittered. "David can take a Hansom cab to the tailor's," she reasoned. "And there's nothing wrong with a yellow phaeton. Why, I wouldn't mind being seen driving it," she claimed.

"I'm not letting you drive a phaeton in London these days," George argued.

"Father," Adeline gently scolded.

"I'm not. I'll not take the chance that some young buck is going to decide he wants to ride off with your mother," he claimed. He held out his hand to Elizabeth as his gaze darkened. "Kidnap her for ransom," he murmured as she took his hand. "Kiss her senseless," he whispered, his manner growing more serious. "Have his wicked way with her," he finished as Elizabeth blushed and gave her daughter a grin and a wink.

"Please, whatever you do, don't pay the ransom," Elizabeth whispered.

"Mother," Adeline said on a sigh. She watched as her parents, hand-in-hand, hurried out of the parlor and headed for the stairs leading up to their apartments.

Her hands went to her hips as she huffed. She didn't have to imagine what they were about to do. She'd lived in Bostwick House long enough to know that when they behaved as they had been doing the past few minutes, they were headed to bed. Or to somewhere they would enjoy one another's company. Unclothed. Or clothed, maybe, depending on what furnishing might be involved.

At least they were still in love with one another. They hadn't taken lovers like some other aristocrats their age. Hadn't resorted to behaving like strangers over the dinner table.

Angling her head to one side, Adeline regarded the tea service a moment, glad Elkins had seen to a fresh pot not long ago. She was about to pour herself another cup of tea when a quiet knock sounded from the threshold.

She turned, expecting to find the butler. Instead, Ertuğrul leaned in. "I hope I'm not disturbing you, Lady Adeline," he said.

She blinked. "Not at all. Please, come in." She waved to an adjacent chair. "By the way, I'm not a lady."

He paused and angled his head. "If not a lady...?"

"A miss is all. But you can call me Adeline. Would you like some tea?"

His steps hesitant, Ertuğrul made his way in her direction. "Yes, actually, if it's not too much trouble."

"Oh, not at all. How do you take it?" She concentrated on pouring the tea.

"With milk, if there is any?"

"Of course there is," she replied as she poured a dollop into his cup. "How was billiards?" She handed him the cup on a saucer.

"Thank you," he said with a nod. "We had a spirited match but no winners. Your father is most excellent at bank shots," he remarked as he watched her refill her teacup and add a lump of sugar.

Adeline chuckled. "I'm well aware," she replied.

"We've spent entire evenings practicing them in anticipation of David's return. Father was convinced he'd been playing every day while he was on his Grand Tour." She took a sip of her tea. "Do you play a similar game where you're from?"

Ertuğrul shook his head. "Not exactly," he replied. "I fear I didn't have much time for such pursuits." He dipped his head. "I cannot help but think my presence means you've lost the opportunity to spend time with him," he said by way of an apology.

Waving him to join her on the settee, Adeline said, "Oh, not to worry. David would have his attentions if you weren't here. Even so, given the time of the year, I best spend my evenings helping Mother with replies to all these invitations." She waved toward the escritoire. "We worked on them the entire time you were in the billiards room, and there are still several that need responses."

Ertuğrul's eyes rounded. "I've interrupted," he said, about to rise.

Adeline held out a staying hand. "Not at all. My parents have gone up to the their apartments. My mother will finish them in the morning," she said. She took a sip of tea and added, "I understand you'd like to go to the British Museum. Father says we can take the coach."

"If it's not too much trouble," he replied. "I should probably practice my dancing, but... there is so much to do and see here in London—"

"Do you know how to waltz?" she asked.

Ertuğrul furrowed a brow. "Of course."

"Good. There will be two of those. No need to be concerned about knowing the Scottish Reel as Lady Weatherstone—she's the hostess of tomorrow's ball— she never has a Scottish reel on the schedule," she explained. "So if you're inclined to ask her to dance, you might suggest that one just to gauge her reaction. She *loves* it when younger men ask her dance to dance. The rest... you'll probably remember when you see them performed."

Chuckling softly, he said, "You seem to think I've been to an aristocrat's ball before."

Adeline inhaled softly. "Haven't you? Whilst you were at Cambridge?"

He was about to respond before he dipped his head. "There were district balls, of course. I... I attended but did not dance."

"Why ever not?" she asked before a hand went to her mouth. "Oh, you're probably a Muslim. Do you... do you dance?"

A grin split his face. "Yes. Yes, of course we dance," he replied. "But... when I was last in England, I was probably the only Muslim in England. Although there might have been some of the sailors that worked for the East India Company who stayed in the port cities," he explained. "I knew I wasn't the first Muslim to attend Cambridge, though, because one of my professors explained that he'd had a Persian student years before."

"You must have felt terribly lonely," Adeline remarked.

He considered the comment a moment before he shook his head. "Actually, it wasn't much different from living in the sultan's palace. Sons are always very sequestered from one another," he explained. "Once I was old enough, I spent my time with my tutors. Occasionally saw my sister and my... mothers." He winced when saying this last, as if he was embarrassed by the arrangement.

"I do hope you're not going to feel overwhelmed by the crush tomorrow night," Adeline murmured.

Ertuğrul furrowed his dark brows. "Crush?" he repeated, obviously confused by the word.

"Oh, the *crowd*," she said by way of clarification. "There will be a lot of people there."

"So I've been told."

"You'll be welcomed, though. The Weatherstones might be old-fashioned, but they're the very best hosts."

He took a sip of tea. "I seem to remember Sultana Charlotte saying something about them. An older couple, are they not?"

"Positively ancient," Adeline said before she tittered. "Lord Weatherstone is very proud of his gardens. He's all about planting the very latest in unusual blooms."

"Blooms?"

Adeline straightened on the settee. "Flowers. This time of the year he'll have tulips and jonquils. I don't know about the roses, but he has an entire garden devoted to roses."

Ertuğrul angled his head to the side. "They are your favorite, are they not?"

Adeline inhaled softly as she eyed him with suspicion. "I suppose they are," she admitted. "There are so many colors, though, it would be hard to choose just one as my favorite." She noticed his teacup was empty. "Would you like more tea?"

His gaze darting to his cup, Ertuğrul gave a start. "Is there more?"

"Of course. Elkins brought up a new pot a short while ago," she said as she set her saucer on the low table in front of the settee and took his from him. She moved to where the tea service was set up. "He's a very attentive servant."

"I understand your father asked you about the museum? He... he may have volunteered you—"

"He did, and I don't mind accompanying you one bit. I haven't been since they opened another hall in the newest wing. The entire museum has been under construction for years, you see," she replied as she filled his cup and added the milk.

"Construction?" Ertuğrul repeated, his interest apparent. "What sort of construction?"

"Oh, the very latest," she enthused. "Concrete floors, a cast-iron frame filled in with London stock brick, and Portland stone on the front layer of the building." She handed him his tea.

"Go on," he encouraged.

She chuckled. "Really, you needn't seem interested on my account—"

"But I am," he insisted. "Construction of the latest palace and two universities has been my... *life*... these past few years. David can attest to it since he's been so involved as well."

Adeline returned to her seat. "Well, I'm of an age where I've been able to watch the expansion happen since I was a very young girl. I've seen a field be replaced with rows upon rows of giant Portland stone blocks. Entire wings rising from the ground," she said in wonder. "When it's done, it will be a quadrangle building with enormous steps and Greek columns and a pediment."

"How far from now will that be?" Ertuğrul asked. If he'd been in charge, it would have already been done. His father would have demanded it be finished in a reasonable amount of time.

"About ten years, I think," Adeline replied. "I should still be alive to see it."

A slight guffaw escaped the sultan's son. "Have you seen anything of this new construction actually finished?" he teased.

Adeline dipped her head. "Not the West Wing yet, but once, I was able to go into the East Wing. About twelve years ago. They had completed the King's Room, you see. Three-hundred feet long, thirty feet wide, and forty-one feet high," she said, barely able to hide her enthusiasm. "Due to its enormity, it required cast iron beams to hold up the ceiling," she explained. "Because it was so heavy due to the ornamentation."

"It sounds quite impressive," he remarked. "Why only once?"

She inhaled to respond and then angled her head to one side. "It was opened for an inspection, but then it was closed to the public." When she noted Ertuğrul's look of confusion, she said, "It was built to house the king's library, you see, but you have to have a special ticket to gain access." Her eyes rounded. "Which I'm sure we could arrange."

Ertuğrul straightened. "I would be very interested," he replied. "You mentioned a new wing?"

She nodded. "I've no idea how many exhibits have been set up in it yet, but it's as large as the East Wing."

He drained his tea and regarded her with a grin. "What time must I be ready to depart?" he asked.

She tittered. "We'll go after breakfast, which will probably be set up in the breakfast parlor by nine o'clock."

"Where will I find this breakfast parlor?"

Adeline's eyes rounded. "Oh, you haven't yet had a tour," she realized. "Well, it's on the ground floor, one door down from the dining room. You'll smell the bacon before you..." She clamped her mouth shut, wondering if anyone had informed the cook that their guest wouldn't be eating any pork.

"Although I won't be eating it, I can still enjoy the aroma," he said with a grin.

"I'm sure our cook will have something else available by way of a meat course for the morning," she replied. Her gaze went to the mantel clock. "Oh, dear. It's nearly midnight," she said as her eyes rounded. "I apologize for keeping you up so late."

He chuckled. "It is I who should apologize," he countered. "I didn't mean to keep you so long."

"I don't mind. I could talk about the museum for hours, but I think you already know that."

Rising from the settee, Ertuğrul offered a hand. Adeline took it and allowed him to help her up before she placed her arm on his and they made their way out of the parlor. "About tomorrow night... what must I do to reserve some dances with you?"

"With me?" Adeline replied in surprise.

"Do you not dance?"

She inhaled to respond and finally said, "I do, but we're allowed only two with the same gentleman."

"Can the waltz be one of them?"

Adeline felt the oddest flip in her stomach, which had her nearly missing a step on the stairs. "I suppose. Could I request that your other waltz be with Lady Rose?"

He allowed a shrug. "I shall dance a waltz with Lady Rose. That is, if her card is not already full."

"I'm quite sure she'll have a line or two for you," Adeline said with a great deal of satisfaction.

CHAPTER 13
A DUCHESS DOTES ON A DAUGHTER

eanwhile, in the parlor at Ariley Place

"You were terribly quiet during dinner," Helen said as she poured a cup of tea and handed it to her daughter.

Rose took the dish and placed it on the small side table next to the chair into which she had fallen only the moment before. She really wished she could be back in the dining room with her father, enjoying a glass of port while listening to him go on about tomorrow's opening of Parliament.

She couldn't recall feeling as bored as she was at the moment. Surely it wasn't as boring down in the dining room.

Learning her brother would be attending Parliament had her wondering if William's head would grow too large for his neck. The writ in acceleration, a sort of summons, merely enabled him to attend the House of Lords using courtsey titles whilst the duke was still alive.

Earl of Waverley.

Her brother was an earl. It was a courtesy title, nothing more, but it still made him an earl.

"I am still not addressing him as 'Waverley' when we're here at home," Rose announced.

Helen tittered. "Is that what has you bothered?"

Rose gave a start. "I suppose," she admitted. She wondered if her father had talked to her mother about their earlier conversation. His undivided attention, even if it had only been for fifteen minutes, had both calmed and alarmed her. As a duke, he could use his influence to force some poor unsuspecting young man into marrying her.

Well, not a *poor* man, surely, but someone who wouldn't dare thwart Ariley's plan for her future.

"If you're concerned your father is going to compel some poor earl to marry you, I have it on good authority he is not," Helen announced.

Rose straightened so fast in her chair, she nearly injured her neck. Staring at her mother, she struggled to close her mouth. "He spoke with you about it?"

The duchess pulled her head back, which had a second chin appearing for only a fraction of a second. "He frequently speaks with me, darling. He has to. He insists on sharing a bedchamber," she replied on a huff. "He did mention before dinner that he was tempted to use his influence to push a certain young man in your direction, but I informed him he had better not do such a thing."

"Oh?" Rose replied, wondering who the young man was he had in mind.

"Sometimes they push back, and the results are not what you expect."

Not sure if she felt relief or disappointment at hearing this last, Rose took a sip of tea.

"You must decide, Rose," her mother said. "You must make a decision as to who you wish to marry—"

"Whom."

"—and then you must pursue him until he catches you."

Rose blinked, not sure if the duchess was aware of what she had said. "I'm supposed to chase him until he catches me?" she asked in confusion.

A most beatific smile appeared on Helen's face. "Yes. Exactly."

Furrowing her blonde brows, Rose gave her head a shake. "You say that as if you think it will work," she murmured.

"Oh, I know it will." At her daughter's questioning expression, Helen added, "Because it worked for me."

Rose blinked again, this time giving her head a quick shake. "With Father?"

"Indeed."

Scoffing, Rose said, "Father wanted you from the time you were both much younger. You didn't have to chase him."

Helen sobered. "Did he tell you that?"

Nodding, Rose said, "Right before dinner. Have you noticed he tends to spend a good deal of time woolgathering these days?"

Her mother inhaled softly, and her good mood seemed to dissipate. "He's being reminded of situations from his youth by his children," she stated, her comment sounding like an accusation.

"William and I are hardly children—"

"And yet you too often behave like children," Helen accused. "This afternoon was a perfect example."

The memory of a gold pillow flying through the air flashed before her mind's eye. "I'm sorry," Rose replied, dipping her head. "I didn't care for the way you and William were talking about me when I was sitting close enough to hear you," she added on a huff.

"He's worried for you is all," Helen said in a quiet voice.

"Why? He should be worried for himself. He's going to join Parliament tomorrow. He's not courting anyone."

"No, but he has the list," Helen stated.

"The list?" Rose repeated. "What list?"

Her mother rolled her eyes. "The list of eligible young ladies who are daughters of the aristocracy and who are not yet betrothed and live here in London and who are between the ages of eighteen and twenty-four years."

Rose stared at her mother a moment, allowing the requirements to repeat themselves in her head. "That's terribly specific," she replied.

"Oh, indeed. But it narrows the list down to a manageable size. He has only the Season to decide. Once he chooses, then we can arrange a marriage for the autumn or winter."

Wincing, Rose realized that her mother had moved her marriage plans from her to her brother. "I hope his young lady will agree to those arrangements."

"Well, why wouldn't she? Whoever he chooses will be a duchess some day," Helen announced cheerfully.

Rose suddenly felt very sorry for whomever her brother would choose for his wife. What if the poor girl —not that she'd be poor in the sense of wealth but rather poor in spirit—didn't wish to be a duchess? "Not every young lady is looking to wear a coronet, Mother," she said on a sigh.

Helen stared at her as if she'd grown a second head. "They do if they've been raised right," she countered.

Despite her mother giving her the perfect opportunity

to claim that she wouldn't wish to be a duke's wife, Rose merely regarded the duchess with a wistful expression. "I'm beginning to understand why Adeline wants to be a spinster."

From the way her mother reacted to that particular word, Rose thought she might have put voice to a curse.

"You don't wish to be a duchess?" Helen asked in alarm.

Rose shrugged. "It's not as if there's a duke in need of a wife, Mother, so it hardly matters if I do or do not."

Helen inhaled sharply. "But there are heirs to dukes who aren't yet married. Huntington's boy Tiberius, for one."

"He was born the same year as me," Rose stated. "He'll be just like his father and marry when he's in his thirties."

Helen screwed up her face in concentration. "Michael Statton," she suddenly announced. "Somerset's heir. The older brother has lost his place in line for attempting to poison his father, and now Michael is the heir-apparent."

Rose simply stared at her mother. She had never met the man, and she was fairly sure her mother hadn't, either. He lived at the ducal estate in Wiltshire, his trips to London to visit his sister, Victoria, and her husband, Thomas Grandby, mentioned in *The Tattler* after he had already departed the city.

Before her mother could suggest any marquesses, she drained her tea and said, "We'll see how the ball goes, Mother. Surely any gentleman who wishes to court me will make an appearance."

Her brows furrowing, Helen nodded. "I'll be sure to invite those two heirs to your ball as well as the Marquess of Billingsley," she said, rising from the settee.

She took her leave of the parlor, as if she intended to write the invitations immediately.

"One week," Rose said aloud, referring to how long it would be before most of the aristocracy descended on Ariley Place for her parents' ball.

The ball they were throwing in her honor.

Nothing like announcing to the world you are desperate to be rid of your daughter, she thought as she struggled out of the upholstered chair.

Shaking out her skirts, Rose reached for her crutch and was about to leave the parlor when the butler appeared on the threshold carrying a silver salver.

"What is it, Jarvis?" she asked.

"A missive was delivered by a Bostwick House footman a moment ago. It's for you." He glanced around. "I offered it to your father first, but he said it wasn't necessary that he read it since it's from Miss Adeline."

Heartened that Adeline had been thinking of her, Rose helped herself to the note. "Thank you, Jarvis."

Limping back to her chair, Rose unfolded the note.

My dearest Rose,

I know we spoke of taking tea on the morrow, but I have only just learned that I will be spending most of the day in the company of our new houseguest at the British Museum.

I know the museum is not your favorite place, but if you have not made other plans and wish to meet a prince of the Ottoman Empire before the Weatherstone's ball—a rather handsome young man (even if his hair is a bit long)—perhaps you might pay a visit to the museum, too?

Ertuğrul is spending the Season in London, and I have learned he is in search of an English wife! Oh, Rose, but who better than you to become a future sultan's queen? I have assurances from him that he will dance a waltz with you!

I do hope to see you before the ball. If I do not, then I shall find you in our usual spot with the potted palms.
Sincerely yours,
Adeline

Rose reread the missive before she straightened in the chair.

A sultan's heir? She remembered her father mentioning the man's arrival and scoffed. Why ever in the world would her best friend think she would be interested in marrying a sultan's son?

She grinned as she refolded the note, deciding she could at least meet the man. There would be some *caché* in having already conversed with him when they came upon one another at the ball. From her missive, it was apparent Adeline had already arranged for him to dance with her, which assumed the man knew how to dance.

She winced at the thought she would have to take her wheeled chair to the museum. Her leg wouldn't hold her up during the ball if she walked on it during a visit to the museum.

About to pen a note to let Adeline know she wouldn't be joining her, Rose reconsidered. With her brother and father scheduled to be in the House of Lords all day, perhaps an outing to the museum was in order.

Even if she didn't care to stare at all the bits of junk neatly arranged with their beautifully penned cards, detailing their origin and year of creation, Rose could admire the Greek statuary of naked men.

If she was expected to marry, then she may as well learn what she must.

CHAPTER 14
BREAKFAST CAN BE A
LEARNING EXPERIENCE

The following morning
Making her way down the second floor corridor from her bedchamber, Adeline slowed her steps when she sensed someone was nearby.

The feeling was the same as the night before, when she had discovered Ertuğrul admiring the statue that stood near the top of the stairs.

Pretending preoccupation, she settled her gaze on the Aubusson carpet runner before her and continued her slow pace. As she expected, Ertuğrul was standing before the statue, his attention on one of Aphrodite's arms.

"Good morning," she said as she stutter-stepped to a halt. She dipped a quick curtsy.

Looking as if he'd been caught stealing a biscuit in the kitchens, Ertuğrul bowed. "Good morning," he replied. When he straightened, his eyes darted to the statue. "You have caught me admiring this lovely lady again," he said. "I have seen a few versions of her, but never this one."

"You can hardly be blamed," Adeline remarked. "She's a goddess. Apparently perfect in her female form," she added as she gave the marble a cursory glance. "Otherwise, why would so many sculptors use their skills to depict her in such seductive poses?"

Ertuğrul blinked, unsure of how to answer.

"It was a rhetorical question. Were you on your way down to breakfast?" Adeline asked.

An unmistakeable look of relief crossed Ertuğrul's face. "Uh, yes. I feared I might be going down too early, though," he said.

"Not at all. I'm sure David is already down there." She sniffed the air, detecting the faintest hint of fried bacon. A momentary reminder that Muslims didn't eat pork had her once again hoping there might be other options available on the breakfast buffet.

"Will you still be joining me for my visit to the British Museum today?" he asked as he turned toward the stairs. He offered his arm, and Adeline gave him a grin as she placed her arm on his. "That is, if you're not too concerned with the wild horses?"

Adeline furrowed a brow. "Wild horses?" she repeated.

Ertuğrul blinked. "Uh, perhaps I misheard your father? He said wild horses couldn't keep you away from the museum. I assumed that meant we might encounter some on our journey there?"

Lifting a hand to her cover her mouth, Adeline struggled not to laugh at the sultan's son. "It's... it's merely an expression one uses to indicate they cannot be deterred from doing something they wish to do," she explained. "So, yes, I still intend to join you today. That is... if you don't mind?"

"I do not, of course. I should like a guide, as I've not been there for many years," he explained. "Is it true the exhibits have doubled in number?"

They started their descent down the stairs as Adeline tittered. "More than that. Besides the one floor of an entire wing that is devoted to the King's collection—the one I mentioned isn't usually open to the public—there are exhibits in the new wing."

Ertuğrul frowned. "Will we be allowed to see the King's collection?" he asked.

Adeline gave him a grin. "Fear not. One of the employees is a friend, and if he is there, we shall be allowed in."

The comment had his brows furrowing even more. "Employee?"

Adeline inhaled softly. "Oh, Mr. Wellingham is a... a curator, I believe is the word? He is in charge of cataloging the Ancient Greek artifacts when they arrive at the museum."

"Wellingham?" Ertuğrul repeated, obviously recognizing the name. "Did he attend Cambridge, by chance?"

"Indeed he did. His given name is Gabriel. He actually answers to Gabe." Adeline's eyes rounded. "Were you classmates?"

Ertuğrul shook his head. "The name is familiar, but I cannot be sure."

"He is the son of the Earl of Trenton," Adeline said, thinking that might help with recollection. "Although he is not the heir." For a moment, she had a thought that in the Ottoman Empire, Gabe very well could have been the heir, even though he was illegitimate. If the sons of a sultan were born to concubines, then they were all illegitimate.

"I look forward to meeting him," Ertuğrul said as he paused on the threshold of the breakfast parlor. George was already seated with a full breakfast before him, his attention on that morning's edition of *The Times*. David was at the sideboard loading a plate with coddled eggs.

"Ah, you found us," George remarked as he glanced up and lowered the paper.

"I had the benefit of a guide," Ertuğrul replied as he nodded. "I thank you for arranging her services for my outing to the museum today."

"Adeline will not steer you wrong," George said. "The town coach should be pulling up to the curb at any moment," he added.

"I'll ride with you two on the way to my tailor's," David said as he set his loaded plate on the table and then took a seat. "I'll catch a Hansom cab to return here."

Handing Ertuğrul a plate, Adeline indicated he should help himself. "A footman will see to your drinks. Just let him know what you'd like. Coffee, tea, chocolate..."

Their guest regarded the line of covered dishes. "You go first," he encouraged.

Chuckling, Adeline said, "All right, but you're our guest."

"I wish to see how it's done," he whispered as he leaned closer to her.

The scent of spice and leather wafted past Adeline's nose, momentarily replacing the smoky odor of bacon. She inhaled and grinned. "Of course." She selected a few items and made sure to leave the cover off the dish of glazed pheasant. She could never remember the fowl being served for breakfast in Bostwick House, so she knew her mother must have said something to the cook about their guest's dietary restrictions. Her father would have apprised her of the details. "The pheasant is my favorite," she said in a quiet voice.

Ertuğrul helped himself to a breast and recovered the

dish. "Do ladies hunt for pheasants here in England?" he asked.

"I'm sure there are some who do," she replied. "But I cannot imagine they would do so with a fowling gun. They are far too long and unwieldy."

"So... a bow and arrow then?" He opened the dish containing baked beans and regarded it a moment before spooning some onto his plate.

Adeline nodded. "Yes. You'll find most of my sex enjoy archery, even though some should probably not be allowed to engage in the sport." She giggled. "One of my friends is quite unable to aim her arrow straight. She nearly shot a footman last year." Her attention went to where his hand was about to lift the next lid, and she noticed an engraved silver ring on the base of his thumb. "Is that a bow ring?"

"It is," he acknowledged, apparently surprised she knew of its use. "A gift, from my father."

"I've heard of them but never seen one before. It's gorgeous," Adeline murmured, leaning closer in an attempt to see the details. "What is that design?"

"Our tughra," he replied, holding up his hand so she could examine the ring more closely. "A sort of... signature."

"Like a monogram?"

He seemed to consider the word a moment before Adeline pointed out the embroidered initials on the edge of the cloth that lay beneath the dishes. "Like this?"

"Indeed," he said. "I cannot help but notice that you, too, wear a ring. From an admirer, perhaps?"

Adeline beamed in delight as she turned to make her way to the table. "You might say that," she murmured. When she saw his quizzical expression, she added, "My father gave it to me for my birthday last year."

At hearing he was part of their conversation, George arched a brow. "I fear the jewelers here in London all know me by name," he said with a grin.

"But neither of us is complaining," Elizabeth announced as she breezed into the breakfast parlor. Although her hair was usually caught up in an elaborate coiffure, this morning her mahogany locks were caught in a ribbon on one side beneath her ear. The wavy hair spilled down in a mass of curls in front of her shoulder.

Both David and George immediately stood and bowed, but it was Ertuğrul who pulled out a chair for the viscountess.

"Good morning, my sweet," George said as he leaned over and kissed her on the cheek.

"Morning, Mother," Adeline and David said in unison.

"Good morning, my lady," Ertuğrul said as he pushed her chair from behind.

"Would you like me to fill a plate for you?" George asked.

Elizabeth beamed in delight. "Please, do, darling. I am *famished*," she replied, batting her eyelashes as she grinned.

If anyone had their attention on George, they couldn't miss the rising color on the viscount's face. Ertuğrul certainly noticed, but he quickly turned his gaze on his food, reminded of how his father behaved with Sultana Charlotte.

"How did you sleep, Ertuğrul?" Elizabeth asked, before taking a sip from the cup of chocolate a footman had set before her.

"Very well, my lady. The bed is most comfortable."

Her smile widening, Elizabeth regarded the sultan's son a moment before she said, "I must admit, it is a joy to have another male at the table. I've been missing my younger son ever since he left for school."

Ertuğrul turned to David. "You have a younger brother?" he asked in surprise.

It was David's turn to display a red face as his father and mother both stared at him in disbelief while Adeline held a hand to her mouth as she tittered.

David straightened in his chair. "I've told you about Daniel on a number of occasions," he claimed indignantly.

Ertuğrul grinned, apparently well aware there was a younger Bennett-Jones boy.

Elkins appeared at the door and cleared his throat.

"Yes?" Elizabeth said as George set a plate filled with toast points and coddled eggs before her.

"The town coach has left the mews and should be in front of the house in a few minutes, my lady."

When Ertuğrul looked as if he was about to rise from the table, David held out a staying hand. "The coach will wait for us," he said. "Take your time with breakfast."

"Speak for yourself," Adeline said. "Ertuğrul and I are anxious to get to the museum." She turned her attention on the şehzade. "Aren't we?"

Having finished most of what was on his plate, Ertuğrul nodded. "I am," he agreed.

David rolled his eyes. "Addy," he scolded.

She grinned. "I have to run upstairs for a bonnet and a shawl, but thanks to mother allowing her lady's maid to see to me first this morning, we needn't wait for my hair to be done."

Elizabeth sipped her chocolate before aiming a flirtatious gaze in her husband's direction. "I'm about to allow you to have her all the time," she said in a teasing voice. "I hardly have use of her these days."

George looked up from the newspaper. "Nonsense, my sweet. Someone has to sew all those buttons back on your corset," he said with a straight face, his attention turning back to an article in *The Times*. "The tip of my fencing sword was a bit sharper than I thought."

David blinked while Adeline rolled her eyes, as if she had heard the same comment on other occasions. Ertuğrul's look of alarm was directed to David.

"They were probably playing pirates last night," David whispered. "Nothing's changed around here, it seems."

"Highwayman," George murmured, his gaze still on the newspaper.

"Highwayman?" David repeated in a whisper.

"I stopped her coach... the bed... and stole all her jewels. And her clothes, of course."

Left speechless, David stared at his father.

"Don't look at me like that. It was *her* idea," George murmured. "A good one, too. Now I have jewels I can bestow on her every day for the next week."

Rolling his eyes, David felt heat suffuse his face as he stared at the remains of his breakfast.

Leaning over so he was closer to David, Ertuğrul said, "Father pretends to be a Saracen with Sultana Charlotte. I have never heard her complain."

David stared at Ertuğrul. "How do you even *know* that?" he asked in shock.

Ertuğrul's gaze darted to George, who had a grin on his face despite his apparent attention on the newspaper. "I believe they are proud of their prowess and merely need someone with whom to share news of their conquests." When David gave him a quelling glance, Ertuğrul added, "We would do well to learn from them. To ensure our wives do not wish to bed another."

Elizabeth glanced at Adeline, who was doing her best

to keep a straight face and her eyes on her plate. "It's best they learn these things *before* they are wed," her mother whispered. "Otherwise lessons can be terribly costly."

Adeline's eyes widened. "Did father do something costly?" she said in hoarse whisper.

"No!" Elizabeth responded. "Of course not. I was referring to *others*. Your father is the model of a perfect husband. Always has been." Her gaze darted to George, who looked up from his paper to regard her with an expression of bemusement. "What is it, darling?" she asked.

"Whenever I see you like this..." He motioned to her hairstyle. "I am simply reminded of our first night together," he said in a quiet voice.

Elizabeth inhaled softly. "Oh," she responded, sounding breathless. She visibly swallowed. "Well, it's about time you three be off, don't you think?" she asked as she turned her gaze on her son and daughter. "The museum will be opening at any moment, and your tailor isn't going to wait for you all day," she added in a scolding voice.

"Yes, Mother," Adeline replied as she rose from the table. The young men immediately followed suit, bowing before they all took their leave of the breakfast parlor.

George chuckled softly as he set *The Times* on the table. "I think we may have shocked all three of them," he whispered as he took one of her hands in his and kissed the palm.

"*Educated* them, don't you mean?" she countered, one of her brows arching suggestively.

"As long as we don't discover a Saracen in our daughter's bed," he replied with a wince.

Elizabeth blinked. "What would be wrong with that?" she asked in a teasing voice.

"That's enough naughty talk from you, you harlot," George accused as he rose from the table, pulling her up with him. "I'll be taking your virtue in the library," he added before his lips took purchase on her bare neck.

"Oh!" she replied in delight as they hurried from the breakfast parlor and rushed up the stairs.

Neither one was aware when Adeline, David, and Ertuğrul took their leave of Bostwick House.

CHAPTER 15

AN AFTERNOON AT THE MUSEUM

n hour later

As the Bostwick town coach pulled onto Great Russell Street, Ertuğrul stared out the window. "Is this really still the largest building project in all of Europe?" he asked in awe.

"That's what they claim," Adeline replied. "I am quite sure it's paltry compared to your recent projects, though," she added. They had dropped off David at Jeffrey Garth's shop New Bond Street a half-hour earlier and had been enjoying a conversation about the young men's involvement in the building of the new palace in Constantinople and the empire's only two universities.

Although she had developed a sense of David's role from his occasional letters to their father, Adeline hadn't realized the sheer scale of the projects Ertuğrul had under his charge until that morning. She had a thought that if he had overseen the museum's expansion, and had the workforce available to him that had built the newest Ottoman palace, the museum would have been finished long ago. "These additional wings have been under construction since the year after I was born," she complained.

When Ertuğrul's expression indicated he was unaware of how long that might be, she said, "One-and-twenty years for me. The East Wing was completed about twelve years ago, but it took some time to move in all the artifacts from King George the Fourth's library."

"That's the wing that may not be open to us?" he asked as they pulled up in front of Montague House. "It was completed when I was last here, but…" He shook his head. "It's all so different with this new wing."

"The West Wing," she agreed. "It's coming along nicely."

He gasped, which had Adeline following his line of sight to see what had him alarmed. "Oh, they are preparing to demolish the original museum next year," she explained. "To make way for a new building and a colonnaded portico that Mr. Smirke has designed. I'm told it will make the museum look as if it's a Greek temple. I'm sure there is a drawing of the plans inside if you're interested."

He grinned. "Oh, I am interested," he murmured.

The coach slowed as it crossed the pavers that filled what had become a courtyard and pulled up to the stairs at the front of the main entrance.

"Is there any illumination now?" Ertuğrul asked before the coach door opened. "As I recall, it was rather dark inside." He stepped out and turned to help Adeline. "The galleries were lit by whatever light came in through the windows."

"There is no gas lighting, and still no candle chandeliers," she replied. "They fear the damage that would be caused by a fire, you see, so it is good that we are blessed with a sunny day."

A quick glance up showed clear skies, and the spring air had already begun to warm. "Lord Weatherstone will be pleased by this fair weather. I understand his gardens are not to be missed," Ertuğrul commented as they made their way to the entry.

Adeline wondered how the sultan's son had learned about the Weatherstone gardens and decided David must have told him. Perhaps her brother had even made recommendations regarding the plantings at the new palace based on what he knew of Lord Weatherstone's back gardens. "They are quite remarkable," she agreed.

"Are they lit at night?"

She inhaled softly. "His lordship usually has Japanese lanterns strung out across part of them," she replied. "But there are areas that remain unlit."

When Ertuğrul noticed how color suffused her face, he chuckled. "Purposely, it would seem?"

"For couples. Like my parents," she murmured before glancing around. "Where would you like to start?"

He regarded her with an odd expression for a moment. "Oldest exhibits first? Work our way forward in time?"

"Egypt," she stated with a grin. "I admit I am fascinated by the stories of ancient civilizations."

They hurried off to the Egyptian Hall, and the two marveled at the ancient artifacts, including a sarcophagus, a large vase, and a marble sculpture of a sphinx. Standing before a statue of Cleopatra, Adeline attempted to match the queen's expression and giggled when Ertuğrul did the same next to a bust of Julius Caesar.

They both sobered in front of the marble of Alexander the Great. "It's amazing he was able to accomplish so much, and he only lived to age thirty-three," Adeline commented. "How old are you?" she asked, her gaze turning from the bust to study Ertuğrul's olive-skinned complexion.

"I was twenty-three on the first day of spring," he replied.

Adeline blinked. "Is that all?" she asked in alarm.

He turned to regard her with a look of uncertainty. "You think I look older?"

Blinking again, she shook her head. "No. Forgive me. It's not that," she replied. "It's all the things you've managed to accomplish," she said in awe. "What you've been responsible for. At such a young age."

"Which is probably why I feel old," he said with a grin.

She gave him a wan smile as she readjusted her shawl. "I admit I was a bit surprised you would come to England for your holiday. Of all the countries in the world, why you would choose ours—"

"Sultana Charlotte might have had something to do with it," he said, pausing at the entrance to the hall containing the Townley Collection. "My father is a changed man because of her."

Adeline noted the way in which he made the comment, as if he was glad of Charlotte's arrival and subsequent position within the empire. "You were not bothered that an English woman apparently upended his entire life?" she asked. She had been curious as to what others might have thought of Charlotte's presence. What they might have thought when Sultan Ziyaeddin I made the dowager duchess his wife. The two hadn't known one another very long, and yet they seemed incandescently happy together.

"Not at all," Ertuğrul said. "Especially when she... *advocated*, I believe the word is, on my behalf. Even though I did not expect nor ask for such consideration from her."

Adeline chuckled softly. "She is a *mother*, much like my own. Fiercely protective. Determined that fairness overrule might."

"But she was not *my* mother," Ertuğrul commented. At seeing Adeline's arched brow, he added, "Well, not at the time, at least."

"She is your stepmother, which for her is the same." They moved into the next hall. "So... I am still curious. Why did you really decide to come to London? Are you truly here to find a wife?"

He shrugged. "I was considering it," he admitted.

"You think taking an English wife will change you as it did your father?"

He dipped his head. "I don't want to be changed as much as I don't wish to be what my father had become before Charlotte arrived." He winced, as if he had struggled with the English words. "Did that make any sort of sense?"

Adeline angled her head to one side. "I think I understand," she replied. "Much like a king, responsibility must weigh heavily upon him. Sharing that with a capable queen—a sultana—can only help."

"Indeed," he said. He was about to say more, but a young woman was rushing in their direction. Or rather, the footman pushing her wheeled chair was doing so, apparently at her insistence.

"Rose," Adeline whispered in surprise. Not having received a response to the note she had sent to Ariley Place the night before, Adeline had forgotten her friend might join them.

"There you are," Rose said as she waved for the footman

to slow down. When the chair halted, she gripped the servant's arm and stood as if she was doing so from a parlor settee. "Addy," she said as she approached. "I feel as if I've been rolling through the annals of time searching for you."

"You no doubt have," Adeline said as she embraced her friend. "I'm so glad you could join us so that I could be the first to introduce you to our guest." She turned to face Ertuğrul. "Emir Ertuğrul Effendi, may I have the honor of presenting my very good friend, Lady Rose Burroughs?"

Ertuğrul immediately bowed. Reaching for her hand, he brushed his lips over the back of Rose's white gloved knuckles. "Your ladyship. It is an honor to meet you," he said as he straightened.

Rose regarded the sultan's son a moment before she said, "And you, Your Eminence. I take it you are the reason Mr. Bennett-Jones has been away for so long? Three years, two months and ten days, wasn't it?" she asked with a pleasant expression.

Hesitating a moment, as if he was having trouble translating her words, Ertuğrul said, "I fear I cannot take the blame for his first year away from London," he replied. "But he was invaluable to the empire for the last two. I apologize if his absence was troubling for you."

Her eyes rounding, Rose quickly shook her head. "Oh, you misunderstand, sir. I was merely teasing you," she said as she displayed a brilliant smile and waved a hand that came to rest on his arm.

Adeline watched the interplay, shocked that her friend would even attempt to tease a visiting dignitary. Whatever could she be thinking? Or was she flirting? "Ertuğrul has come for the Season and, of course, will be attending the Weatherstone's ball this evening," Adeline commented lightly, hoping Ertuğrul wasn't offended.

Impressed by this bit of news, Rose said, "So good of you to accept their invitation, as I hope you'll accept the invitation to attend my ball next week. Sometimes there are never enough unattached men at these entertainments, but I hear tonight's will be well attended."

Recognizing the hint that he should secure a dance in advance, Ertuğrul asked, "If your ladyship's dance card is not yet full, might I request the first waltz of the evening?" He held out his arm as if to indicate they should continue their tour of the museum.

Rose blinked, her gaze darting to Adeline for a moment. "Why, yes. Yes, of course, sir. I would be honored. Might I introduce you to my father, the Duke of Ariley, this evening?" She placed her arm on his and allowed him to lead her to the first statue.

Ertuğrul shrugged. "Indeed. Am I to understand you also have a brother? And a mother?" His gaze was no longer on the duke's daughter, but rather on the marble, *Discobolus*.

Adeline struggled to keep a straight face as Rose continued her study of the sultan's son, apparently in an attempt to avoid looking at the statue of a nude man in the process of throwing a discus. "Why, yes. William is this very day joining Parliament as the Earl of Waverley," she said, feigning pride as she arched a brow in Adeline's direction. "And my mother will be there, of course."

"Then I shall ask her to dance as well," Ertuğrul said as he moved them to the statue of *Townley's Venus*.

Rose beamed in delight. "Shall I tell her when I return home? Or would you prefer she be surprised?" From her anxious manner, it seemed she would have trouble keeping the news a secret from the duchess.

Ertuğrul turned to regard her with an expression of

worry. "I do not wish to vex her, so... whatever you think is best."

"Oh!" Rose answered happily. She suddenly sobered. "And what of the supper dance? You'll want to be sure to secure a partner for the second waltz."

Adeline inhaled softly, shocked her friend would be so bold. Did Rose expect the sultan's son would ask her for *both* waltzes? She had to suppress the streak of annoyance she suddenly felt.

When Ertuğrul turned to her, she expected him to ask what would be appropriate. Instead he said, "I already have a partner for the supper dance, but... I am aware of someone who will wish to fill that line on *your* card," he added as he turned his gaze back on Rose.

"You are?" she asked, her blue eyes rounding with curiosity.

"Indeed. I expect he will find you early in the evening to make his intentions known."

Rose exchanged a quick glance with Adeline. "Oh, well, I cannot imagine who *that* might be," she said as a wash of pink colored her cheeks.

Unable to hide her sudden amusement—who else could it be but her brother, David?—Adeline raised a gloved hand to her lips. "But of course you can, Rose," she said, briefly wondering why her brother would wish to dance with Rose.

Her good humor abated when she noticed Ertuğrul staring at the statue of Venus. His thoughtful gaze was much like it was when he was studying the statue of the Greek's version of the goddess on the second floor of Bostwick House.

The oddest sensation shot through her belly, and Adeline gripped her shawl more tightly in an effort to hide what she was sure would be apparent to anyone who might be watching her.

For a moment, she wondered why she would feel jealous of the carved marble. Ertuğrul was a friend. Her brother's friend. Why should she care that he found statues of Venus or Aphrodite so intriguing?

Apparently Rose noticed Ertuğrul's perusal of Venus as well, for when she realized she was no longer the object of his attention, she lifted her chin and angled her head to regard the statue with a hint of derision. "I cannot imagine having such a thick waist," she murmured.

"This is isn't the original," Adeline remarked, ignoring her friend's jibe, "but rather a Roman copy from an earlier Greek version," she said, remembering the details from the last time she had visited the museum and had read the placard describing the exhibit. "And she's had to be repaired since she was moved here in two pieces. Mr. Townley was an avid collector, but I don't believe he was always very law-abiding when it came to acquiring newly-excavated artifacts."

Having learned some of what happened during archaeological expeditions involving his brother-in-law, Ertuğrul chuckled. "Lord James has said as much," he murmured. His gaze lowered to the chiton draped at Venus' waist and over one arm. "Although the fabric is well done, she is not as pleasing to the eye as other renditions of her," he said, his attention moving back up to the statue's hair and face.

Adeline thought it interesting he could be but two feet from the marble and not stare at the pair of naked breasts. Rose certainly was, when she wasn't casting side glances at the şehzade. "What do you suppose caused this discoloration in the marble?" she asked as she waved a hand to indicate areas that appeared slightly stained.

"There's a probably a bit of iron in the marble, and it has rusted over time with exposure to air," he replied. He nodded that they should proceed to the next exhibit.

"Townley's favorite was this one," Adeline said as she moved to stand before the marble bust of a woman. *"The Nymph Clytie."*

"My father says my mother looked like this in her younger years," Rose remarked, angling her head to match the marble.

"You may look like her in a few years," Ertuğrul said, his gaze darting between the statue's wavy haired beauty and Rose. "She is quite stunning."

Rose inhaled softly. "Why, thank you, Your Eminence."

Adeline leaned back and aimed a grin at her friend behind Ertuğrul's back. When she caught Rose's attention, she waggled her brows.

Rose merely rolled her eyes in response before she straightened and strolled to regard the next marble bust. *"Hadrian,"* she read from the brass placard attached to the base. "He obviously had very curly hair and a curly beard," she said with a grin, one of her gloved fingers tracing the hair on the man's chin.

"Don't touch it," Adeline scolded.

Rose shrugged before moving on to the statue of a young woman lounging on the ground. *"The Knucklebone Player,"* she said as she frowned. "Do they play knuckle-bones in the Ottoman Empire?"

"Different versions of it," Ertuğrul replied. "We call it *vek*," he said absently, his attention on a large vase. He hurried over to study the detailed bas-relief carving that surrounded the ovoid shape.

"Oh, we have one of those," Rose said as she moved to stand next to him. "It's marble, but an imitation, of course."

"You say that as if they're quite common," he replied.

"They are," Adeline said on a chuckle. "You'll see many copies of Greek artifacts in the homes of aristocrats who host balls and *soirées*."

"I look forward to it," he said.

"As do I," Rose said, giving the sultan's son an appreciative grin. The sound of a clearing throat had her turning to discover the footman near the entrance to the hall. He was standing next to her wheeled chair and holding up his pocket watch from its chain. "Oh, I had no idea the time had grown so late. I really must be going," Rose said as she turned to face Adeline and Ertuğrul.

"But you've only just arrived," Adeline countered.

"There's a ball tonight," Rose countered. "I have to stop by the modiste's to pick up my gown, and my lady's maid must do my hair."

Thinking her hair looked fine as it was, Adeline knew better than to argue. "I'll find you tonight in our usual place," she said with a grin. "Otherwise you'll find me standing next to Fred." She kissed Rose on the cheek.

Ertuğrul bowed. "I look forward to our waltz this evening," he said before taking her hand. He brushed his lips over the back of it. "My lady."

"Your Eminence," she replied before she turned and hurried off, doing her best to keep from limping. Once she had joined the footman, she settled into the wheeled chair and was gone a moment later.

"I do hope she was not in pain whilst she was with us," Ertuğrul said with worry.

Adeline jerked at hearing his comment, but when she turned to answer him, he was back to studying the vase.

"She is much better these days. She didn't even appear to limp, so I think she must be fully recovered."

When Ertuğrul didn't respond, Adeline moved to a caryatid of a woman holding out a hand, palm up. The card explained how the sculpture had been one of many found at a Roman villa and was dressed to take part in some sort of religious rite.

"Whatever you do, don't give her any money." The male voice had Adeline gasping. She whirled around to discover Gabriel Wellingham standing next to her, his hands clasped behind his back.

"Mr. Wellingham! We were about to come find you," Adeline said as she rose up on tiptoe and kissed the man on his cheek at the very moment Ertuğrul turned from examining the vase.

Gabe grinned and lifted her hand to his lips. "So glad to learn I haven't been forgotten," he said, his gaze going to Ertuğrul. "How do, sir?"

Adeline was quick with the introduction. "Emir Ertuğrul Effendi, may I have the honor of presenting my good friend, Gabe Wellingham? He is the curator I told you about."

At learning the identity of the young man who looked as if he could have been Cupid in his younger years— Gabe still had curly blond hair and, although his cheeks were no longer rounded by youth, his blue eyes hinted at mischief—Ertuğrul seemed to visibly relax. "It's good to meet you, sir," he said as he held out his right hand.

Gabe's eyes rounded. "Emir Ertuğrul, it is an honor," he said in awe as he shook the hand. "I recall your arrival in Cambridge about the time I was completing my studies. I think you must have been the youngest student at the time." He turned his attention on Adeline. "How is it *you* are in the company of a şehzade?"

Giggling, Adeline said, "Because Ertuğrul is our guest at Bostwick House. He and David are friends, you see."

"Ah, I had heard rumors that Bennett-Jones was back on English soil. Good to know he made it... in one piece, I take it?"

"Indeed," Ertuğrul replied. "I understand you are in charge of cataloguing Greek artifacts here at the museum?"

Gabe chuckled. "I am, when I'm not looking for missing appendages." He pointed to the caryatid's extended hand. Several fingers were broken off where the last knuckle should have been. "I've managed to locate one," he added. "It's not the first time she's lost them."

"Oh, dear," Adeline said. "Can Mrs. Wellingham reattach it?" She knew Gabe's wife worked at the museum repairing and restoring ancient pottery.

"We have a marble restorer for such repairs," he replied. His brow arched. "You said you were about to come find me. Pray tell, what have I done?"

"Oh! Yes. We were hoping you might allow us into the East Wing. To see the King's Collection," Adeline said with a hint of pleading in her voice. "Ertuğrul is most interested, and it's been an age since I was in there."

"I'd be honored," Gabe replied. "Come. We'll bribe the guard," he said as he grinned, which had a dimple appearing in his cheek.

"How much should we give him?" Ertuğrul asked as he pulled his purse from his waistcoat pocket.

Gabe paused. "Oh, I was merely joking, Your Eminence. He'll let you in on my recommendation."

Ertuğrul seemed confused for a moment but joined Adeline and Gabe as they made their way out of the Townley Hall toward the East Wing.

"Will you be at the Weatherstone's ball this evening?" Adeline asked, rather enjoying the fact that she was on the arm of one man whilst conversing with another.

"Wouldn't miss it," Gabe replied. "But we won't stay too late. We must come to work tomorrow, and Frances is..." He waggled his brows as his hands waved in a half circle over the front of his body.

"With child?" Adeline guessed, her excitement apparent.

"Indeed," Gabe said proudly.

"Congratulations," Ertuğrul said. "Do you already have any children?"

Gabe grinned. "This will make three is all. And you? You must have a few by now."

Adeline's gaze darted to Ertuğrul, curious as to how he would react. She hadn't thought to ask him, but perhaps he did have some children with the concubines her brother claimed he didn't have.

The thought had her momentarily annoyed.

His father had probably fathered more than a few babes by the time he was twenty-three.

"I am not yet a father," Ertuğrul stated. "A situation that I hope to change this year or next."

"Ah, so you haven't yet started your harem," Gabe guessed.

Ertuğrul shook his head. "Bennett-Jones and I have been overseeing some building projects that are finally finished, so we came for the Season."

Gabe held up a finger before he approached a man who was standing next to a set of double-doors. After a moment, he returned at the same moment the guard opened one of the doors. "I must return to my office," Gabe said, "but you can stay in there until the museum closes."

Adeline and Ertuğrul said their farewells and moved into the hall, both looking to their left. "Oh," Ertuğrul murmured in awe.

"Where would you like to start?" Adeline asked as a grin split her face.

He glanced about and then looked up. "It appears we'll have daylight for a few more hours," he said.

"It will close before it gets dark," Adeline replied. "But we can always come back another day. We can start at this end and work our way to the end on this side of the hall," she suggested. "Then move to the other side and continue."

"Challenge accepted," Ertuğrul said with a grin.

Unlike the rest of the museum, they had this wing all to themselves. After a few minutes of perusing the exhibits, an awareness crept over Adeline. She was alone with a young man only two years older than she. Alone in a hall large enough to accommodate two or three townhouses. Despite the sheer size, the situation felt as intimate as if they had been locked into a bedchamber together. Their occasional comments were kept to near whispers, which only magnified the effect.

"Even if I started now, I do not believe I could collect as many books and whatnot as your king amassed in his lifetime," Ertuğrul murmured as he studied a clock.

"If you did, do you have someplace where it could all be displayed?" Adeline asked as she stared at an array of colorful butterflies.

"I suppose I could arrange to have something built," he replied on a chuckle. "Turn it into a museum."

With only the sounds of his boot heels and her skirts swishing as they rounded row after row of display cabinets, the two worked their way to the other end of the hall, marveling at the splendor of the exhibits.

"We should go," Ertuğrul said suddenly.

Adeline looked up from a display of small pistols. "What's wrong?"

"There is a ball tonight?" he reminded her as he held up his pocket watch.

"Oh!" Adeline replied, immediately directing him to the nearest doors. "Thank you for noticing. Mother will wonder what's become of us."

The two left only a moment before a guard approached informing them the museum would be closing in a few minutes. Finding the Bostwick town coach among those lined up along Great Russell Street proved easy—it was the only one bearing a gold crest on the door.

A few minutes later, and they were safely ensconced inside as the driver did his best to return them to Bostwick House before six o'clock.

CHAPTER 16
A COACH RIDE REVEALS MUCH

A few minutes later

"It was so fortunate Mr. Wellingham found us this afternoon," Adeline remarked as she settled into the squabs. "Instead of me having to ask a museum employee to deliver a note to him on our behalf."

"Indeed. I found him to be very amiable," Ertuğrul remarked. "I look forward to meeting his wife. A potter, did you say?"

"Yes. Her name is Frances Longworth. She came to London from Stowe, where all the very best pottery is made. Besides her skills in repairing pottery, she is an artist in her own right. She takes commissions to do beautiful paintings on porcelain objects."

"Perhaps I should start with one of her pieces when I build my collection," Ertuğrul said on a chuckle.

"Your wife will be pleased to receive such a treasure as a gift," Adeline replied, her gaze briefly directed out the window as they crossed an intersection. Although she didn't want to seem anxious, she knew there would be little time to dress once they reached Bostwick House.

"Lady Rose is fortunate to have you as a friend," Ertuğrul said from his side of the coach. Although he would have preferred sitting next to Adeline, he had taken the bench that faced away from the direction of travel since it seemed the proper thing to do. On the way to the museum, David had sat next to her.

"Thank you," Adeline replied. "I know she is nervous about tonight, so I apologize on her behalf if she seemed... preoccupied." In reality, Adeline had thought Rose's behavior was strange. She was usually far more relaxed in the company of new friends. Far more curious than she seemed while they toured Townley hall.

What if she had decided she didn't like the sultan's son? Could that even be possible? When the two stood together, they made the perfect couple, both more handsome than they had a right to be. Both from wealthy families. Both born into situations of responsibility.

"She seemed quite pleasant," Ertuğrul commented. "I understand from your father that there is to be a ball for her next week? I thought she might tell us more about it today. I would think such an event rather momentous in a young lady's life."

Adeline glanced out the window in an effort to determine how much longer their trip might be. She had to dress for that night's ball. Have her mother's lady's maid do up her hair. "She is modest is all. Her parents are hosting the ball in her honor."

"Is that... customary?"

Inhaling softly, Adeline said, "When a girl has her come-out, yes. The duke and duchess hosted a ball for her back then, but that's been some years ago, so I think they merely wish to remind the *ton* that she is not yet betrothed."

"I find it curious she is not already married," Ertuğrul

said. "A duke's daughter? I would have expected such a fine woman to have been claimed when she was much younger."

The words were said as if the şehzade was suspicious, and Adeline interpreted them as such even as a streak of jealousy had her wincing. "Me, as well."

"What is it?"

"I wonder if perhaps there is more to it," she said, not meaning for the sultan's son to overhear her.

"Something more to it?"

She glanced up, struck at seeing Ertuğrul's expression of curiosity. "It's just that... usually the young men here in England will wait until they are older to marry, but something happened a few years ago—"

"All those young men who married at a younger age?" he guessed.

Adeline's eyes widened. "Why, yes." She was about to ask him how he knew and realized David would have told him. "Seven of our male friends, including Mr. Wellingham, married during the spring that year. All very suddenly."

"Because they feared their first choices for wives would not be there to marry when they were older," he explained.

Adeline gave a start. Seven young men married seven young ladies they apparently didn't wish to lose to another, and yet Lady Rose wasn't among them. "Said as if you were here when it happened," she accused.

"Your brother would read the letters from your mother. He was usually quite happy to learn whatever news she shared, except he told me there was the one time he wished he hadn't received her letter. That was before he came to the Aegean palace to rescue Sultana Charlotte."

"Three years ago," Adeline said, realizing it would have been exactly three years ago since so many of their mutual friends had wed. "He and Lord James had only been gone a couple of months when all that happened. He must have felt affection for one of the young ladies."

"My father sensed his... disquiet," Ertuğrul said. "He offered him a concubine from his harem."

Adeline struggled to keep an impassive expression on her face. "Oh?"

"One of the virgins. My father had several concubines he never took to his bed—they were gifts, you see, so he had to accept them—but he hadn't yet made arrangements for them to marry outside of the household."

Obviously the şehzade was unaware that their topic of conversation was entirely inappropriate, but her curiosity had Adeline hoping he would say more.

"Did he accept the sultan's offer?" she asked lightly.

Ertuğrul shook his head. "He has never said, and I have not asked."

Adeline did her best not to let out a 'huff' at hearing Ertuğrul's lack of curiosity on the matter. Men were supposed to be worse gossips than women. "I wonder if he fell in love with her?" Adeline whispered before her eyes widened. "Do you suppose—?"

"No," Ertuğrul said firmly. "He has always wished to marry an English girl. In fact..." He replayed part of the conversation that had occurred during billiards the night before. "Your father had a list of available young ladies—"

"My father?" she interrupted, almost at once realizing he must have assembled it after their discussion in the study.

"Yes, and I am quite sure David has one of them in mind to court."

Adeline waited with baited breath, hoping he would divulge a name. "And?" she prompted.

"Well, David has always known he must do his duty. He knows he must remain in England, even though my father has assured him there would be a position for him in Constantinople if he returned with me."

Disappointed he didn't share a name, Adeline decided she would learn soon enough who might one day be her sister-in-law. "And what about you?" she asked.

Ertuğrul shrugged. "I, too, must do my duty. It is different for me because I do not *have* to take a wife, although I would prefer to, but I must return to my father's palace. I am in charge of the government buildings in the empire, and I cannot see to those from outside of the empire."

"Of course not," Adeline agreed. They sat in companionable silence for a moment before she noticed his brow furrowing. "What has you bothered?"

Leaning forward, Ertuğrul said, "I could not help but hear you mention to Lady Rose that you would be meeting her in your usual place this evening. Might I learn where that is so I can claim you for the second waltz?"

Adeline blinked. "The second waltz?" she repeated. From what he had told Rose, Adeline had a thought her mother and Ertuğrul would be paired for the second waltz, which, after she thought about it another moment, was ridiculous since her father always danced the supper dance with her mother.

Ertuğrul nodded. "I meant to ask you earlier, and then Lady Rose..." He allowed the sentence to trail off.

"I would be honored," Adeline replied. She straightened on the bench. "I can usually be found standing with the wallflowers."

He stared at her a moment. "Wallflowers?" His eyes darting to one side, as if he was struggling to sort the appropriate translation, Ertuğrul finally gave his head a shake. "There is a papered wall featuring flowers in the ballroom?" he guessed.

Adeline giggled. "Wallflowers are the young ladies—and some not so young—who do not have many dance partners. We line up near the wall where Lord Weatherstone is sure to have his prized potted palms on display." A reminder she would be standing a good deal later that evening had her considering what slippers she might wear. Although her feet hadn't bothered her too much while they stood before the myriad exhibits, she knew her usual dance slippers would not be comfortable.

"I cannot imagine you not having dance partners," Ertuğrul murmured.

The oddest sensation coursed through Adeline at that moment, and she almost said, "Bless you," but thought better of it. "As Lady Rose mentioned, there are never enough men willing to dance at these entertainments, and so those who have any sort of..." She paused and winced. "Infirmity or who aren't blessed with pleasing countenances are left to stand and watch."

"Infirmity?" Ertuğrul repeated, his brows furrowed as if he didn't recognize the word.

"Oh, uh. A withered arm, or a club foot, for example."

Ertuğrul considered this information for a moment. "You seem especially concerned for those who are less fortunate than you."

Adeline angled her head to one side. "I am. I suppose because my mother has been so with her charities for wounded men."

"Do you meet these wounded men?"

Not sure of his reason for asking, Adeline shrugged.

"But of course. I work in the office with Mother a few days every week. I search newspapers for positions that might suit them and help them complete their applications if they are unable to write." She paused and allowed a grin. "I sometimes even go with Mother when she meets an employer. Some will not take a man with an infirmity unless they can be assured he can do the work, so Mother bribes them."

Ertuğrul blinked. "Bribes them? You mean—?"

"She pays them to hire our clients, as an insurance of sorts."

He blinked again. "From where does she get the funds?"

Adeline's grin widened. "We are a charity, so we have benefactors. When Mother started, she used her own pin money. But then Father—before he had even met her—learned she had helped his best friend—"

"Baron Streater," Ertuğrul guessed, remembering the conversation in the billiards room.

"Yes, him. He is missing his right arm, you see, but he could perform his duties as a bank clerk without one. So my Father starting providing funds, as did her father, and..." She shrugged. "It just grew from there. And now some of the funds come from the men who have been helped. When they can afford to do so, they reimburse the charity for the money that was spent to make them a suit of clothes or to repay us for the bribe. As a result, we have never had to turn anyone away for lack of funds."

Apparently impressed, Ertuğrul settled into the squabs and regarded her with a curious expression. "I should like to visit your charity," he said.

"You would be welcome to do so," she assured him, glancing out the window again.

"What is it?" he asked.

"Oh, I merely wish to see where we are. I fear Mother will not be pleased with me having spent so long at the museum."

"I will take the blame," Ertuğrul stated.

Adeline giggled. "Well, you can try, but she knows I will not leave the museum until I am forced to do so."

Ertuğrul grinned. "We are of like minds on that account." He lifted a finger to his brow and scratched it, the bow ring at the base of his thumb glinting in the late afternoon light.

Remembering the beautiful design on the ring, Adeline wondered if he wore it all the time. There was a moment when she imagined it sliding over one of her nipples, the cool metal sending shivers of delight through her breasts and belly. A moment when she wondered how his lips might feel if he were to kiss a nipple. To draw it further into his mouth and suckle it. And then repeat the entire process with her other nipple.

How would that cold metal feel against the rest of her skin? If he pressed it into her flesh, would the tughra leave its mark? Branding her as his?

She imagined the sensation she would experience as he drew his hands down her torso. Down her thigh and to her knee to bend it before he moved his mouth to kiss the inside of her thigh. *Maybe kiss her down there.*

She wasn't supposed to know about such things, of course. But how could she not when her mother made salacious comments to her father during breakfast about their lovemaking the night before?

Everyone in the household knew her father and mother enjoyed one another. They would have had to be blind given both were so open with their affections. So teasing with one another before they raced up the stairs to enjoy another round of lovemaking.

For the longest time, Adeline thought everyone's parents were madly in love with one another. It wasn't until she was in finishing school that she learned some barely spoke to one another. Or they were so polite in mixed company, they came off as aloof in their feelings.

If she did get married, she thought she would prefer an attentive husband. One who would tease and taunt and take her to his bedchamber in the middle of the day. Surely that would be better than a husband who behaved as if he were merely a friend.

No friends, she decided.

If she was to marry, it would be to a man who had no qualms about showing his passion. No qualms about proving his passion. Whose eyes would darken, making his intent known without any words needing to be spoken.

Much like Ertuğrul's were doing this very moment.

Adeline gave a start, realizing almost at once that the coach had come to a halt. Wrapping her shawl more closely around her, she gave the sultan's son a nod. "I do not wish to be rude, but I really must rush up to my room to change clothes," she said in an effort to hide her embarrassment over what she had been imagining.

He allowed a shrug. "I understand," he said. "I will be right behind you since I must do the same."

Sure her face was bright red, Adeline wondered at his look of bemusement and remembered he couldn't possibly have read her thoughts.

So why then did his thumb tap against his thigh in an anxious tattoo?

CHAPTER 17
THE BEGINNING OF A BALL

An hour later
"Who is Fred?"

David leaned to one side and regarded Ertuğrul's reflection in his mirror. "Fred who?"

The sultan's son moved farther into David's bedchamber, shifting his shoulders as if he found the traditional *kaftan* he wore too small. The navy garment, made of very fine wool and embroidered with gold and red thread, rivaled any of the formal clothing aristocrats wore to balls. Beneath it he sported a long gold waistcoat, the buttons looking as if they were amber gemstones. The baggy legs of the white şalvar were gathered at the ankles into gold cuffs. Gold slippers with pointed upturned toes completed his court attire. "While we were at the museum, your sister told Lady Rose that she would find her standing with Fred."

Pausing as he attempted to thread a cuff link through the hole in his sleeve, David turned and regarded Ertuğrul with a frown. "I have absolutely no idea," he murmured. He cursed under his breath, and Ertuğrul hurried over to take the cuff link from him. He completed what David had been attempting to do and stepped back.

"Lady Rose obviously knows him," he remarked.

David gave Ertuğrul the other cuff link, but the mention of Rose had him straightening. "I hope he hasn't claimed a waltz with her," he said.

Ertuğrul gave a start. "You wish to court Lady Rose?"

"Do you?" David countered.

The sultan's son lowered his gaze. "I only met her this afternoon. I do not believe I spent enough time in her company to know one way or the other." He winced. "I claimed the first waltz with her." At seeing David's look of alarm, he narrowed his eyes. "You do wish to court her."

David sighed loudly. "It's been three years since I last saw her."

"Much can change in three years," the şehzade remarked. "As have you."

A grimace passed over David's face. "When I left, there were three girls I thought to court when I returned. Two of them have since married," he explained as he watched his friend finish with the cuff link. "I don't know what I'll do if Rose ends up with someone else."

"I shall not pursue her," Ertuğrul promised. "If there is a polite way in which I can grant you the waltz I have—"

"No, don't change anything," David said as he held up a hand. "With any luck, she won't have promised the supper dance to anyone," he added.

"She hadn't when we spoke with her earlier this afternoon," Ertuğrul said.

David seemed to visibly relax. "Please, don't tell anyone in the family I am considering Rose. I haven't even seen her—"

"She's very comely," Ertuğrul stated. "Which had me wondering if there is some other reason than her accident that she has not yet wed."

David considered his friend's assessment. "She's a duke daughter. Ariley would have run off the fortune hunters and, well..." he shrugged. "I might have mentioned my interest in her prior to my departure. Perhaps..." For a moment, he had a thought that Ariley might have dissuaded other potential suitors on his behalf. He shook his head, deciding that was merely wishful thinking. "I'll never be more than a viscount."

"He must respect you," Ertuğrul murmured. "Like you, even," he added on a tease. He suddenly sobered. "Or do you know something he wishes to keep secret?"

David blinked, almost immediately realizing what his friend was insinuating. "I do not," he replied on a huff. "Nor would I blackmail the man to get his daughter." His gaze dropped to Ertuğrul's shoes and slowly lifted. "You're dressed better than most of the women who will be there tonight," he accused. "And all the men, damn you."

Ertuğrul winced. "This is probably the only time you'll see me wearing traditional Turkish garb," he said. "I hadn't planned to, but your mother claims Lord Weatherstone's guests will be disappointed if I don't appear royal enough."

David chuckled. "If all the eyes are on you, then they won't be on me, and that's exactly the way I like it."

Giving him a frown, Ertuğrul followed David out the door and down the steps.

George and Elizabeth were already in the hall, the viscount placing a black velvet mantle on his wife's shoulders. "We're not late, my sweet. They will be along at any moment, and..." He looked up at the sound of the

Ertuğrul and David descending the stairs. "Here they are," he added, the change in his voice causing Elizabeth to turn and gape in wonder.

"Your Eminence," she said as she dipped a deep curtsy.

"Your ladyship," he replied as he bowed. "You are a vision," he added before taking her hand to his lips.

George cleared his throat. "That's enough practice. You'll do fine this evening," he said with a smirk. "Did you see your sister up there?"

David shook his head. "I saw the lady's maid go in right after she returned from the museum."

Moving to the base of the stairs, George was about to call up when the hurried but slight *thump thumps* of slippered feet sounded from above. "David, help your mother into the coach. We'll be along shortly."

When Adeline finally appeared on the last flight of stairs, George inhaled softly. "You look like a fairy tale princess," he said, knowing the tease would annoy her. Instead of the usual white ballgowns she had been forced to wear during her first few Seasons, which did nothing for her complexion, Elizabeth had announced that this year, she could wear a gown in a pale color. The full blue silk skirt was enhanced with a series of darker blue furbelows above the hemline with miniature versions along the neckline and at the edge of the gathered sleeves. Long white silk gloves ended just above her elbows.

But it was her hair that made her appear far older than her one-and-twenty years. A series of curls had been ironed into her hair, outlining an otherwise messy bun atop her head, all except for one curled lock that hung down and rested on her shoulder.

"Oh, Father. Can you believe what Perkins has done

to me?" she complained, referring to her mother's lady's maid.

George chuckled. "I'll see to it she receives a raise in pay."

Adeline gave him a quelling glance. "I'm not taking a wrap tonight."

"All right," he said as he escorted her out the door. "You'll have to sit between the boys. There's no room for your gown and your mother's on the same side of the coach."

Elkins nodded as the two took their leave and watched with a suppressed grin as Adeline struggled to push her skirts into the coach. Once the horses had pulled the coach away from the curb, he closed the door as he chuckled.

"*H*ave dresses grown wider whilst I was gone?" David asked as Adeline wedged herself between him and Ertuğrul.

"Obviously," Adeline replied once she was seated. She watched her father take his place next to his viscountess and realized she could take a breath.

A breath awash in an odd combination of spice, amber, leather, Bay Rum, and lime.

After a moment, she determined that all three men wore different colognes. The one to her right smelled the best, however, and she turned her head in that direction to discover Ertuğrul regarding her with the same bemused expression he had left her with. "Your gown is lovely, Miss Bennett-Jones."

She blinked. "Thank you, Your Eminence. Your suit is gorgeous, " she countered, barely able to see much of it given how packed they were in the coach. From the little she could see by the light of the coach lanterns, the embroidery appeared exquisite.

Did all the men in the empire wear such beautiful clothes for formal occasions? And smell so good?

She grinned at the thought of Lord Weatherstone hosting a ball in the Ottoman Empire. Hosting a ball for Ertuğrul. She could just imagine the sun setting over the majestic palace of the sultan, its red and gold hues reflecting off the intricate mosaics and the grand marble columns. Inside the palace, Ertuğrul would be preparing for the ball that was to be held in his honor.

As the night grew closer, he would anxiously await the arrival of a mysterious stranger who had been promised to him as a surprise guest.

Lady Rose.

Little did Ertuğrul know that this stranger would soon be the cause of a destructive and passionate romance between him and the beautiful viscount's daughter who had also been invited to the ball.

Adeline blinked.

From where had that last thought come?

"Addy?"

Jerked out of her reverie, Adeline stared at her brother, who was no longer sitting next to her but was staring at her from outside the coach door. "What?"

"Ertuğrul cannot get out of the coach until you do," he said on a huff.

"Oh!" She hadn't even been aware that the coach had stopped, let alone started. She caught a glimpse of Weatherstone Manor through the window, not surprised to find it was ablaze with lights. "Forgive me."

Adeline allowed her brother to help her down and turned to watch the şehzade follow. She inhaled softly at seeing his attire by the light of the lanterns that lined the path to the front door. In the ballroom, he would practically shimmer given all the gold he wore.

When he offered his silk-covered arm to her, Adeline hesitated and then tittered as she placed hers atop his. "I feel like an underdressed queen," she murmured in a teasing voice.

"Unless I am invited to an event hosted by your queen, I won't be wearing this again," Ertuğrul said under his breath.

"You look so dashing, though," she replied. "And if it's any consolation, there will be men here dressed like peacocks." She tittered again as his face betrayed his confusion. "You'll see what I mean."

As was usual for Weatherstone balls, Lord and Lady Weatherstone formed the start of a receiving line which included their son and heir, Sebastian, and their daughter-in-law, Vivian.

"Vivian—Viscountess Cougham—is my sister's best friend," Adeline whispered to Ertuğrul.

"You refer to Christina?" he guessed, remembering David had only two sisters.

"Indeed."

He nodded his understanding, apparently pleased he had something to say to the tall brunette who stood next to the even taller Viscount Cougham.

George handled the introductions, and Adeline watched in delight as Lady Weatherstone fawned over Ertuğrul's clothes. When he asked if she might join him for the Scottish reel—if she hadn't already promised it to someone else—she looked positively crestfallen. "There isn't one scheduled, but I may have to have the orchestra add one," she replied.

Glancing over at her brother, Adeline noticed how he was having trouble suppressing his amusement. He had obviously told Ertuğrul to ask for that particular dance knowing full well the Weathertones never offered a Scottish reel at their balls.

Once through the line, George informed the announcer as to their identities, the man's eyes widening at learning a sultan's son was among the guests.

"What's happening?"

Adeline leaned closer to Ertuğrul. "He will announce us and then we make our way down the stairs," she murmured. "I merely try not to look too frightened that I'll trip and fall flat on my face."

She made the comment so seriously, Ertuğrul placed his other hand on her arm and said, "I'll catch you before that happens."

At the very moment her mouth opened to mention that he would be descending the stairs by himself, the announcer stated, "His Eminence, the Emir Ertuğrul Effendi of the Ottoman Empire and Miss Bennett-Jones."

*E*rtuğrul glanced over at Adeline before he led her down the stairs, nodding first to the left and then to the right in acknowledgement of the smattering of applause that sounded from those already in attendance.

For a moment, he felt a bit overwhelmed by the excitement and grandeur. Everyone appeared dressed in their finest attire, the women in beautiful gowns, their hair adorned with turbans or feathers or glittering tiaras, and the men in tailcoats and waistcoats of every color. Apparently, the ones wearing the bright colors were the peacocks.

Vaguely aware of the announcer calling out his host's names and David's, Ertuğrul was momentarily relieved he hadn't had to make the descent by himself. A quick glance at Adeline showed she displayed a pleasant expression, although her color was high with what he assumed was nervousness.

Halfway down the stairs, he took note of the lighting. Several chandeliers, candelabras, and wall sconces cast the large room in a golden glow. Although the dancing hadn't yet begun, music filled the air from a small orchestra set up in one corner. A table off to one side held a huge punchbowl, and several footmen carrying salvers bearing champagne moved through the growing crowd.

By the time they made it to the bottom of the stairs, conversations and laughter had already resumed, the air abuzz with energy.

"Now what do we do?" he asked as they stepped aside to make way for the rest of the family to join them.

"You're with me," David said as he headed off into the crowd.

Ertuğrul glanced back at Adeline. "What about you?"

"Wallflowers, remember?" she replied with a grin, indicating the end of the room where a line of potted palms stood in front of a mural depicting a scene of nymphs in a forest. A number of young ladies stood in small clusters, their heads dipped in quiet conversation.

Nodding his understanding, Ertuğrul remembered her description of wallflowers and wondered how she had aligned herself with those who stood on the sidelines and watched. From his time with her that afternoon, he would not have thought her awkward or uncomfortable in a crowd. In fact, from the way the other young ladies greeted her, it was evident she wasn't shy.

"Would you like champagne?"

Giving a start, Ertuğrul realized David must have asked the question twice. "I don't drink spirits," he said.

"Suit yourself," David replied, helping himself to a glass from a footman's tray. Before he could take a drink, his gaze lifted to the top of the stairs. "She's here."

The booming voice of the announcer called out some new arrivals, and most of the heads in the room looked up to see the Duke and Duchess of Ariley descend the steps followed by Lady Rose and her brother, William, Earl of Waverley.

"She did not look like that this afternoon," Ertuğrul remarked. Dressed in an ivory satin ballgown trimmed in Belgium lace, her hair adorned with a jeweled tiara, Lady Rose was a diamond of the first water. She had been every year since her come-out. With her chin held high and lips curled in a wan grin, she appeared positively regal.

"She's looks like a damned princess," David said before draining his champagne in a single gulp.

Ertuğrul turned to regard his friend with a look of confusion. "Is that not good?"

"I don't want to have to vie for her attentions with twenty other blasted bucks," David groused.

"I doubt you will have to do such a thing. Especially if you were to go to her right now and request the supper dance." He was about to ask why there would be any bucks in the ballroom but thought better of it. Surely their hosts didn't allow wildlife indoors.

Apparently deciding Ertuğrul had the right of it, David made his way back to the base of the stairs, bowing to the duke and duchess before stepping forward to offer his arm to Rose.

"Bennett-Jones," William said in surprise, pausing on the bottom step. "You're finally back."

"I am," David acknowledged. He turned his gaze onto Rose, determined to secure the supper dance before he lost his nerve. "Lady Rose, it's very good to see you again," he said as he reached for her gloved hand. Although he recognized her immediately, there were differences in her appearance. She had matured into a lovely young woman.

"Mr. Bennett-Jones," she said as she dipped a curtsy. "I trust your trip went well?"

"I feared I was gone too long."

"I should say so," she replied on a huff.

"Please don't hold it against me, my lady," he said in a quiet voice. "I should hate to learn I have lost your good opinion."

She lifted a shoulder and dropped it in an exaggerated shrug. "Three years, two months and ten days is far too long to be away from civilized society, Mr. Bennett-Jones," she stated, her gaze darting about as if she was looking for someone.

Disappointment settled over David like a wet blanket. Apparently, he had missed his opportunity with the duke's daughter.

Then it hit him.

Three years, two months and ten days.

She had kept track of his absence. "That's rather specific," he countered. "Accurate, too," he added as he brows lifted.

Pretending nonchalance, Rose merely shrugged again, which only drew his attention to the expanse of milky white skin that showed above her neckline. To the hint of décolletage created by a pair of breasts he had thought smaller when he last saw her.

His gaze drifted back up to discover her jawline was more defined, her cheekbones more evident. The eyes that had one time regarded him with mischief—they had occasionally played together as children—were now regarding him with an unspoken challenge.

"You missed me," David murmured in surprise.

About to deny his claim, Rose lifted her chin and thought better of what she was about to say. "Maybe."

"May I have the honor of dancing the second waltz with you?" He reached for her dance card and the pencil that hung from it.

Her eyes rounding, Rose paused a moment before she removed the card from her wrist. "It's the supper dance," she said as if in warning.

"I am well aware," he replied as he wrote his name on the card, grinning at seeing how she had written Ertuğrul's name—*Airtoorool*. "Where will I find you?"

She glanced toward the line of potted palms. "I'll probably be standing over there with Fred."

At the mention of Fred, David blinked. "Fred?" he repeated.

"Your sister's palm tree," she replied as she rolled her eyes. "There's always one she seems to favor at these balls."

David's chuckle turned into a full-throated laugh.

"It's not that funny," Rose said, flipping open her fan as if to hide behind it.

"Probably not," he agreed. "But I know someone who will be very relieved to learn it's merely a potted plant and not some bloke over six feet tall."

Rose grinned despite her attempt at remaining annoyed. "At least plants don't tend to disappoint, Mr. Bennett-Jones."

"David, please," he replied. "And I shall do everything in my power to ensure you are never disappointed in me." Before she could respond, he bowed and took her hand in his once more. "I look forward to our dance."

She curtsied and hurried off.

Expecting Ertuğrul to have paid witness to the exchange, David turned and discovered the sultan's son was no longer nearby. A quick glance around, and he found him surrounded by a curious assortment of aristocrats, including James, Duke of Ariley, and his wife, bravely introducing himself.

Since he wished to speak with the duke, David joined the men and Lady Ariley.

"Ah, Bennett-Jones," Ariley said as David bowed. "It's good to see you're safely back in London."

"Thank you, Your Grace. Ertuğrul and I arrived only just yesterday. As such, I fear His Eminence has not yet secured many dances for this evening."

Ariley chuckled. "He has already claimed one with my duchess," he said. "Not the supper dance, though. That's mine," he said as Helen gave him an appreciative glance.

"If you'll excuse me, Your Grace, I will take my leave to seek dances with the wallflowers," Ertuğrul said as he bowed.

Ariley and the others bowed, grinning as they watched the sultan's son make his way to the wall featuring a line of potted palms.

"That's rather sporting of him," Ariley said with a grin. "He even asked my permission to dance with my daughter."

David inhaled softly, a streak of jealousy causing him to wince. He had to remind himself that Ertuğrul had promised not to court Rose. "Which is why I seek your company on this evening, sir. I, too, wish to dance with Lady Rose. The supper dance, if you'll allow it."

Ariley regarded him with an assessing glance. "You are always welcome to dance with Rose," he said. "I thought I had made that clear several years ago."

His eyes widening at hearing the duke's response, David said, "Thank you, sir. Since it's been so long, I thought it best I ask again."

"I understand you've become somewhat of an expert in the manufacture and installation of mosaics," Helen said. "Are you available for a consultation with my decorator?"

David blinked. "Uh, of course, Your Grace. I would be happy to help. What are you wishing to have done?" he asked, thinking she might be after a small hunting scene in a vestibule or the billiards room.

"The floor in our Red Room," she replied. "It's our largest salon. I wish to change the name to the Greek Room, and I want it to be as if I was walking into the salon of a rich Greek merchant. An ancient one, of course. And there would be columns of deeply grained marble, and Grecian couches, and rich fabrics, and statuary. Lots of statuary."

Noting the duke's look of alarm at hearing his wife's list of ideas, David said, "Of course, ma'am. I believe I can be of assistance. There are some sources for gorgeous mosaic tiles in north Africa. Very affordable." He suppressed a grin when he noticed the duke's look of relief.

"You are planning to attend our ball next week, are you not?" she asked. "We would be honored to have the emir attend as well."

"Of course, Your Grace. My mother informed me of your ball when we returned to London yesterday. We would not miss it." He noticed the music had ended and another dance was about to start. "Oh, forgive me. I have promised this dance to someone."

"Enjoy your evening," Ariley said, arching a brow. "I hear the gardens are especially lovely tonight."

"I shall be sure to take a tour, Your Grace." David bowed and backed away, relieved he hadn't lost the good opinion of the Duke and Duchess of Ariley.

As for the suggestion he take a tour of the gardens, he was fairly sure the duke didn't intend for him to tour them by himself.

So why did he think it would be difficult to escort a certain young lady among the early spring blooms?

CHAPTER 18
THE WALLFLOWERS

t the other end of the ballroom
By the time Rose made it to end of the ballroom where most of the wallflowers had already gathered, the first dance had begun. The longways dance required the clusters of those in conversation to step to the sides of the ballroom to clear a path for those who had secured partners.

"There you are," Adeline said a she turned around. One of the other young ladies had nodded upon seeing Rose threading her way through the crowd.

"This hasn't happened since my very first ball," Rose said as she held out her dance card.

Adeline furrowed a brow as she glanced at the white pasteboard card. Her eyes widened. "You have nearly every line filled," she commented in awe, her attention going to the line for the supper dance. She immediately recognized David's scribble of a signature.

"I don't understand," Rose said. "I was approached by nearly every young buck in the ballroom from the base of the stairs until I got here. Starting with your brother."

"Why is it you don't sound pleased?" Lady Lucy asked. "I would be thrilled to have half of my lines filled," she added as she showed her card. Only four dances had been claimed, but two of those had been reserved by the future viscount Mark Cunningham.

"Something tells me you'll be a future viscountess," Adeline whispered happily. "Rich, too."

"I am merely surprised is all," Rose said as Lucy displayed a brilliant smile of excitement at hearing Adeline's assessment.

"As am I," Lady Patience remarked, waving her nearly filled card. "Pleasantly surprised. It's all this 'first ball of the Season' excitement."

"Actually," her sister, Faith Fulton, said as she held up a finger. "It's because there won't be a card room open until after the supper dance."

"What?!" The chorus of surprise had the ladies giggling when those standing nearby turned to regard them with various looks of censure and amusement.

"It was Lady Cougham's suggestion, and Lady Weatherstone agreed, of course, because she positively *adores* Vivian," Hope Batey explained.

Adeline grinned at the thought of her sister Christina's best friend ensuring there would be more young men to dance if they didn't have a card room in which they could hide during the ball. "I suppose the library is open, though." She glanced around in search of her maternal grandparents. Everyone knew the Marquess and Marchioness of Morganfield enjoyed a tryst at some point during a ball.

A chorus of titters followed her remark. Older couples seemed to favor the library over the gardens when it came to prearranged liaisons, probably because it contained a large leather sofa. Only one couple could occupy the library at a time, though, which meant some of the more amorous aristocrats were forced to find an alcove in which to carry on their illicit *affaires*.

The chatter around her suddenly quieted, and Adeline noticed how the young ladies began dipping deeper than usual curtsies. She turned to discover Ertuğrul bowing.

"Ertuğrul," she said as she hurried to join him. The inhalations of breath behind her reminded her that she hadn't yet told the wallflowers about the sultan's son. "May I have the honor of introducing you to my friends?" she asked.

"I would like that very much," he replied, grinning at the young ladies who now stood in a straight line between two potted palms. They looked as if they had become part of the decorations given the painted mural behind them, although their expressions ranged from shock to humor. "And I hope to secure a dance with every one of you."

Adeline gave him an approving nod, her gaze darting to Rose. "Emir Ertuğrul Effendi, this is..." Adeline began as she moved to the left end of the line, "Lady Lucy Turnbridge, daughter of the Earl and Countess of Fennington..." She paused as he took Lucy's hand and kissed the back of it. "The Ladies Patience and Faith Fulton, daughters of the Earl and Countess of Wadsworth..." Adeline rolled her eyes as the emir kissed their gloved hands and examined the dance cards hanging from their wrists. "Miss Hope Batey, daughter of the Viscount and Viscountess Lancaster..." She did her best not to titter at seeing Hope's eyes round into saucers as the emir kissed the back of her hand. "And, of course, Lady Rose, whom you have already met. His Eminence is our guest at Bostwick House for the Season."

The girls murmured greetings as Ertuğrul asked them

if they might afford him a dance. When he straightened from having completed their cards, he glanced around. "I understand there may be a challenger for my affections somewhere nearby. Where is Fred?"

Rose gasped and covered her mouth with a gloved hand as the other young ladies once again burst out into a fit of giggles.

"He's right here," Adeline said with a grin as she waved to the nearest potted palm. "Please don't challenge him to a duel, though. He's completely defenseless. Can't hold a pistol, and he's rot with a sword."

"But he's a good listener," Rose said with a shrug.

"He never argues," Lucy commented.

"And he's one of Lord Weatherstone's favorites. He's always right here, year after year," Faith added, her hands clasping together as she lifted them to her chest and angled her head to one side.

Ertuğrul blinked as he regarded the plant that was barely taller than he was. "Well," he said as he placed his hands on his hips and puffed out his chest. "I suppose I can grant him a reprieve this one time," he said, trying to remain as serious as possible. He chuckled though, apparently relieved. He turned to Adeline. "Might you have another dance available for me on this night?"

Adeline gave a start. "Are you quite sure *you* have an opening?" she teased.

He took her card and the small pencil and wrote an 'E' in script on two lines, one of them the supper dance. "Not any longer," he said proudly. He leaned in closer, "Which means I don't have to try and remember the names of all these men who insist on speaking with me about matters of the empire."

"Ah, politics, you mean?" she guessed.

"Exactly. I know about our buildings, is all." He realized the last dance was ending and moved to escort Faith to the end of the line for an English country dance. The rest of the young ladies watched with amusement when they departed.

Well aware Rose stood at her side, Adeline said, "Well, what are your thoughts on our esteemed guest?"

Rose glanced over at her and shrugged. "He's very pleasant," she remarked.

Adeline winced. "Oh, dear. Perhaps the first waltz will improve your opinion of him," she replied. She had such high hopes for her friend and the sultan's son. When they had been standing together only the moment before, they looked positively regal together. "I couldn't help but notice my brother's signature is on your dance card."

Dipping her head, Rose examined the card before allowing a shrug. "He was the second to claim a waltz," she said. "The supper dance."

Adeline considered the comment. "Were you surprised?"

Rose regarded her with a furrowed brow and then allowed her gaze to sweep the ballroom. "Truth be told, I had hoped to speak with him this evening. Scold him, rather, which I did quite thoroughly."

It was Adeline's turn to give a start. "Whatever for?"

Prevented from answering when a young man bowed before her, Rose curtsied and gave Adeline a quick shrug before she hurried off to join the dance already in progress.

About to return to stand with the remaining three girls—Adeline was curious as to what gossip they might have heard since their last tea together—she discovered they were all on the arms of young men and headed in the direction of the dancing.

Sighing, she moved to stand next to Fred but was intercepted by her brother before she made it two steps.

"Dance with me," he ordered, offering his arm.

Startled, Adeline went with him. They had barely joined the line when he leaned closer and said, "I must discover what you know." The dance, already in progress, forced him to step away and in front of another partner, so Adeline couldn't ask what he was about until the steps once again brought him near to her.

"Know about what?" she asked.

"Lady Rose." Then he was behind her and off to the partner to her right for the next part of the set. She nodded politely to an older gentleman who was now in front of her. Glancing down the line, she discovered Ertuğrul was performing the steps as if he'd been doing them his whole life.

How could that be?

Had he danced whilst at Cambridge more than he had admitted?

Or had her brother given him last-minute lessons that evening?

"Is her card full?"

Adeline blinked, shocked to find her brother was once again paired with her. "Mostly, but I think she still had a line or two empty. What's this about?"

"Is anyone courting her?" he asked before the dance once again took him to another partner and left her with Gabe Wellingham.

"We meet again on this day," he said with a grin.

"Indeed. How is Mrs. Wellingham? I did not see your arrival."

"She is home this evening. She's begun her confinement," he managed to say between labored breaths. "I wished to inform Father and Mother, and I knew I would find them here," he explained. "With any luck, I'll be a father again in the next few days." His brilliant smile had Adeline giggling.

"Do give her my regards," she said before her brother was once again in front of her. "I was hoping Ertuğrul might court Rose," she said. The look on David's face had her missing a step. "What's wrong?"

"He promised he would not," David said when the dance had him drawing closer to her.

For a moment, confusion had Adeline wishing they could have just remained with Fred to have what was becoming a very disjointed discussion. "But no one is courting her," she argued.

At that point, David missed a step, grabbed Adeline's hand, and pulled her out of the line.

"Pardon me," Adeline said by way of apology to the older gentleman who had been about to take her hand. She allowed David to pull her along if only because he was clearing a path for her through what had become a crush.

When they reached a clearing nearing the French doors that led to the gardens, David stopped and regarded her with an expression of anger mixed with uncertainty.

"Whatever is wrong?" she asked, wishing her gown's skirts weren't so wide. She had to lean over in order to keep their conversation private.

"Lady Rose. You saw her today?"

Adeline nodded. "She came to the museum. I sent her a note last night letting her know I would be there."

"How long was she there?" he asked, obviously disturbed by the news.

"Not long," she said with a shrug. "Spent some time

with us in Townley Hall and then took her leave. What's wrong?"

For a moment, David didn't look as if he would give her an answer, but he finally sighed. "Hopefully nothing," he said. "She... did not greet me as I hoped upon her arrival this evening."

Adeline furrowed her brows. "What did you expect, exactly? You've been gone for three years—"

"Three years, two months and ten days," he said on a huff.

Remembering Rose's comment at the museum earlier that afternoon, Adeline narrowed her eyes. "That's rather specific," she murmured. "And exactly what Rose said to me."

David gave a start. "To me as well," he admitted. "So, she *is* she angry with me?"

Adeline blinked, slowly realizing why David seemed so upset. Of all the eligible young ladies, she hadn't thought *he* would be interested in Rose Burroughs. Although he had known her since they were young children, she was a duke's daughter. He was a viscount's son. He would never be more than a viscount. "Did you... did you make some sort of promise to her before you left on your Grand Tour?" she asked.

He shook his head. "Of course not."

"Did you write to her?"

Angling his head to one side as he gave her a quelling glance, David didn't respond.

"It was just a question," she said as she scoffed. After a moment, she added, "If she is angry with you, she has not put voice to it. At least not to me."

"So what prompted her to say what she did about how long I was gone?"

Adeline stared at him for a time before a slow grin

appeared. "Apparently, our dear Lady Rose missed you," she murmured.

"I have the duke's permission to dance the second waltz with her."

Inhaling softly, Adeline remembered Ertuğrul had written his signature twice on her own dance card, but she hadn't examined the card to determine which dances he had claimed. She lifted her wrist and regarded the card with a chuckle. "It seems I will be waltzing with Ertuğrul at the same time." Well, he had said he wished to dance the supper dance with her.

"The duke informed me the gardens were not to be missed," David remarked as he arched a dark brow.

"Oh, I hear the early spring blooms are…" Adeline stopped speaking, her eyes rounding as a grin once again split her face. "Oh, David. He's given you permission to…" She stopped again, wondering if Ertuğrul expected to tour the gardens with her.

"To what, do you think?"

"Well… kiss her, of course. Ask her to go riding in the park with you. Ask if you might escort her in Rotten Row. Ask her to… to marry you," she added on a whisper.

"Well, let's not get ahead of ourselves," he said.

"Why ever not? Isn't that what you want? *Her?*" Adeline challenged.

David inhaled to answer but dipped his head. "I don't yet know for sure," he replied.

"How can you not know?" she challenged. "You either love her or you don't."

"I've been gone three years, two months and ten days," he reminded her. "And she is *not* pleased with me."

Adeline's fists went to her hips. "So… make her pleased with you," she argued. "Take her to the gardens, kiss her senseless, and…" She clamped her mouth shut, shocked at what she was telling her brother to do to her best friend. "Make her my sister," she whispered.

She lifted her eyes to meet her brother's and was surprised at what she saw in them.

Humor.

Well, and a bit of fear.

CHAPTER 19
THE FIRST WALTZ

A half hour later

When Ertuğrul approached Rose for the first waltz of the evening, he had expected her to behave much like she had upon their meeting in the British Museum.

He had found the duke's daughter pleasant enough, but her behavior had been aloof, almost proud. Familiar with roses—they were one of the most coveted flowers in Anatolia—he decided she was only living up to her name. Every rose came with thorns, and it was apparent Lady Rose had them.

Instead, the duke's daughter seemed happy to see him, her eyes bright as they took their places around the empty circle of ballroom floor that had formed once the last dance had ended. Remembering his lessons, he placed a hand at her waist and held the other aloft, pleased when her own gloved hands landed on his shoulder and in his hand. A quick glance around the ballroom showed they were but one of dozens of couples about to engage in a dance that had at one time been considered scandalous.

Why, he had never been able to discern. Partners were held so far apart—probably because the ladies' skirts were so large—there was no way any illicit behavior could take place.

When the strains of the three-count music started up from the five-piece orchestra, he gave a nod and led her into the first three steps.

"If I start to fall, will you catch me?" Rose asked.

Ertuğrul furrowed a brow. "I am not that poor a dancer," he replied.

"Oh, I was not insinuating that you were," she said with a shake of her head. "I was in a carriage accident, you see, and my leg was broken. Sometimes it seems as if it's not completely healed."

"Does it pain you to dance?" he asked, his brows furrowed in worry.

"Not yet," she assured him, giving him a wobbly grin.

"I will catch you, of course, but if dancing should cause you pain, please inform me. I will do my best to maneuver us out of the circle without drawing too much attention."

Rose grinned. "Thank you." She circled under his arm, and when her hand was once again on his shoulder, she asked, "Did you enjoy your afternoon at the museum?"

"Oh, very much," he replied, his gaze darting about to be sure they weren't going to collide with another couple. "Mr. Wellingham joined us shortly after you left and gave us access to the East Wing."

Her eyes widening, Rose said, "Isn't that closed to the public?"

"Indeed," he said, and he had to wait a moment while

she twirled beneath his arm to add, "But it seems Miss Adeline has some sway with the curator."

"Oh, I rather imagine it was you who swayed Mr. Wellingham, Your Eminence," Rose countered. "How could he turn down such a request by an important dignitary?"

Ertuğrul chuckled softly. "I am not yet a sultan, my lady," he said. "Which is why I don't wish to mislead any of the young ladies into thinking I am a... a good catch? I think that is what they call it?"

Rose's pleasant expression faltered. "But you are an emir, which would suggest you have some position of importance in your country."

"True," he agreed. Once again, it was time for Rose to go under his arm, and halfway through the turn, she seemed to stutter-step. Her eyes were wide when her hand went to the top of his shoulder and gripped it, as if she needed his support to keep her upright.

"Apologies," she whispered.

"Are you in pain?" Ertuğrul immediately scoped out the area around them, looking for a break in the crush where he might dance them out of the circle.

"No. No, I'm fine. I think I may have stepped on the hem of my gown is all," she replied.

"If you're sure," he said. At her nod, he struggled to think of what they might talk about. David had warned him he needed to converse whilst dancing. "May I inquire as to your thoughts on marriage?" he asked. "Specifically, who on the list you're most interested in courting?"

Rose stared at the sultan's son, doing her best to keep her mouth from dropping open at the bold query. "The list?" she repeated. She nearly cursed at having to go under his arm again, but was ready to resume the conversation immediately after she had her hand back on his shoulder. "What list?"

Ertuğrul blinked. "The list of eligible young aristocrats who have completed university, returned from their Grand Tours, and are not already married," he replied. "And for you, a duke's daughter, I would expect they must be sons of higher positions within the aristocracy, or a prince, perhaps?"

Rose blinked. "That's rather specific," she replied, doing her best not to offend the emir by tittering. He had a point, though. There was a list, even if she had avoided confronting the issue since the end of the last Season. "As for sons of higher ranking aristocrats, there really aren't that many at this time," she added, "so I have no expectations in that regard."

Curious if she might divulge her preference, Ertuğrul pressed the issue. "Surely you have someone in mind, and if you do not, might I make a recommendation?" he asked.

For a moment, Rose feared he was going to suggest himself, and she was relieved when she was once again sent under his arm. She knew the music was coming to its end. Perhaps she would be saved from having to provide an answer. "That all depends, sir."

"On what?" Ertuğrul asked, his dark brows furrowing.

"Your motivation, I suppose."

He glanced about, noting how the other couples movements had slowed now that the music was fading. "Hope for a friend, is all," he said in a quiet voice.

"A friend?" she repeated in surprise.

Ertuğrul was about to mention David's name, but a young man had approached and was bowing to them.

"Pardon, sir, but I'm here to collect Lady Rose for the next dance."

The sober manner of the man had Ertuğrul thinking he was used to getting his way. "Of course, my lord," he said with a nod.

Rose dipped a deep curtsy to Ertuğrul's bow. "Thank you for the dance," she said before turning to Mark Fitzsimmons. "How do, Lord Chamberlain?" She took his proffered arm and gave Ertuğrul an apologetic glance before she was whisked off to start the cotillion.

CHAPTER 20
THE SECOND WALTZ

An hour later

"I never thought I would welcome the sight of Fred so much in my life," Rose said as she joined Adeline next to the potted palm. She glanced around, surprised to discover the other girls were missing from their usual posts. "I haven't danced this much since my come-out."

Adeline grinned. "You looked as if you were enjoying yourself, and that's what's important," she said as she stood on tiptoes in an attempt to see over the crowd. "And apparently, Patience, Faith, Hope and Lucy are having a good time, too. I haven't seen them since the first waltz."

"They went to get punch. Or rather, they were escorted there," Rose murmured, her brows waggling. "I do believe Viscount Chamberlain has chosen his candidate for Viscountess Chamberlain," she added, referring to Lady Lucy. "The supper dance is next."

"It is?" Adeline asked in alarm. Although she hadn't danced as much as the other young ladies, she had enjoyed her evening watching the comings and goings of various couples as they made their way through French doors leading to the gardens.

Perhaps they were unaware they were being watched. Or perhaps they didn't care if they were spotted. Although she hadn't been keeping track of the length of time certain couples spent out of doors, it was evident most of the men were having their way with the ladies. Only the older couples returned before the younger couples, most complaining it was too cold to be in the gardens without a wrap.

None of the younger couples made similar remarks, which had Adeline thinking they were either impervious to the cold or were so engrossed in their liaisons, they didn't notice.

She was about to ask Rose how her leg was holding up when her brother David appeared. "Adeline," he said with a nod. He turned to Rose and bowed. "I've come to claim the second waltz, my lady."

Rose dipped a curtsy and, giving Adeline a quick glance and a grin, she placed her hand on his proffered arm and disappeared into the crush.

"They make a very handsome couple," a male voice said from behind and to her right.

Adeline gave a start and turned to discover Ertuğrul making his way in her direction. "I suppose so," she replied as she grinned. "Have you enjoyed yourself?"

He nodded, "Indeed. This is a very strange ritual, but there is much joy in it," he said. "I have come to the domain of the wallflowers to claim the supper dance."

"Oh!" she replied. "I'd almost forgot." She couldn't help but notice the flicker of disappointment that crossed Ertuğrul's face. "It was to be *this* dance, I mean. The evening has flown by."

Apparently Ertuğrul took some solace in her comment, for he offered his arm. "Shall we?"

Adeline placed her arm on his and they merged onto the dance floor using the same path that had been cleared for her brother and Rose. "What has been your favorite dance so far?" she asked as she placed a hand in his. Despite her gloves, she could feel the warmth of his hand and the intricate embroidery of his kaftan against the pads of her fingers.

"The waltz, if only because there aren't as many steps to learn," he replied. The music started, and after three counts, he moved them into the inner circle of dancers. With so many couples engaged in the second waltz, the outer circle had grown too large, making it necessary for a few couples to dance in the middle.

"I've never been in the middle before," Adeline said with some excitement.

"I worried we might collide with another couple," he said, keeping his attention as much on her as he did on those around them.

"Did that happen during the first waltz?" she asked in alarm.

He chuckled. "No, but I think I may have caused Lady Rose to... stumble a bit."

"Her leg gave out?"

"No. She claimed she stepped on her hem."

Adeline glanced to her left, easily finding her brother leading Rose. "Oh, that's to be expected," she replied. "Especially if she dipped too low to go under your arm." The very moment she made the comment, she was sent beneath his. Given their height difference, it wasn't necessary for her to bend to one side to fit under his arm.

"You are easier to dance with," Ertuğrul said.

"Thank you," she replied as she allowed a brilliant

smile. "All this dancing must have increased your appetite. Are you hungry?"

"I am. Am I right to assume the term 'supper dance' means there is a meal associated with it?"

She chuckled. "A buffet, actually."

He furrowed a brow. "I do not think I recognize that word."

"Imagine lots of different foods all lined up on a long table with empty plates at each end. Like how our breakfast is served in the morning, but... much more in the way of food choices."

"Will there be lobster rolls?"

Adeline scrunched her nose. "Yes, and lobster cakes."

"You don't like lobster?" he asked in surprise.

"I used to. But it's so common, and not always well done," she explained. "The Weatherstones' cook does a decent job of it, though. The specialty here is the roast beef, and there is usually a curry dish or two since the Weatherstones visited India a long time ago."

They danced in companionable silence for a time before Ertuğrul noticed a few couples had danced their way out of the outer circle and into the crowd. "Where do you suppose they are going?" he asked.

"To eat," Adeline replied. "There are always those who wish to be first in line for the food."

"What is this I hear about a card room?"

She grimaced. "Ah, the reminder that we shall lose half of our dance partners," she remarked. "There is a separate room set up with tables for playing card games. Whist, mostly, but there will be some others. The men like to gamble, so they will play for money."

Ertuğrul seemed to think on her explanation for a time before he asked, "Do you think I will be expected to join them?"

Adeline considered the query for a moment. "Has anyone challenged you to a game?"

He shook his head. "Not that I know of."

"Good. Then you shall be free to dance or go to the gardens should you wish."

"The gardens seem as if they are a very popular spot this evening," he repeated. "Can they be that large?"

Tittering, Adeline said, "Probably not by your standards, but they are the most remarkable gardens in all of Park Lane."

"Isn't it too dark to make out the plants?"

Adeline's titter turned into a giggle. "Most couples don't go out there to admire the flowers so much as they look for a dark place in which to engage in..." She clamped her mouth shut.

Ertuğrul's eyes darted to one side. "Kissing?" he guessed.

Already warm from the dance, Adeline knew the color in her cheeks deepened. "Probably."

His gaze followed a young couple as they hurriedly made their way in the direction of the French doors. "Making love?" he suggested.

Adeline's eyes widened. "Perhaps, although I'm not sure there's really any place out there it can be done... comfortably," she said in a quiet voice.

"I suppose not. Which is why there is the library."

"Ertuğrul!" she scolded, even as her grin widened to a brilliant smile. "Who told you about the *library*?"

The sultan's son sobered. "David might have mentioned your... grandparents. They tend to spend some time there, do they not? I couldn't help but notice Lord Morganfield's color seemed especially high when your mother introduced me to him."

"He didn't," Adeline replied with a scoff.

"Lady Morganfield is especially lovely. I would never have guessed she was old enough to have grandchildren of yours and David's age."

"Oh, that's because she's Italian," Adeline said. She was tempted to add that it helped the marchioness made frequent visits to the library, but thought better of it.

Ertuğrul grinned. "You have her eyes," he said.

Adeline inhaled a bit deeper than the dancing required. "Thank you."

A moment later, and the final strains of the supper dance faded. Once Adeline had curtsied to Ertuğrul's bow, they headed for the supper room.

CHAPTER 21
THE GARDENS

*M*eanwhile...

Even before the music for the second waltz was halfway complete, David sensed Rose was having difficulty. Spying an opening in the crowd, he said, "Stay with me, and don't be alarmed," he warned.

Rose blinked. "Whatever are you going to...? Oh!"

Despite the momentum that would have sent her sprawling if not for David's strong lead and subsequent hold on her as he danced them out of the circle, Rose managed to slow to a walk and to do so without limping.

"I apologize, but I was concerned your limb might be experiencing some discomfort after so much dancing, and I didn't wish for you to be in pain," he explained as he escorted them towards the French doors.

"My limb is fine," she replied, about to insist that he resume the dance. What if someone saw their hasty retreat from the dance floor? A twinge of pain had her wincing and she decided David had made the correct move. "But I appreciate your consideration." Outside the doors, she inhaled deeply in an effort to settle her labored breathing.

"I hope you don't mind," David said as he led them away from the doors and along the pavers leading through the gardens. "I haven't been in these gardens for a very long time, and I've been told Lord Weatherstone has made improvements." He glanced over at her, surprised to discover she had threaded her arm around his and her other hand was lightly resting on his forearm. Perhaps he had guessed right and her leg was about to give out on her.

"Over three years, two months and ten days, I imagine," she gently chided, a teasing smile showing when David glanced over at her with a furrowed brow.

When he saw she was smiling, he chuckled. "It has been at least that long," he agreed.

They walked slowly through the dark gardens, the swish of Rose's skirts against David's leg the only sound they made. The early spring air was alive with the sound of crickets and the sweet scent of flowers. The shadows of the back garden's three trees danced across the grass as they passed beneath them, moonlight and a few Japanese lanterns providing enough light to follow the well-worn pavers sunk into the cut lawn.

Stopping every now and then to admire the beauty of the night and the stars twinkling above, David was filled with a deep sense of peace as he took in the romantic atmosphere of the garden.

He could only hope Rose was experiencing the same sense of peace. The same sense of calm that had settled over him ever since they had stepped out of the waltz.

A breeze ruffled his hair, which had him shaking off the reverie he'd been experiencing for the past few minutes. "Are you cold?" he asked.

"It is a bit chilly out here," Rose replied. Although she wore long gloves, her upper arms were bare as were the tops of her shoulders. The ivory satin gown's sleeves, edged in a thin satin ruffle, were ruched and barely rested on the edge of her shoulder. The fitted bodice was lower cut than most of the gowns the young misses wore, but given she was no longer a debutante, it was appropriate for the formal occasion.

David immediately stopped walking to undo the fastenings of his top coat. He shrugged out of it and draped it over Rose's shoulders, heartened when she surreptitiously sniffed the superfine wool collar and grinned.

"Does it smell of my cologne?" he asked.

"You've been wearing this scent for as long as I can remember," she replied.

"But do you like it?" he pressed.

She nodded. "Of course. You would not be David Bennett-Jones if you wore a different cologne," she chided.

Warmed by her words, David once again offered his arm. "I shall be sure to have Floris save the recipe for the rest of my life," he said on a chuckle.

They walked in silence for a few more steps before David glanced around and said, "Is it my imagination, or are the hedgerows shorter than they used to be?" At one time, it was possible for couples to hide behind the hedgerows and engage in a round of kissing before returning to the ballroom.

Rose giggled. "They are shorter because Lord Weatherstone has become shorter these past few years," she said.

"He has become rather crooked," David agreed. "He's

made other changes as well. Wasn't there a statue and a fountain back here somewhere?"

"Are you referring to Cupid?" she asked as they passed beneath an ivy-covered trellis.

"You know of him?" he asked, a streak of jealousy reminding him that she was his age. That she had no doubt been in the gardens with other young bucks over the years he wasn't in London.

"I come out here every year, if not during a ball, then during one of Lady Weatherstone's *soirées*," she said. She gently pulled on his shirt sleeve so he turned to the right. They followed the faint sounds of splashing water until they reached the white stone fountain.

Cupid was still mounted atop the center column, his bow loaded with an arrow as if he was poised to shoot some poor unsuspecting soul.

A circular bench surrounded the pool, and he led them to it. Rose took a seat, obviously relieved to be off her feet for a few minutes. David sat next to her, careful to leave a few inches between them lest they be spotted by someone.

The last thing he wanted was to be a topic of gossip in the next issue of *The Tattler*.

"When you've come out here during a ball... who usually accompanies you?" he asked, trying not to sound jealous.

Rose turned and regarded him with an expression of bemusement. "Do I detect a hint of jealousy?" she teased.

David's gaze darted to a nearby tree and then to a daffodil. "If you do?" He clasped his hands together and rested his elbows on his knees.

Giving a start, Rose angled her body to better face him. "I would be surprised since I have known you almost my entire life, and you've never seemed the jealous type before." She paused a moment before asking, "Did something happen while you were in Turkey?"

He straightened. "Did it? I mean... did someone court you? Make you an offer?"

Inhaling softly, Rose was torn between showing annoyance at hearing his query or removing herself to the ballroom. "Not that it's any of your business, but yes, I was courted by someone." She almost enjoyed seeing the future viscount's reaction. "He was a fortune hunter, though, and I declined his offer."

"A duke's son?" he asked. "A prince or—"

"He was the third son of the an earl, if you really must know. He's left for the Continent, apparently chased out by all his vowels." She said this last with a good deal of derision, and for a moment, David was glad he hadn't accepted any of the offers he'd had to join some other gentlemen in the card room that was due to open at any moment.

Then he remembered what happened to young ladies who were courted by older men, sometimes before they were betrothed. "Did he take your virtue?"

"David Bennett-Jones!" she scolded. "I am a duke's daughter. My father would have shot him if he'd tried anything like that."

Looking suitably chagrined, David dipped his head. "I am sorry that happened to you," he said. "I mean... the courting. By a fortune hunter."

"Why are *you* sorry?" she challenged, unable to suppress the subsequent *huff* she'd struggled so hard to hide all night whenever her dance partners had attempted inane conversations.

He inhaled and let the breath out in a *whoosh*, his frustration evident. "You deserve better, my lady. You deserve the best," he amended.

Rose inhaled softly at hearing his words. "It's kind of you to say so."

"Which is why I never asked if I might court you," he said, ignoring her comment.

Holding her breath at hearing his confession, Rose stared at him in shock. "You are better, David. Better than most of those reprobates in that ballroom. At least... you were before you left on your Grand Tour," she added in a quieter voice.

Although he was heartened to hear her assessment of him, David shook his head. "I am a viscount's son. I am never going to be more than a viscount."

Rose's gaze darted to the same daffodil that he had been staring at earlier. "You say that as if it's a poor circumstance."

"Isn't it?"

Unable to discern his meaning, she glanced over at him, studying his profile by the dim light of a nearby lantern. Understanding suddenly dawned on her.

She was a duke's daughter. He would never be more than a viscount.

"There are far worse situations in which to find your-self, David," she argued. "You could be a pauper. Or a tailor. Or one of the Fitzwilliam twins," she said in a quiet voice.

David gave a start. "What's wrong with the Fitzwilliam twins?" he asked in alarm.

She scoffed. "Nothing, really. But I still can't tell them apart. I cannot even imagine being courted by one of them. I'd never be sure which one was taking me riding and which one was meeting me in a rose garden for a tryst."

Despite her serious expression, David couldn't

suppress the chuckle that erupted a moment later. "So you learned what happened with their mother, I take it?" he commented, remembering a story his mother had told him about the boys' father and his twin brother.

"I beg your pardon?" Rose asked, her eyes rounding.

David's grin slowly faded. "Lady Norwick... the original Fitzwilliam twins? The younger twin apparently courted her but she ended up married to the older twin. She couldn't tell them apart," he explained with a shrug.

"How awful!" Rose replied, her eyes rounded in shock.

"Oh, it turned out all right in the end," David assured her. "She ended up married to the right one when the wrong one died in some sort of traffic accident. The current Earl of Norwick is the one who fathered Duncan and David, and it's Duncan who will inherit."

Rose stared at David for a long moment before she said, "In the end, a man's title doesn't really matter."

He swallowed, wondering if she was giving him some sort of hint or permission to pursue her. Deciding he would take a chance and attempt a kiss, he couldn't when nearby laughter had him rising to his feet. "I should escort you into the supper room," he said as he held out a hand to help her up.

"All right," she said, although there was a hint of disappointment in her voice.

They had taken only three steps from the fountain when an older couple appeared in the clearing and immediately came to a halt.

"Is that you, Rose?"

Inhaling sharply, Rose turned to discover her mother and father standing hand-in-hand next to the fountain. "Hello," she managed.

"Ah, Bennett-Jones. So good to see it is *you* escorting

my daughter," James, Duke of Ariley, said. "Did you enjoy the waltz?"

"Very much, Your Grace," David answered as he bowed. "I brought Lady Rose out for some air, but we're headed back inside to partake of the supper."

"Well, you needn't hurry back in," the duke countered. "The line is no doubt rather long at the moment. You can take your time. Enjoy Weatherstone's latest additions to the gardens."

David blinked. "Additions, sir?"

Helen took over and said, "The west side gardens are magnificent. You really must see the tulips. We've only just come from there."

Glancing over at Rose, David said, "Well, if you insist, we'll head over there right now."

"Do enjoy the evening," Ariley said as he took off his top coat and placed it on his wife's shoulders. "Thanks for the reminder," he said in a quieter voice, nodding to what David had done with his own topcoat.

"You're welcome, Your Grace. Have a good evening." David offered Rose his arm and they stepped back under the trellis. Behind them, the duke and duchess were once again laughing, apparently taking up where they had left off when they encountered David and Rose.

Rose suddenly giggled.

"What is it?" David asked, following a set of pavers that led to the west end of the house.

"I think that fountain is where they first kissed," she said. "And if I'm not mistaken, they're probably doing it again right now."

Relaxing now that they were out of her parents' sight, David chuckled. "You sound jealous," he accused with a grin.

"Maybe I am," she replied. There was no humor in

her voice, and David took the hand that rested on his arm and lifted it to his lips. He kissed the back of it.

Rose stopped in her tracks and stared up at him. "Why did you do that?"

David swallowed. "I wanted to do far more," he whispered. "Back at the fountain. Say more. Learn your thoughts on the matter."

About to respond, Rose was suddenly aware of faraway voices and soft giggles. A stream of couples was exiting the ballroom by way of the French doors. Gripping David's hand, she pulled him along the path to the west side until the house hid them from view. Given the lack of tall hedgerows and the openness of the newer garden, she didn't think they would be interrupted.

"What was it I said?" David asked when they were far enough away and had slowed their steps.

Rose turned and placed a hand on his chest. "Tell me the truth, David. Are you attempting to encourage me into a... a courtship with the sultan's son?"

David blinked. "What? No!" he replied as he stared down at her. "Not that... not that it would be wrong, of course. He's the equivalent of a prince. You deserve a man with that sort of station in life."

Scoffing, Rose dropped his hand. "Would you stop with the talk of titles and for just one minute think of me as a... as a *woman?*"

Jerking his head back in confusion, David regarded her with a furrowed brow. "All right, Miss Burroughs—"

"Rose. Call me Rose."

He placed a hand over the one she still had pressed to his chest. "Does that mean you can do the same for me, Rose?"

She audibly sighed. "Yes, Mr. Bennett-Jones—"

"David," he interrupted. "Call me David," he insisted, even though she had been doing so most of the evening.

"I don't care if you're a viscount's son."

David closed his eyes a moment, as if he was determining the right thing to say. "Then does that mean you would allow me to kiss you?"

He wasn't prepared for what happened next. For her to suddenly be pressed against the front of his body, for her arms to wrap around his neck, and her face to be mere inches from his. For her lips to touch his.

His opened more from shock than from his intention to kiss her, but he managed to capture her lips at the same moment his hands encircled her waist.

At first, the kiss was slow and gentle. Only a hint of passion existed as their lips moved in perfect harmony, melting into one another's. A moment later and he lost any awareness of their surroundings. Lost himself in the sensation of the soft pillows of her lips pressed to his.

David felt her heartbeat increase against his chest, its rhythm matching his as warmth surrounded him. When he finally pulled away, the effects of the kiss lingered. Aware his cock had responded to her even before she had launched herself at him, he was glad her skirts and petticoats would prevent her from feeling his arousal.

"I suppose that means the answer was yes," he whispered.

She blinked but didn't pull away. "Yes," she agreed.

Determined to pour every ounce of passion into his next kiss—he knew he wouldn't be able to put it into words—he once again captured her lips with his own. As if a fire had ignited between them, the gentle touch quickly deepened, the intensity increased, and for several moments, he was lost. As their lips moved in perfect sync with one another, first his tongue and then hers explored and tangled in tentative touches.

At the same time, one of Rose's hands slid into his hair, her gloved fingers ruffling the silken strands. One of his hands moved to the small of her waist to pull her harder against his body while the other moved up and over the swell of her breast.

While the kiss seemed to last an eternity, it was less than a minute when they both broke away and stared at one another.

"I really wish I wasn't starving right now," David whispered as his breathing slowed.

Her eyes rounding in delight, Rose grinned. "I suppose that depends on what you're hungry for," she teased.

"Well, food, of course," he replied, realizing too late she was hoping for a different response. "Because, although I am hungry for something else, I don't dare try anything more out here. With you."

Rose swallowed and lowered her feet back to the ground, but she kept her arms around his neck. "Do you wish to go back inside?" she asked.

He shook his head. "No." He placed his hands on either side of her face, much like he had seen the sultan do with Charlotte, and placed a kiss on her forehead. He allowed his lips to linger there before he reluctantly pulled away. "But we've been out here too long. I don't wish for your reputation to suffer on account of me," he murmured.

Rose blinked and glanced around, as if she had forgotten where they were. "Of course," she whispered.

He offered his arm, but before he led her back around the house, he pondered what to say. What to do next. He remembered what his sister had told him to do.

"Would you like to go riding with me in the park tomorrow afternoon? I could come by at two-o'clock," he offered.

She nodded. "I'm supposed to have tea with your sister at three—"

"She'll understand," he interrupted. "I'll make her... understand," he stammered.

Rose giggled. "All right. Two o'clock. But Father will probably require a groom to ride along with us," she warned.

David grinned. "Perhaps not," he replied.

"What makes you say that?" she asked as they approached the French doors leading back into the ballroom.

"I believe I have your father's permission to court you," he said.

Rose stared up at him in confusion. About to ask when he would have managed such a feat, she couldn't when they were once again amongst the crush of attendees, surrounded by fine fabrics, the scents of perfumes and colognes, and the strains of orchestral music.

CHAPTER 22
THE END OF ONE NIGHT

*A*n hour later, in the Bostwick town coach George Bennett-Jones held onto his wife's gloved hand as she stepped up and into their coach. Ertuğrul and Adeline were already settled into the squabs, engaged in a quiet conversation.

"Where's David?" Elizabeth asked once she realized he was missing.

"He said he's going to walk home," Ertuğrul replied.

Her eyes widening, Elizabeth turned to George, but he had already lifted a hand to pat hers. "It's all right. He spoke with me. He needs some time to himself," he murmured.

"But... what about footpads?" she asked in alarm.

"Bostwick House is not that far away," he assured her. "He'll probably get there before we do."

Ertuğrul leaned closer to Adeline. "Does he usually walk home from balls?"

Adeline shrugged. "Sometimes. Especially if they're in Park Lane. My father is right when he says David will probably arrive before we do. We only live a few houses away."

Remembering it hadn't taken long to get to Weatherstone Manor, Ertuğrul nodded his understanding. "Should we have walked?" he asked, barely nodding in the direction of George and Elizabeth. The two were murmuring quietly, and from the way their bodies were angled, he didn't think they were discussing the ball. Before he could avert his eyes, he paid witness to George nibbling on one of Elizabeth's ears.

Trying hard to suppress a giggle, Adeline held a gloved hand around one side of her mouth and said, "Perhaps we will next time."

Ertuğrul grinned at her antics. He had a thought that she might have drunk too much champagne during the supper. Although she had never seemed reserved around him from the moment they met, she had behaved on this night as if they had become especially close.

Close friends or something more, he didn't yet know. Didn't yet know if he was ready to know.

Despite having danced nearly every dance at the ball —almost every one with a different partner—he hadn't felt as comfortable with any of the other young ladies as he had with Adeline.

He knew the reason of course.

They had spent hours in each others' company at the museum. Their shared interests had much to do with their easy banter during the waltz. The more time they spent together, the more enamored he had become of her.

Even if nothing more than friendship developed between them, he looked forward to the next morning, when he would deliberately stand in front of Aphrodite in anticipation of her finding him. Look forward to her chiding him about his interest in the half-naked statue. Look forward to their descent to the breakfast parlor.

Curious as to what she thought of the evening, he turned to ask her and discovered her head resting against his shoulder. A quick glance at George, and he realized his viscountess was sound asleep in his arms.

George shrugged. "They tend to do this after all the balls. And the theatre," he whispered hoarsely. "If you're uncomfortable with her like that, you can simply push her away."

Ertuğrul's eyes widened. "Oh, no sir. It is fine. She is fine." Sure his face was bright red, he was glad for the darkened interior of the coach.

A moment later, and they were in front of Bostwick House.

*M*eanwhile, in the Ariley town coach
"I don't think I'm as ready for this Season as I thought," Helen, Duchess of Ariley, said as she stepped into the Ariley town coach. Her feet sore from wearing new slippers, she practically fell into the light blue velvet squabs as she sighed in relief.

The coach's new coat of black lacquer fairly gleamed under the light of the moon, the Ariley coat of arms emblazoned in gold paint on the door. "I do believe I know what you mean," James replied as he helped his daughter into the coach. "First day of Parliament followed by the Season's biggest ball does remind one of their mortality."

"It reminds me of why I haven't missed courting," Rose said on a huff.

She was followed by William, who remained uncharacteristically quiet as he settled onto the bench next to Rose.

Their departure from Weatherstone Manor appeared to have signaled a sort of permission for others to take their leave, for a quick glance out the coach window showed a steady stream of couples emerging from the manor house.

When the hall clock had struck one, those in the grand ballroom had begun to bid their farewells to one another, but it was another hour before James and his family thanked their weary hosts and made their way towards the waiting coach outside.

William knocked on the trap door above him. A moment later, four matching black horses, their muscular builds and glossy coats a testament to their care and training, lurched into motion. The chatter of ball-goers faded, replaced by the sound of the coach wheels and clattering of hooves on cobblestone.

"Did you not have a good time?" Helen asked of her daughter.

Rose straightened in the squabs. "Oh, I did. I danced more than usual, but I was reminded there are some young men in this town who seem to have forgotten their dance lessons."

"Who stepped on you?" William asked.

Inhaling softly, Rose said, "No one, actually."

"How is your leg, darling?" her mother asked. "Did it cause you pain?"

Remembering what David had done during the second waltz had her realizing her parents hadn't paid witness to his maneuver. Perhaps they had already stepped out to the gardens. "Hardly at all," she replied.

"I trust Bennett-Jones was a perfect gentleman this

evening?" James asked. "I apologize if we interrupted your discussion at the fountain."

William scoffed as he turned to regard his sister. "*You* were with Bennett-Jones near Cupid?" he asked in disbelief.

Rose glared at him. "I was, yes. And there's no need to apologize. We were simply taking the air," she added, turning her attention back on her father. "Thank you for the recommendation regarding the gardens on the west end of the house. I think I shall have to see them during the day to appreciate their colors."

Truth be told, she had barely noticed the early spring flowers. Her attention had been entirely on David, and apparently his was on her, for she couldn't remember anything but the kiss they shared.

Kisses. They had kissed twice.

Had he thought her fast for practically initiating the first one? She didn't know what had possessed her to nearly launch herself against the front of his body, to touch her lips to his.

Yet, he hadn't hesitated in returning the kiss.

Had he thought he required her permission? Waited for her to make the move that sent them into a few moments of kissing bliss?

No one had kissed her like that before. No one had slipped their tongue into her mouth before. No one had pulled her so close she could practically feel their arousal through her skirts.

"You'll want to awaken by noon," Helen said, interrupting her reverie. "If you're to be ready to go at two o'clock."

Rose blinked. "What's this?"

"Your ride in the park," her father stated. "Bennett-Jones informed me of his intentions to take you riding. I gave my permission, especially because your grey walker could use some exercise," he added, referring to the horse she had been riding since she was a young girl.

"Oh, of course," she replied. She would have to send a note to Adeline to let her know she wouldn't be joining her for tea. "Will we go riding in Rotten Row at five o'clock?"

"You can ride, darling," Helen stated. "Your father is taking me on his phaeton." She beamed in delight and batted her eyelashes, as if she was still a young miss looking forward to her first ride with a suitor.

"Careful, my sweet, or you'll shock our children," James teased.

Both Rose and William scoffed in unison.

"You're rather quiet tonight," James said, his gaze going to his son. "Waverley," he added with a grin. "I don't know that I'll ever get used to calling you that."

William shrugged. "It's been a long day," he murmured.

"I didn't see you dancing," James remarked.

"But I did," his son insisted. "The cotillion and the English country dance. Played cards."

Helen gasped, but James reached over and gave one of her hands a gentle squeeze. "Don't worry. He didn't lose," he whispered.

She sighed softly, her eyes closing as she settled her head against the duke's shoulder.

Once James knew she was sleeping, he directed his gaze on his son. "So what really happened tonight?" he asked.

William glanced out the coach window in an attempt to determine how much longer they had before they would arrive at Ariley Place. "She wasn't there," he stated.

"Who wasn't there?" Rose asked, straightening in the squabs.

Inhaling deeply, William directed a look of annoyance at his father. "Lady Eva."

Rose's eyes rounded. "She'll be back in time for my ball," she replied. "Are you... are you planning to court her? Because if you are—"

"I'd rather you not say anything to her," he remarked, cutting her off before she could offer any sort of assistance. "She's been gone all winter. She may already be married with two children and a dog," he groused.

Despite the seriousness of his son's comment, the duke chuckled. "It doesn't happen that fast," he said, although looking back at his situation reminded him that sometimes it had felt like that with his first two daughters. "Besides, Lord and Lady Sommers only left London a few weeks before Christmas," he added, referring to Lady Eva's parents. They had taken their daughter and their niece, Lady Helen Tennison, to their country estate in Shropshire. "I have it on good authority the baron is due back in Parliament before the week is out."

When William noticed Rose's happy expression, he asked, "What are you beaming about?"

Rose sighed. "Although I would have dearly loved to have Adeline as a sister, I do believe Lady Eva will be an acceptable substitute."

William stared at her a moment. "Adeline?" he repeated. "But she would never do. She's merely a viscount's daughter," he added.

Inhaling sharply, Rose turned to stare first at her brother and then her father, immediately reminded of what David had said to her that night in the gardens.

I am a viscount's son. I will never be more than a viscount.

Despite the dim lighting inside the coach, she could

see the wince the duke displayed at hearing his son's comment.

"Unlike a hundred years ago," James said in an even, clipped tone, "the Ariley dukedom is in good stead. There is no need for your marriage to be one of financial or political importance."

William furrowed his dark brows. "What are you saying, Father?"

James sighed softly, his hand covering one of his wife's. "Marry for love, dammit." He paused before turning his gaze squarely on his daughter. "Both of you."

His attention going from his father to Rose and then back to his father, William allowed a huff. "Well, this certainly changes things," he said. He settled into the squabs, a grin lifting his cheeks.

All at once, Rose realized Lady Eva wouldn't be her sister.

CHAPTER 23
BREAKFAST AFTER A BALL

The following morning
Only an hour later than usual, Adeline awoke and quickly dressed, refusing the lady's maid offer to do her hair. "I'll leave it down for now. I don't want to be late for breakfast." In reality, she wanted to hear everyone's comments about the ball the night before.

She emerged from her bedchamber and headed down the corridor toward the stairs. In her haste, she nearly collided with Ertuğrul near the statue of Aphrodite.

"Oh, my apologies, Your Eminence," she said as she stepped back and curtsied.

Ertuğrul's initial grin turned to a frown. "There's no need for formality betwixt us," he said. "Is there?"

She dipped her head. "Of course not. Old habits, I suppose. I do wish to apologize for... for having fallen asleep on you last night in the coach." When she replayed the words in her head, she winced and a blush heated her cheeks.

It was Ertuğrul's turn to dip his head. "As I mentioned last night, I did not mind." he said. "You're always welcome to sleep on my shoulder." At noticing her blush, he added, "Your hair is very long. Very beautiful. It reminds me of the copper from Cyprus."

Now glad she had dismissed Perkins, Adeline said, "Thank you." She took a steadying breath. "Were you going down for breakfast?"

Ertuğrul nodded. "Yes. I'm anxious to hear all the stories from the ball. And you?"

"I practically live for them," she said on a giggle.

He offered his arm, and she took it. "I am glad I was merely an outsider last evening," he commented. "It gave me a chance to observe as well as participate, although I do wonder how I was judged."

Inhaling softly, Adeline said, "I hadn't thought anyone was judging you," she replied. "I think most were merely curious is all." Halfway down the stairs, she asked, "Did you enjoy it, though? You must have danced nearly every set."

"I might have missed one," he said as they approached the breakfast parlor. "But I do think the supper dance was my favorite."

Adeline grinned as a blush once again colored her face. "It was mine as well." She couldn't say more as three pairs of blurry eyes turned to regard them. "Good morning," she said before making her way to the sideboard.

Ertuğrul greeted the others, an expression of amusement appearing when his gaze stopped on David. "Did you ever go to bed?"

David grimaced. "For a few hours," he replied, before nearly draining his coffee. "The walk home did me good, though. Gave me time to think."

"About?" Adeline prompted as she joined them at the table with a plate filled with coddled eggs and toast. A footman delivered a cup of tea and waited for Ertuğrul to give his order.

"The Season, I suppose. And how some people were so different while others hadn't aged a bit," David said. "I was only gone... three years, two months, and ten days," he added, remembering Rose's pointed comment on the matter.

The precise length of his absence had Adeline arching a brow—she knew exactly who had first said those words—but she didn't say anything in response.

"How was your supper dance?" Ertuğrul asked, his dark brows waggling.

"Short," David replied. "Lady Rose was experiencing some discomfort, so I danced us out of the circle."

"Is she all right?" Elizabeth asked, tearing her attention from the correspondence that had been delivered earlier that morning.

Before David could answer, Elkins appeared at the door bearing a silver salver with a note on it. He cleared his throat.

"What is it, Elkins?" George asked, looking up from a copy of *The Times*.

"A footman from Ariley Place has delivered a note."

David and George both gave a start, as if they thought the message might be for them, and they both frowned when the butler added, "For Miss Bennett-Jones."

"Oh, that will be from Rose," she said as she plucked the note from the salver. "I invited my wallflower friends for tea this afternoon."

David furrowed his brows, and Ertuğrul noticed, but he merely pretended indifference as Adeline opened and read the short missive.

"Is Lady Rose all right?" Elizabeth asked again.

Adeline nodded. "She is, but she won't be joining me

for tea. Apparently, she's accepted an offer to go for a ride in the park this afternoon."

"Oh, her mother will be thrilled," Elizabeth commented, unaware of both Ertuğrul's and Adeline's pointed glances in David's direction. "I think the duchess was beginning to think her daughter would end up a spinster."

"Nonsense," George murmured, although he was reminded of the Duke of Ariley's comments on the matter of his grown children's lack of spouses when they had last met at White's. "She's on a list that's rather short," he added.

Elizabeth gave a start. "What list might that be?"

"The list of all the young ladies who were born between eighteen-seventeen and eighteen-twenty-three who are not yet courting anyone," George replied, ignoring Adeline's slight gasp. "And who live here in the capital."

Considering the conditions for a moment, his viscountess furrowed a brow. "That's terribly specific," she commented. Her gaze fell on her daughter before she suddenly turned to her husband. "Is Addy on that list?"

George grimaced. "Of course she is."

Ertuğrul leaned closer to Adeline and whispered, "It's not me." At her look of confusion, he added, "I'm not the one taking Lady Rose for a ride in the park."

Adeline managed a slight shrug. Although she was sure Rose would be riding with David, she found it surprising he would even try to court the daughter of a duke. Still, the assurance that it wasn't Ertuğrul who was to ride with Rose had a sense of relief settling over her. "Do you ride, though?" she asked, a combination of annoyance and embarrassment at hearing she was on a list making it hard for her to keep her voice light.

"I do," he replied. "Do you?"

"Yes, of course."

"Perhaps we can go some afternoon. When you're not hosting your friends."

Before Adeline could respond, George set aside the newspaper and said, "We'll take a drive in the park this afternoon for the parade in Rotten Row at five o'clock," he announced. "Go in the barouche and get some air before we have a quick dinner and then head to Worthington House for tonight's *soirée*."

"Cook is making a cold collation for us this evening, so we won't be starving when we get there," Elizabeth said.

Murmurs of agreement circled the table, but David said, "Since it will be a tight fit with five of us in the barouche, I'll probably ride a horse this afternoon, if it's all the same."

His father shrugged. "We have several mounts who could use the exercise," he said by way of agreement. "In the meantime, I'm off to Westminster."

He kissed Elizabeth on the cheek and took his leave of the breakfast parlor. Once he was gone, she leaned forward and said, "I cannot believe he didn't ask you, but I will. What happened at the ball last night? I want to hear everything," she said as she splayed her fingers in anticipation.

David, Adeline and Ertuğrul all exchanged quick glances. "We were hoping you would tell us," Adeline said.

Scoffing, Elizabeth pretended disappointment. "Oh, if I must." She proceeded to describe what she had seen and learned the night before.

Although it might have been of more interest to those who actually knew any of the people she mentioned,

Ertuğrul thought the gossip was still entertaining to hear. He found her delivery amusing, and despite the seriousness of some of what was said, she showed restraint in her descriptions. Nothing mean-spirited was said unless it was about a known rake.

David and Adeline obviously knew everyone she mentioned for they laughed when appropriate and appeared worried at hearing of someone's troubles. He was reliving his waltz with Adeline in his head when his name was mentioned.

Ertuğrul glanced over at Adeline. "Who was this?" he asked.

"Lady Lucy. She was quite happy to dance with you," Elizabeth repeated. "She's rather shy, so your attempt to dance with all the wallflowers was noted by many and was well appreciated."

Ertuğrul shrugged. "It... it was my pleasure, my lady," he replied. "I should be happy to do it again at the next ball."

Even as he said the words, he had the impression a certain young lady didn't appreciate hearing them.

CHAPTER 24
A COURTSHIP BEGINS

Later that day

After a brief search of his wardrobe, David found a tweed riding jacket and breeches that still fit. A short struggle with Elkins' assistance ensued before he managed to force his feet into a pair of Hessians. Standing before the cheval mirror in his bedchamber, he decided he was as ready as he would ever be for his first day of courting Lady Rose.

The sun was shining brightly when David entered the mews behind Bostwick House. A chestnut gelding whinnied softly as a groom hoisted a saddle onto him.

"Afternoon, Thompson," he said as he stood before the horse.

"Good to see you back, sir," the groom replied, barely pausing as he secured the leather straps of the saddle.

"Good to be back," David commented. "I don't recognize him," he added as he regarded the horse, the white blaze in the center of its forehead a common feature among the race horses that had been bred at the Bostwick property in Sussex. He was larger, too, his muscular frame suggesting he hadn't been bred for the racecourse.

"This would be Ares, sir. Your father's riding horse. He suggested I saddle 'im for you seein' as how yours is out to pasture down south."

David winced, realizing his absence from London had meant his regular ride would have lacked attention and exercise. "Ares," he said. "Are you up for a ride in the park?"

A series of nickers suggested the horse looked forward to the outing.

"I'll be gone a long while, I expect," David said as he mounted the gelding. "If I don't return before the parade in Rotten Row, then it's because I've gone directly there from my appointment."

"Very good, sir."

David tested Ares as they departed the mews, keeping the horse moving at a comfortable canter until they were out in Park Lane. Then he gave him the rein as they headed north toward Ariley Place.

He found a groom holding the reins of an Irish Walker in front of the large Georgian townhouse. "Would that be Lady Rose's mount?" David called out as he approached.

"Indeed, sir," the servant replied at the same moment the front door opened to reveal the reason for David's presence.

"Your punctuality is to be commended," Rose said as he dismounted and hurried to take her hand to his lips.

"As is yours, my lady," he replied. She was dressed in a bright blue riding habit of wool. The fitted bodice, decorated with black frog enclosures and a small collar, reminded him of the night before, when he had held her waist in his hands as he kissed her. "How are you on this fine day?" After he kissed the back of her kid-gloved hand, he leaned forward and kissed her cheek.

Rose inhaled softly, her gaze dropping to regard his riding clothes with appreciation. She dipped a curtsy. "I will admit I wished I might have been able to sleep another hour or so," she replied as she made her way to her horse. "But the sun is good to see."

"Was your family the last to leave the ball?" he asked. Although the groom would have bent and interlocked his hands so she could more easily mount the sidesaddle, David waved him off. He placed his hands at her waist and easily lifted her onto the saddle, ignoring her gasp of surprise.

He couldn't help the odd annoyance he felt when he imagined her dancing with other young bucks after he had taken his leave of Weatherstone Manor. The walk home had been necessary, though. The cool night air helped tamp down his ardor. Once he'd had a taste of her in the gardens, the supper foods hadn't satiated his appetite for her one bit. He knew if he stayed, he would suffer worse.

Hooking her leg around the pommel while David ensured her booted foot was in the stirrup, Rose watched as he easily mounted his much larger gelding. "We were not the last to leave," she replied, "but I could not help but notice your departure. Did something happen?"

David gave a start, which had his horse heading for the street. "It is more what might have happened if I hadn't left when I did," he replied, his brows furrowing when he noticed the groom didn't have a mount. Rose's walker had already moved alongside his.

About to ask what he meant, Rose looked back to follow his gaze. "Father informed me I didn't require a chaperone when I am with you."

His eyes rounding, David gave a shrug. "I suppose I should take that as a compliment of my honor?" he asked. Given what he would have liked to do with her at the ball the night before, he didn't feel as if he had earned the duke's trust.

"He likes you, David. He always has," she replied.

"And you?"

Despite the bright sunlight, the color in Rose's cheeks visibly reddened. "I have known you since we were children," she reminded him. "So... yes."

Grinning, David decided to save the rest of his topics of conversation until after they were well into Hyde Park. They entered through Cumberland Gate at the northeast corner, the sound of hooves on the trail mixed with the rustling of leaves and birds chirping in the trees.

David led the way when the path wasn't wide enough for both horses, maneuvering confidently around other riders and pedestrians while Rose followed closely behind on her gray mare.

As they rode, they talked about the ball, enjoying the freedom of the open space and the beauty of the park. They stopped and dismounted to let their horses graze on the lush grass. In the distance, Kensington Palace provided a stunning view.

Taking up the reins of both horses, David led them to a bench set against a hedgerow, the sounds from the nearby Serpentine muted by the leaves rustling in the breeze.

Tying the reins into the branches of the hedgerow, David ensured the horses could reach the grass before he joined Rose on the bench.

"I left after the supper dance because if I had stayed..." David paused and swallowed. "I would not have been as honorable as your father thinks me."

Her eyes rounding at hearing his confession, Rose straightened on the bench. "What would you have done?" she asked. When he seemed as if he wouldn't answer, she said, "I am not a young miss, fresh from the school room." When he still appeared reluctant to respond, she added, "In fact, I might wish to hear such a confession, especially if it's a compliment of sorts. I don't hear many of those these days."

"Rose," he breathed.

"After you left on your Grand Tour, it was as if I was suddenly an old maid—"

"Rose, no," he murmured.

"—and the only man who showed me favor turned out to be the fortune hunter I told you about."

David winced. "I did not mean to stay away so long. If I had known then that your father..."

Rose inhaled softly. "Go on," she encouraged. "Please, tell me. Whatever it is."

"Promise you won't think less of me?"

Her brows furrowing, Rose took a deep breath. "I promise."

"All right. I lusted for you," he stated, ignoring how her eyes rounded. "Part of the reason I left with Lord James was because I thought time would change me. That by the time I returned, you would have married someone, and once I knew I couldn't have you, I would lose interest, or my ardor would have cooled, or I would have met someone else."

Dipping her head, Rose placed a hand in front of her face in an attempt to hide her open mouth. His admission was as shocking as it was welcome. "Do you still? Lust for me?"

"Of course," David replied. "I thought I made that clear last night."

She lowered her hand as she regarded him and then swallowed. "What would you have done to me last night? If you hadn't left?"

He winced and then glanced around as he if thought someone might be eavesdropping. "Escorted you to an alcove, or an empty bedchamber, or the library, or... or back out to the gardens. Kissed you senseless. Maybe done more."

Gasping, Rose displayed a blush and said, "I would have let you." She suddenly sobered. "I suppose that makes me sound rather fast."

He shook his head. "I know you said you're not a young miss, but I would have ruined you, Rose," he warned. "Thoroughly."

"I would have let you," she replied in a whisper.

Swallowing, he shook his head. "Knowing you would be forced to marry me?" he countered. "As I said last night, I am never going to be more than a viscount."

Remembering what her father had said in the coach very early that morning, Rose chuckled softly. "My brother and I were informed at two o'clock this morning that we are not to marry for financial or political reasons."

David furrowed his brows. "The duke said that?"

She nodded. "Father said—in no uncertain terms—that we are to marry for love." One brow furrowed as she considered his earlier claim. "However, he didn't say anything about lust."

Blinking, David cleared his throat. "I wish to court you properly, Lady Rose."

The claim had Rose experiencing a mix of excitement and disappointment. "I am not getting any younger," she warned.

"But you're certainly becoming more beautiful," he countered.

"David," she murmured softly. "You might have started with that," she teased. After a moment of shared silence, she dipped her head. "Will you tell me why you stayed away so long?"

Giving a start at hearing the query, David inhaled and let the breath out in a *whoosh*. "When James and I departed, we had an itinerary that had us taking two years to explore the entirety of Italy, the island of Sicily, the mainland of Greece and some of the islands," he explained. "We were on Rhodes when we learned about Lady Charlotte and the pirates, and... turns out, she didn't require saving, but then James met Sevinc—Ertuğrul's twin sister—and they married and left on their wedding trip. I would have returned to England then, but Ertuğrul and I had begun to work on plans for buildings, and the sultan invited me to stay on... so I did." He took one of Rose's hands in his. "I didn't think I had any reason to come home. At least, not right away."

Rose gave a start, his words reminding her she hadn't made her regard for him more apparent. "So... was the trip worth it?"

The words were said in such a quiet voice, David barely heard them. "On the one hand, I don't regret it—I have experienced situations no other man here in England has had," he replied.

"Beautiful women, I suppose?" She couldn't help the tinge of jealousy she felt at the thought of him with exotic women in faraway lands.

David gave a start. "What? No," he claimed as he shook his head. "I mean, there are beautiful women there, but none I was interested in," he said.

"Did you bed any of them?"

His eyes rounding in shock, David regarded her with disbelief. "Rose," he scolded.

"I'm merely curious," she said. "I hear Turkish women learn how to make love to a man as part of their education. Is it true?"

His mouth opening and closing much like a fish, David struggled with how to respond. "I've heard the concubines in a harem learn those skills, but I don't know about the rest," he stammered.

He knew about those skills, but not because he had bedded one. He had been in the company of a concubine for an entirely different reason, though. One he hoped would help him when it came to bedding his future wife.

"Did a concubine make love to you?"

He shook his head. "No." He rolled his eyes. "Ziyaeddin offered me one once. One who was apparently still a virgin. But I refused as politely as I could."

Rose regarded him with disbelief. "Why?"

He inhaled softly and then said. "Because she wasn't you."

Rose stared up at him for the longest time before she blinked. He had her in his arms a moment later, his lips capturing hers in a soft kiss. "I wish I could make love to you this very minute." He glanced around, glad to discover no one had paid witness to his public display of affection.

"You're going to have to propose marriage for that to happen," she warned in a whisper.

He grinned. "As a duke's daughter, aren't you the one who has to propose marriage to me? Seeing as how I'm merely the son of a viscount?"

About to agree, Rose remembered hearing that Elizabeth Carlington had been the one to propose before she married George Bennett-Jones. She scoffed. "David Bennett-Jones, if you think for one minute you're going to receive a proposal of marriage like your father did, well..." She inhaled and displayed an expression of indecision.

What if someone else proposed during the Season? What if there was someone else who wanted to marry her? If she accepted the proposal and later changed her mind, her chances for another betrothal would be even less than they were now.

Despite her obvious annoyance with him, David hadn't left her at the fountain or on the dance floor. He had accepted every scolding word she had said as if he had already said them to himself.

Memories of the night before flitted before her mind's eye. Memories of his kisses. Of how he had held her. Of what she had dreamed about him early that morning.

"Well, then, I suppose you are going to," she said in a whisper, realizing he really believed she had to be the one to propose marriage. "Will you marry me?"

David blinked as a chuckle escaped. "Did you... did you just propose to me?"

"I did, but your window of opportunity to answer is closing very quickly," she warned on a huff.

"I will," he replied, his look of awe remaining for several seconds. "I will marry you. Yes," he added, his look of shock still evident.

"What is it?" she asked.

He inhaled. "I think I'm in love," he whispered.

Rose slapped a glove against his shoulder as her eyes rounded. "With whom?"

Blinking again, he finally chuckled. "With you, of course."

Grinning in delight, Rose slapped him again with the glove. "You'd better be," she warned before he once again pulled her into his arms. "Don't tell Adeline," she said after a moment.

"What? Why not?" he asked, placing a hand at the edge of her cheek.

Rose glanced away. "She's determined to see to it that Ertuğrul court me while he's here in England," she explained. "She seems to think that we should marry."

"Well, that's not going to happen," David claimed. At her look of worry, he added, "Because I already had Ertuğrul's assurance that he wouldn't court you. I made him promise."

She straightened in his hold. "You did?" she asked in awe.

"Of course. I wasn't going to let my best friend marry the woman I'm in love with," he insisted.

A brilliant smile appeared before Rose kissed him. "What do we do now?" she asked when he finally ended the kiss.

He pulled his pocket watch from his waistcoat. "Care for a ride in Rotten Row? The parade will be starting in about an hour."

Her eyes rounded. "We've been gone that long?" she asked in disbelief.

"We have. I'll have to return you to Ariley Place right after, though. We have a *soirée* to attend at eight o'clock."

"As do I," she replied.

"Should we tell our parents?"

Rose shook her head. "What if we were to wait until my ball. It's only a few days, away," she suggested. "Father can announce it before the supper dance."

"You'll dance with me?" he asked.

"Well, of course," she said, about to slap the glove

against his shoulder. He intersected her hand with his own and lifted it to his lips.

"You're not going to change your mind?" he asked with suspicion before he placed his lips on the back of her bare fingers.

She inhaled softly. "Are you going to change yours?" she countered.

He laughed. "I'm not," he assured her. He kissed her fingers again. "But given our ages, perhaps we shouldn't wait too long to wed?" he suggested.

"Are you saying I'm old?" she asked on a huff, pulling her hand away.

He retrieved it and kissed the palm. He shook his head. "I'm not getting any younger."

"Promise me you won't tell the men at your club that you're marrying an old maid."

He frowned. "I'm not marrying an old maid, so why would I tell them such a thing?" At seeing her look of worry, he tightened his hold on her. "Do you think you could ever love me?"

She shook her head. "I don't see how," she replied before a brilliant smile appeared and she giggled. "If you could have seen your face just now," she teased. Sobering, she wrapped her arms around his neck and kissed him. When she finally pulled away, she sighed. "I'll admit, I am in lust with you. Will that be enough?"

David chuckled. "It will do," he replied. "For now." He swallowed. "Tell your parents," he said suddenly.

Rose dipped her head. "I will." At his look of surprise, she added, "I wouldn't have been able to keep it a secret for three days."

They remained on the park bench a few minutes before they finally straightened and glanced around as if they had forgotten where they were.

The two retrieved their horses and made their way south to Rotten Row, both aware they would remember this ride forever.

CHAPTER 25
AN AFTERNOON IN THE PARLOR

*M*eanwhile, *back at Bostwick House*

Well aware Ertuğrul had paid witness to the arrival of her four guests for tea that afternoon—he had paused in his climb up the stairs as Elkins saw to their wraps—Adeline reminded him he was welcome to join them should he wish for a cup of tea and a biscuit. He deferred even as he seemed intrigued by the offer.

"Is it usual for a man to join a lady's tea party?" he asked in a whisper.

Adeline tittered. "No, but you would be welcomed. You've met everyone," she reminded him. "Danced with them. But I certainly understand if you're not comfortable among so many young ladies."

Ertuğrul wasn't sure if she was teasing him or not. Perhaps she didn't know he had spent his early years in a harem. Although there had been another boy or two with him back then, he had been surrounded by concubines, servants, and female relatives of the sultan. "I might be more comfortable than you wish me to be," he warned, waggling his brows. He resumed his climb up the stairs,

Adeline's expression of confusion bringing a grin to his lips.

Finally pulling her gaze from his retreating backside—did the young man have any idea how his thigh muscles moved beneath his doeskin breeches?—Adeline inhaled softly and turned her attention on the four women who Elkins was escorting to the front parlor.

The elegant salon was brightly lit, both from the front window as well as from the gas-lit chandelier that sparkled as if it was made of diamonds. The group of five young women sat in comfortable upholstered armchairs, sipping tea and nibbling on delicate biscuits. Dressed in their finest day gowns, adorned with bows, lace and frills, they were still basking in the glow of the prior night's ball.

"Was that you I saw talking to Lord Waverley last night?" Lucy Turnbridge asked with a pointed glance at her hostess, her green eyes sparkling with mischief. "He seemed quite taken with you."

Adeline scoffed. "I think you have me confused with someone else," she replied, not remembering having even seen William Burroughs at the ball. "He's truly a lord now, at least according to my father. He was offered a writ of acceleration, and now he's in Parliament."

"If Rose was here, I'm sure she'd tell us he's grown too big for his breeches," Patience Fulton muttered.

"I spoke with him," Hope Batey announced. When all the others turned their eyes on the daughter of the Viscount Lancaster, she visibly blushed. Casting her eyes downward, she added, "Oh, it was nothing, really. I just asked him about his travels."

Lucy turned to Faith Fulton, "And what about you, Faith? Mother said she was sure she saw you in the company of Lord Waverley. Said he appeared quite smitten with you," she claimed.

Faith shook her head, her honey-brown curls bouncing around her reddening face. "Me? I'm a wallflower. He is handsome, but whatever would he see in *me*?"

"An earl's daughter, perhaps?" her sister, Patience, asked rhetorically. "We could ask Rose if she were here. Where is she?" she added, helping herself to a biscuit when Adeline held out the salver to her.

"I received a note from her during breakfast. She was asked to go on a ride in the park." Adeline explained as she waggled her brows.

A collective gasp had the young women giggling. "With whom?"

"I think I know," Adeline admitted, "but I'm quite sure I'm not supposed to say anything."

A collective groan resulted in another round of giggles. All at once, the room went silent.

With her back to the door, Adeline straightened in her chair and directed a questioning glance in Faith's direction.

"Your Eminence," Faith said, immediately coming to her feet.

The other young women followed suit, huge smiles on their faces.

Adeline turned to regard the şehzade with a grin. "How do, Your Eminence?" she asked as she waved him into the room. "I believe you've already met everyone," she added as she poured him a cup of tea.

"Ertuğrul, please," he said as he bowed. The girls all curtsied in unison. "I trust you all had a pleasant evening last night?" he asked as he took the chair that had been meant for Rose.

"All because of you," Lucy said happily.

For a moment, Ertuğrul looked a bit befuddled. "I can hardly imagine how one dance would make for an entire evening's enjoyment," he replied.

Most of the women giggled. "Everyone saw you come to our end of the ballroom last night. By coming to sign our dance cards, you had all the young bucks rather jealous," Patience explained. "As a result, I had partners for nearly every dance."

"Me as well," Faith said.

Hope straightened. "You managed to cause William… I mean Lord Waverley… to realize he had some competition," she said, her eyes nervously darting about the room.

"Hope?" Adeline whispered hoarsely, curious as to why the viscount's daughter—and daughter to the woman who was the matchmaker at *Finding Wives for the Wounded*—seemed so anxious.

"I take it Lord Waverley made his intentions known last night?" Ertuğrul asked with a grin. "I could tell he wasn't happy with me when I handed you off to him for the second waltz."

The bold question had all the other young women gasping in shock. "Hope?" Patience prompted, her mouth still open.

"He hasn't asked me to marry him. Not exactly," Hope blurted. She dipped her head. "I'm only a viscount's daughter, though, so I really don't think he will continue to court me."

"Court you?" several repeated in surprise. "How long has he been courting you?"

Hope winced. "Only a few weeks. We've kept quiet about it because… well, it's been our secret. But after last night..." She sighed. "I'm only a viscount's daughter," she repeated.

"Your mother was a countess before she married your father," Adeline stated, as if that made all the difference.

"He... he said he would speak with his father and send a..."

The sound of a clearing throat had them all turning to discover Elkins standing at the door with a silver salver.

"What is it, Elkins?" Adeline asked.

"A footman delivered this note for Miss Hope. He apologized for its late delivery. He tried first at Stanton House but was told Miss Hope could be found here."

Another collective gasp had Ertuğrul chuckling softly as Hope came to her feet and plucked the white envelope from the salver.

"Who's it from?" Faith asked in excitement.

"It has the Ariley seal on the back. I can see it from here," Adeline remarked. She dared not seem too happy in the event the missive brought disappointing news.

Hope stood holding the note as if it might explode. "I don't think I dare open this," she murmured, a look of worry replacing her happy expression of only a moment ago.

"My lady, may I offer you any assistance?"

All eyes turned to the sultan's son, and Hope rushed to stand before him. "Can you read English? A man's penmanship? Because William's writing is rot," she said in a rush, unaware she had used his given name.

Ertuğrul took the missive from her, slid a thumbnail beneath the wax so that it lifted cleanly from the parchment, and he gave it to her. "An interesting sigil," he remarked as he unfolded the paper. "Do you wish me to read it aloud?"

"Oh, please let him," Lucy begged. "I'm about to die of curiosity."

Hope nodded and Ertuğrul held up the note. "My dearest Faith Hope..." He stopped and glanced up at her in confusion.

"Oh, it's my full name. I go by Hope since there are so many Faiths," she explained as she waved at Faith Fulton. "Please, continue."

He inhaled and read aloud, "Upon our departure from Weatherstone Manor early this morning, I was informed by my father that neither my sister nor I am to marry—"

"Oh!" a collective sound of disappointment filled the salon before Ertuğrul held up a finger. Patience was halfway to standing and then looked as if she might faint.

"—for financial or political reasons. His manner was most sober. He ordered that we marry for love."

A collective gasp of excitement filled the room at the same moment Elizabeth appeared at the door. Standing next to the butler, she gave him a questioning glance.

"A missive for Miss Hope arrived from Ariley Place," he whispered, his presence at the door long forgotten by those who were listening intently to Ertuğrul.

"I heard the 'ohs' and 'ahs' and gasping all the way upstairs. I was beginning to think a Peeping Tom was exposing himself in the front window."

Elkins' eyes widened. "I would never allow it, my lady," he claimed.

"And all those roses out there? Who are they for?"

His gray brows furrowing, Elkins looked confused for the first time in his service to Bostwick House. "Roses?" he repeated in a soft whisper. He left her side, apparently to discover what she was talking about.

Elizabeth's attention returned to Ertuğrul, who seemed to take delight in what he was reading.

"I do not believe I have ever seen my father appear so serious about anything in all my life," the sultan's son continued after the girls had settled down. He furrowed a brow when he noticed Lucy removing a hanky from her pocket. She lifted it to the corner of her eye. "Are you all right, my lady?" he asked in alarm.

"Oh, I cannot help but either be happy or sad. Please, get on with it," she said as she waved a hand in a circle.

Finding the line where he had left off, Ertuğrul placed a hand on his chest and read, "Lady Rose and I have been ordered to marry and to do so with great haste. After our kiss in the gardens last night—"

"Oh!" several of the girls exclaimed in delight, clapping their hands together in their mutual excitement.

"—I am writing to ask if I might have the honor of announcing our betrothal at the ball my parents are hosting in three days' time?" Ertuğrul looked up first at Hope and then at Adeline before he added, "I look forward to your soonest reply. With all my love, Waverley."

Tears were streaming down Hope's face as those around her clasped their hands together and sighed.

"I would never have thought Waverley to be so romantic," Patience whispered loudly.

"Shh!" Faith held up a finger to her lips. "Is there more?" she prompted. "There's always more."

"*Post scriptum,*" Ertuğrul said as he held up a finger. "I know orange roses are your favorite, so please excuse the color of these. There were no orange roses in Chiswick."

"Roses?" Hope repeated. She turned around to discover Elkins standing at the door with a huge bouquet of red roses.

"My lady, these arrived for you," the butler stated in his baritone. "And a footman awaits your reply."

Adeline noticed her mother standing next to the door, and she gave her a watery grin. Elizabeth's attention was on Ertuğrul, though, who was regarding the women around him with a combination of humor and curiosity.

"So he *is* head over heels for you!" exclaimed Lucy, tears streaming down her face.

Patience took one of Lucy's hands in hers. "Whatever is wrong? You're crying as if..." She furrowed a dark brow. "Did *you* have feelings for Waverley?"

Lucy's eyes rounded as she sniffled. "No!" she replied. "I have news as well, but," she sighed heavily. "Chamberlain's proposal wasn't nearly as romantic as Waverley's," she complained. "He didn't even kiss me until after I agreed to marry him."

"You're marrying Marcus Fitzsimmons?" Adeline asked in awe.

Nodding, Lucy's watery grin widened into a smile. "This summer. He promised to take me on a wedding trip to the Peak District."

"Oh, that's wonderful," Faith said as she settled back in her chair. "The Season has barely begun and already two of you have proposals."

"What should I tell the footman?" Hope asked suddenly.

"Yes!" they all cried out in unison.

A collective giggle followed their reply as Hope made her way out of the salon.

Adeline caught sight of Ertuğrul's pointed glance and she furrowed a brow in question.

"Lady Rose has been ordered to marry and to do so with great haste," he repeated in a quiet voice. "I expect we shall be hearing of another proposal during the Ariley ball."

Although his comment wasn't immediately heard by

the girls left in the salon, their attentions all turned to him upon hearing the last line.

"He's only just returned to London," Adeline replied, thinking her brother wouldn't propose so quickly.

"Who?" Patience asked, helping herself to another biscuit.

"My brother, David," Adeline said in a faraway voice. She was sure he was with Rose this very moment. Somewhere in the park. Perhaps he was proposing marriage.

In a matter of minutes, she had learned half her close friends were betrothed.

Patience and Faith exchanged quick glances and gave Adeline a sympathetic shrug. "So, there will just be three of us standing with Fred," Faith said with a sigh.

"Three of us, yes," Adeline replied. She held out the plate of biscuits. "Would you like another?"

Patience deferred as Faith helped herself to a lemon biscuit. Their gazes followed Hope when she came back into the salon, the scent of roses wafting in with her.

"I am glad I did not walk here today," she said with a grin. "There is no way I could carry all those roses home with me."

"I wonder if I'll ever receive roses from Chamberlain," Lucy said as she helped herself to a biscuit and allowed Adeline to refill her teacup.

Her gaze darting to the door, Adeline discovered her mother was no longer hovering beyond it. "You might mention Waverley's betrothal gift when next you see him," she suggested. "He might not know you like roses."

"I would prefer tulips this time of the year," Lucy said as her eyes rounded. "I shall have to remind him of the fact at the *soirée* this evening."

The conversation turned to the other eligible bachelors who attended the ball, with each woman sharing her opinions and observations. They giggled and sighed, like schoolgirls in love, all while Ertuğrul sat and sipped tea. All at once, Lucy seemed to remember he was still there.

"Oh, we're probably boring you with all this chit-chat," she claimed on a giggle.

"Not at all," he replied. "This has been a most educational day," he added. "Might I ask, though, what is Chiswick?"

The girls all exchanged quick glances before they tittered. "It's a town southwest of here," Patience explained. "Where the hothouse nurseries grow all the flowers for the florist shops here in London."

"Ah," Ertuğrul replied, a second before the clock chimed.

"We must depart to dress for this evening," Faith said as she stood. "It wouldn't be good for Patience and me to be late seeing as how our Uncle Benjamin is married to Lord Torrington's sister," she added, referring to Angelica Grandby Fulton and the hostess for that evening's *soiree*.

"They'll be prompt if only because they live next door to Worthington House," Patience reminded her. "We're off."

The rest of the young women reluctantly rose to leave, promising to meet again at the Ariley ball.

Left alone in the salon, Ertuğrul helped himself to the last biscuit as he pondered the upcoming entertainments and all the relations he had learned about during the ball and that afternoon's tea.

Other lists might be growing shorter, but he had only one name on his.

CHAPTER 26
A NIGHT IN THE LIBRARY

The following night

From his carver at the end of the dining room table, George leaned back and regarded the others with a satisfied grin. Although only two of his four grown children were present, he found it interesting that the addition of Ertuğrul to their household for the Season reminded him of when his youngest son was still in residence.

The sultan's son was obviously well-educated. Inquisitive. Curious. He might have seemed reserved—shy, even—upon his arrival, but he had settled into life at Bostwick House as if he had lived there his entire life.

The daily afternoon activity seemed to befuddled him, though. George supposed any outsider would wonder why aristocrats would insist on riding horses or walking or riding in open carriages every afternoon at five o'clock along a dog-legged road on the south side of Hyde Park.

"To see and be seen," didn't seem logical to the young man, but he seemed to enjoy the outings. He had chosen more European style clothing for the rides in the carriage, which seemed to disappoint some of those he had met during the ball two nights before, especially the young ladies on horseback who occasionally rode past their carriage—a few more than once.

"Where might I find more information on the palace in Brighton?" Ertuğrul asked. "Architecturally speaking. I learned of it during last night's *soirée*."

George realized he had missed some of the conversation. "There's a book about a proposed redesign for it up in the library. About its decorations and such," he offered. "We can arrange to go down to Brighton at some point later in the Season so you can see it in person if you'd like. It is one of our few examples of Mogul architecture here in England."

Ertuğrul's eyes rounded. "Truly? I should like that, but reading the book will be most helpful for now."

David glanced up from his dessert. "Are you working on another project?" he asked. "Another building?" His query made him sound as if he wanted to be included in the planning.

Ertuğrul nodded. "Three, actually. My father would like to build smaller palaces for his brothers who oversee some of the outer provinces," he acknowledged. "I saw a drawing of the palace in Brighton in Lord Torrington's study last night and thought it might be a good starting point for a design."

"I know where that book is," Adeline said. "I can show you after dinner. That is, if you're not going to play billiards?"

Ertuğrul looked first to David and then to George, not sure if they had plans for that evening. He had already seen the schedule for the next two nights—the theatre and the ball for Lady Rose—and he welcomed the thought of spending an evening in the library.

"I can play billiards with Father," David offered. "I need to discuss something with him anyway." He had been absent most of the day before, returning to the house only an hour before they departed for Worthington House, smelling of horse and saying only that his long ride in the park was pleasant. He also claimed to have ridden a horse in the parade in Rotten Row while the rest of them had ridden in the carriage, but they hadn't spotted him among the many riders who had joined the first parade of the Season.

As for this day, he had made his excuses during breakfast and left on the phaeton, claiming he had need of more new clothes and cologne.

Elizabeth looked up from her dessert, immediately catching George's eye. He merely nodded, understanding he would be expected to share whatever David talked about with her. If he didn't, she would pester him about it, and he had learned long ago it was best not to keep secrets from his viscountess. "I'm up for one game," George said. "We'll take our port up there."

"Might I take mine to the library?" Ertuğrul asked.

"Of course," George replied.

*A*lthough he had passed by the library several times during his short stay at Bostwick House, Ertuğrul hadn't actually gone into the room. Pausing on the threshold, he took a moment to survey the scene. He inhaled deeply, breathing in the scents of leather bindings and antique pages, vellum and vanilla.

"It's not the largest collection of books in a home, of course, but there are some good ones in here," Adeline remarked when she appeared from behind one of the center bookcases. She held two books in her arms and waved for him to join her closer to the fireplace.

Ertuğrul leaned to one side, shocked to discover that besides the two freestanding bookcases, shelves of books lined two entire walls from the floor to the coffered ceiling. The fireplace at the opposite end of the room featured a wood fire, and the golden glow from it along with two gas-lit sconces made that end of the room bright enough for reading. A large Turkish carpet covered the floor, swallowing up most of the sound. He was still tempted to whisper when he spoke, though.

A velvet covered sofa, similar to one he remembered seeing in the study, wasn't the fussy settee type, but rather a couch with overstuffed cushions and pillows featuring gold tassels. "This looks like what we have in the palace," he remarked.

"It's almost too comfortable," Adeline said as she handed him the book, *Designs for the Pavilion of Brighton* by Humphry Repton. "Now, this shows changes this particular designer had proposed for the palace, but the man who actually got the job must have used it as a guide. That was John Nash."

Ertuğrul opened the book, and awestruck at seeing the color plates inside, slowly settled into the couch. "You've been to this palace?" he asked.

"I have," Adeline admitted, sitting down next to him. "Although, I didn't see all of the interiors at the time. It's free to go into, but you must have a ticket."

The two sat together, both silent for a time as Adeline read a novel. When Ertuğrul turned a page and occasionally glanced her way, he was struck by how different she appeared when she wasn't in the company of her friends or family.

She was a delicate thing, her features refined and

elegant. As was usual, her mahogany hair was piled atop her head, loose tendrils framing her heart-shaped face. Dressed in a cream satin dinner gown, its simple lines and high neckline complemented her natural grace.

For a moment, he was reminded of Sultana Charlotte. Although the two looked nothing alike, they probably shared similar upbringings. Were raised with the same expectations. The same regard for those less fortunate.

Were all young ladies in England expected to spend time in charitable pursuits, though? Charlotte had told him about her time volunteering as a nurse at St. Bartholomew's Hospital, especially when the man who was to become her first husband was recovering from his terrible burns.

Earlier that afternoon, Elizabeth and Adeline had departed Bostwick House to work at her ladyship's charity. Even though England wasn't currently engaged in a war that had soldiers or sailors returning with injuries that kept them from working, the charity was still placing men into employment situations or finding wives willing to marry them.

"Do you like working at your mother's charity? he asked.

Adeline gave a start. "I do." She glanced over at his book. "Why do you ask?"

He shrugged. "Do you work there because you choose to do so, or because your mother requires it?"

Adeline inhaled softly. "I do so because I enjoy it, I suppose. I like helping people," she explained. "Mother doesn't require my presence, but if one day, I end up running it, it's best I learn all the intricacies now so that I might continue her legacy," she explained.

Ertuğrul nodded his understanding.

"What about you?" she asked. "Will you become the

sultan because your Father wishes it, or because you want the responsibility?"

Dipping his head, Ertuğrul considered how to respond. "Because I will not have a choice," he replied. "There is much to do to run an empire," he added. "I will have help, of course. My uncles and my brothers oversee various departments—the army, navy, treasury, food, transportation, the provinces... but I know I will need to make decisions that will affect every one of our citizens."

Adeline listened to the emir's words, her eyes full of empathy and understanding. She could tell he felt burdened by the weight of his future empire, consumed by the enormity of the task before him. "Your father must know you are capable if he has chosen you as his heir," she remarked.

He scoffed before he told her of the time when he didn't think his father wanted him as a potential heir. Didn't want him in his presence. Didn't want him in his palace, even.

Back then, he had always believed Ziyaeddin I blamed him for his mother's death. He had been the second of twins, making an already difficult birth worse. One of the concubines who had taken on the responsibility of feeding the newborns had told him that despite her weariness, Afet had held and fed both he and his sister, Sevinc, before she finally died the day after his birth.

"He didn't really think it was your fault that Afet died," Adeline said in a whisper.

Ertuğrul glanced at her. "He has since told me that he does not, probably because Sultana Charlotte thoroughly scolded him on the matter."

Despite the seriousness of their discussion, Adeline had a hard time suppressing a snort. "She is a duchess," she said with a grin.

"I owe her much," Ertuğrul stated. "Imagine my surprise when my father told me he had decided I was to be his heir. He said he was..." He paused, struggling to find the correct English words to describe what he meant.

"Hard on you?" she guessed.

"Yes," he agreed. "Because he had high expectations for me."

"Do you hate him for it?" she asked in a quiet voice.

Ertuğrul shook his head. "No. I respect him. Very much. He's a good ruler. A man of hope. He is looking to the future. Making changes that are good for our empire," he explained. "I do wish... I do wonder, though, if Sultana Charlotte had not been brought to us by the pirates... would he have ever told me he didn't blame me for my mother's death?"

Adeline leaned closer to him. "I have learned that if you wish to know the answer to a question, you must ask it," she murmured.

Ertuğrul considered her quiet words. "I think I did not do so because I feared the answer," he admitted, his dark brows knitted so he looked far older than his age.

"What's the worst he could have said?"

Ertuğrul blinked. "Yes, I suppose."

Adeline scoffed. "Ziyaeddin surely would have known it wasn't logical to blame you," she insisted. "Besides, who can blame a baby for anything bad that happens in this life?"

Staring at her a moment, he inhaled softly. "He does love babies," he whispered. "He's spoiling Zehra and Ahmet, you must know," he added, referring to his newest sister and brother.

Adeline tittered. "Charlotte will do what she must to keep them from becoming brats," she assured him.

Setting aside her novel, she asked, "Is your father's love of babies the only reason why you have so many brothers and sisters?"

He allowed a grunt. "More because there has always been an expectation a sultan will father as many children as possible."

"Even though only one boy can inherit?" she asked.

He nodded. "The daughters have value, too, though, for they are married off to... aristocrats or other important dignitaries. To important people in other countries."

"Not for love then?" she asked. "Only politics?"

"Not always," he countered.

"So... do you have a harem? I remember you said you didn't have any children," she said, realizing it was a question to which she wasn't sure she wanted an answer.

"Oh, I don't," he replied. "I know that I should have already started a... what do you call it here? A nursery?" he asked.

"Yes."

"But I think I should like to do so with a wife rather than concubines."

His answer surprised Adeline. "But does legitimacy even matter?" she asked, remembering what her father had told her about the children of sultans.

"It's not about legitimacy," he replied, "although you are right that it is not held in the same regard as it is here." He furrowed his brows. "I have seen my father when he's been in the company of his concubines—how he regards them, how he behaves—and I have seen him with Sultana Charlotte. He loves them all, but he is *different* with Charlotte."

"Different?"

He nodded. "Beholden, perhaps?"

"Like how my father looks at my mother?" Adeline offered, her cheeks reddening as she dipped her head.

He chuckled softly. "Like that, yes."

As they finished their discussion, lost in the quiet comfort of the library, Ertuğrul felt something special stir between them, a deep and unspoken connection. Perhaps they were bound by their shared commitment to the betterment of their two worlds, by their mutual belief in the power of love and action, a bond that transcended their disparate backgrounds and cultures.

Or perhaps he was merely in love with her.

Remembering her comment about asking when one wanted to know the answer to a question, he was about to ask her if she might share his feelings when he realized her head was resting against his shoulder.

Glancing down, Ertuğrul discovered that, much like she had the night before in the coach, Adeline had fallen asleep.

Deciding it was best not to disturb her—she might wake up of her own accord—Ertuğrul returned his attention to his book.

He was soon lost in the idea of designing a palace, but not one suited for any of his uncles. One in which Adeline would enjoy living. One from which she could run a charity to help those who had suffered war injuries or accidents that rendered them unable to work. One where their children might grow up learning the importance of empathy, of charity, of caring for others. One with a garden of tulips in the spring and roses in the summer.

Perhaps she agreed with his ideas, for soon Adeline had nestled her head into the small of his shoulder and placed a hand on his thigh.

If he had been the least bit wary of his regard for her

before, he wasn't any longer. Her simple touch and the sound of her soft breaths convinced him of his regard for her.

Settling his head atop hers, he closed his eyes and imagined their future.

CHAPTER 27
A SON CONFESSES

*M**eanwhile, in the billiards room*

"I couldn't help but notice your absence when I returned from Parliament yesterday," George remarked after he took his first shot on the long billiards table. None of his balls made it to any of the pockets, but he wasn't playing to win on this night. "You mentioned you rode in the parade in Rotten Row, but I didn't see you there, either."

David dipped his head. "I was there. On horseback," he replied. "But... I was with someone."

George straightened and turned to regard his son with a furrowed brow. "A woman, by chance?"

Giving a start, David scoffed. "It wasn't like *that*," he replied. "That is, I was... I was with my betrothed." He let out a breath, as if he'd been holding it for too long.

Placing his cue on the green felt, George crossed his arms and leaned against the table, a combination of emotions playing across his face. "This is unexpected, at least so soon after your return," he said. "Best wishes," he added with a grin.

"Thank you." David's eyes darted to the side. "Aren't you going to ask me who it is?"

"Well, seeing as how Grace Foster is already married, I should hope it's Lady Rose. There isn't another young woman on the list for whom you showed as much regard when we talked the other night."

David set aside his cue. "She proposed. In the park yesterday." At seeing his father's widening grin, he chuckled softly. "We've had a bit of a rocky start, and so I told her if she wanted to marry me, she had to do the proposing. Duke's daughter and all," he added with a shrug.

George's chuckle erupted into full-throated laughter. "You'll have a story to tell your son," he said when he finally sobered. "I can just imagine he'll be the one who gets a proposal from a princess."

David blinked. "I think it's a little too soon to be talking about heirs," he said, and then clamped his mouth shut.

Given what he and Rose had done in a townhouse in Green Street earlier that day, it was possible she was already pregnant.

He hadn't intended to take her virtue. Hadn't intended to be alone with her in a townhouse for which she had a key. Hadn't intended to even be in Green Street when he had fetched her from Ariley Place. They were going to spend the day shopping in Jermyn Street, New Bond Street, and make a stop in Ludgate Hill followed by a visit to Gunter's Tea Shoppe in Berkeley Square for an ice.

Rose had other plans, though.

•   •   •

*E**arlier that day***

"Turn right at the next street," Rose said as David maneuvered the phaeton around a dray cart that had stopped in front of a Mayfair mansion.

"I was going to turn at Oxford Street," he replied. "Won't that be faster?" Although it had been over three years since he negotiated the streets of London whilst driving a phaeton, it didn't appear much had changed in the arrangement of the streets in this part of Mayfair.

"We're not going shopping," Rose stated. She pulled a key from her redingote pocket and held it up. "We're going to my townhouse."

"Your townhouse?" David repeated as he had the Cleveland Bay making the turn onto Green Street.

"Well, it's my father's—where he raised his first two daughters—but when I told him I was going to marry you—"

"You already told him?" David asked in alarm.

She gave him a pained expression. "He spoke with me after dinner last night. Wanted to know about our ride in the park," she explained, her hand suddenly on his thigh. "It's that one, with the green door," she added, nodding her head toward a white stuccoed townhouse with black shutters and and green window boxes.

David's eyes widened. "You're sure?" he asked, rather liking how her gloved hand gripped his thigh.

"Well, of course I'm sure," she said. "It's an entailed property of the dukedom, of course, but father always said it would be mine should I wish it, and last night, when I told him what I'd done, he said that since I was the one to propose then I'd best provide a place for us to live."

Rolling his eyes, David scoffed. "We could live at

Bostwick House," he said. There are plenty of bedcham—"

"We will after you inherit," Rose interrupted. "I'll insist on it when I'm your viscountess. But for now, I should like my own household. My own servants." She realized where her hand was and attempted to pull it away, but one of David's gloved hands covered it. "You don't mind terribly, do you?" she asked in a quieter voice.

Halting the horse in front of the townhouse, David gazed up at the façade and let out a low whistle. He glanced over at her and chuckled. "You are a minx, aren't you?"

Rose's eyes rounded. "I don't know what you mean," she said, even as her cheeks reddened.

He leaned over and kissed her temple, glad her felt hat was angled in the other direction. "Of course you don't," he whispered. "And no, I don't mind. In fact, I should like a tour. I'm especially interested in seeing how it's decorated," he added.

A young boy ran up, his cheeks smudged with soot and his trousers appearing far too short for him. "Hold your 'orse for you, guv'nor?"

David chuckled as he secured the reins on the pole. Most street urchins would have addressed him as 'sir' or 'mister,' but he supposed in this part of Mayfair, all men driving phaetons would be aristocrats. He tossed the boy a coin. "Can you stay awhile?"

"Of course, guv'nor. All day if ye need me."

David stepped down and walked around the back of the phaeton to help Rose down. Although she seemed game to use the steep step, he simply took her by the waist and lowered her to the pavement.

"You like doing that, don't you?" she asked.

David offered his arm. "You're as light as a feather,"

he murmured. "But, yes, I do like doing it," he added in a low voice. "Gives me a chance to hold onto you."

Rose inhaled softly, her eyes rounding as she gazed at him.

The front door opened before they stepped onto the bridge that spanned the area to the entry. A green-painted wrought iron fence wrapped the top of the area, preventing someone from falling into it. A quick glance down showed it was swept clean, although it was evident coal deliveries were made there.

"Ah, you must be Thompkins?" Rose said when an older man appeared.

"Lady Rose, it's good to see you again." The butler stepped aside to allow them in.

"Have I made your acquaintance before," she asked in surprise.

He nodded as he took her redingote and David's hat. "His Grace brought you and your brother here when you were quite young. As I recall, he came to claim the rest of what he'd left in the study."

Rose arched a brow. "I barely remember that," she murmured.

"And you must be Mr. Bennett-Jones," Thompkins said as he bowed. At David's look of surprise, he added, "His Grace sent word that you would be touring the house."

"That was very kind of him," David remarked. "I take it you are part of a limited staff given no one lives here?"

Thompkins nodded. "There's only the housekeeper—my wife, Mrs. Thompkins—the cook, and me for now, but I shall see to hiring a larger staff for when you wish to take up residence here."

"Then you must do so very soon, for Mr. Bennett-

Jones and I will be wed by mid-May," Rose said. "Until that time, I intend to claim the mistress suite."

David blinked, but didn't argue. He rather liked that Rose seemed determined to marry quickly rather than opt for a longer betrothal. As for claiming the mistress suite... "Are you moving in today, my sweet?" he asked.

Rose grinned at hearing him call her by an endearment. "My lady's maid has begun packing my clothes," she replied. "I thought perhaps I would move in on the morrow." She didn't add that she would be moving into the townhouse even if they weren't planning to wed. Her father had said he planned to evict her and her brother if they didn't marry this Season, and since she had practically given up on a betrothal, she thought it best to move sooner rather than later.

"I shall contact the agency immediately, my lady," Thompkins stated. "If you don't require anything at this time...?"

"We'll find our way around," David said, giving the butler a sympathetic look. "Lead the way, my lady."

"It's not very large—"

"It's four stories tall," David murmured. "Eight chimneys."

She gasped. "How do you know that?" she asked in surprise as they entered the grand hall.

"I counted them as we drove up," he replied, "and the exterior is in excellent shape. The stucco is newly refinished, there's fresh paint on the window boxes and on the door. The shutters are probably newly painted as well, but we weren't out there long enough so I could examine them."

Rose blinked and grinned as she watched him take in the series of marble busts mounted on caryatids that lined the hall in between the doors. Set against the opposite wall were the stairs to the first floor. There wasn't a central round table but a half-round was set against the wall beneath the stairs, an empty vase its only decoration. The floors were done in large tiles of alternating black and white marble.

"We can play a very large game of chess in here," he said with a grin.

Rose tittered as she led him into the blue-painted front salon. "This will be my room. A place for me to do my correspondence in the mornings."

"Maybe host your friends?" David hinted, remembering how Adeline had adopted a similar room in Bostwick House. "Are you in agreement with the colors?" he asked, impressed by the plasterwork on the ceiling and along the crown mouldings. A simple gas-lit chandelier provided the room's only overhead lighting.

"Do you not like them?" she asked, her brows furrowing as she studied the blues in the carpet and the reds in the upholstery.

"I want *you* to like them," he replied. "Since it is to be your salon."

She dipped her head. "Except for the upholstery on the two chairs, I like it very much."

"Then we shall have the upholstery changed," he replied, agreeing with her assessment. It was obvious the room had been decorated in the last century.

"You're going to be very agreeable, aren't you?" Rose asked as they entered the study.

David stopped short at the threshold. "Very," he murmured in awe. His gaze took in the oak-paneled room and then the oak-coffered ceiling. The light gold wood almost appeared gilded when struck by the light of the study's only window. Beneath his feet, the Aubusson carpet looked as if it was practically new. "Recently redone?" he asked as he finally stepped into the room and regarded the large oak desk with appreciation.

"I don't think so," Rose said as she moved to the two chairs that stood near the fireplace.

"I think I can spend my entire day in here," he said as he examined the books that lined nearly all the shelves of an entire wall.

"You can't," Rose replied. "At least, not today."

David furrowed his brows. Something in her voice had him straightening from the desk. He was about to ask her what she meant, but from the way she looked at him, her blue eyes nearly silver in the light, he swallowed. "You obviously have plans for me to be somewhere else," he whispered.

She nodded. "Master bedchamber. Second floor, I think."

David blinked. "Now?" he asked, stepping away from the desk to approach her. Although he'd been able to keep an arousal at bay since the moment her hand had gripped his thigh on the phaeton, his control was ebbing.

"Please? I'm not getting any younger," she whispered.

He shook his head. "Maybe not, but you're certainly more growing more beautiful," he said as he placed a hand on the side of her face. Remembering how the sultan showed his affection for Sultana Charlotte, he kissed Rose's forehead.

"You have to teach me. What to do. My mother... she told me some of it, but—"

"We'll... we'll learn together," he murmured.

"Will you show me what the concubine did for you?"

David gave a start, stepping back to regard her in shock. "What concubine?" he asked.

For a moment, Rose appeared flustered. "You said the sultan offered you one."

David sighed. "He did, and although I could not refuse the offer, that does not mean I took her to my bed," he said.

For a moment, she didn't appear to believe him. "Did you not find her... lovely?"

"She was gorgeous," he replied with a shrug. "But I meant what I said the other night. She was not you, Rose." He moved his hand up the side of her face and then around to the back of her neck to pull her closer. His lips captured hers in a light kiss. For a moment, it seemed as if the entire world stood still. As if the clock on the mantel had stopped its quiet ticking. As if they were entirely alone in the world.

When he finally ended the kiss, he left his forehead pressed against hers. "For the rest of my days, I shall remember this very spot as the one where I first kissed you in this house," he promised.

Her glazed eyes cleared as she blinked several times. "All right. Where will you kiss me next?"

David's eyes darkened. "In this house? Or on your body?"

Her mouth dropping open in surprise, Rose inhaled sharply. "David!" she responded in a shocked whisper.

"If you're thinking to scold me again," he said as he clasped one of her hands in his, "then I must inform you that you'll be doing a lot of it," he warned.

"What are you saying?" she asked, allowing him to lead her from the study and up the stairs.

He didn't climb them quickly, though. Determined to study the decor in an attempt to keep his arousal at bay, David knew he was losing the struggle when with every step, his cock seemed to understand what was about to happen.

By the time they reached the second floor, he had a

plan for what he might do with the wall colors and where a mosaic could be installed. A thought of how some additional plasterwork would look on the ceiling. When he opened the door to the master bedchamber, though, his only interest was the bed.

"Are you sure about this, my lady?" he asked as he closed and locked the door.

Rose turned her back to him. "Ever since I thought of it very early this morning," she murmured.

"I must have known you were thinking of me," he whispered, remembering how he had been attempting to fall asleep when he realized his arousal wasn't going to allow it.

Every time he thought of her, it responded by hardening, lengthening, until he was so uncomfortable he had to think of something else entirely.

He hadn't been able to at two o'clock in the morning, though.

He'd had to take himself in hand and imagine he was making love to Rose. Imagine what she might look like in the throes of passion. How she might sound as he pleasured her. How she might sound when he brought her to the brink of her release.

He had come before he heard what she might have sounded like when he sent her over the edge.

He wouldn't make that mistake today. He was determined to know. Determined to learn what he must do to pleasure her. To make her his. To keep her his for the rest of their lives.

David regarded the short row of buttons down her back. He had a thought to simply rip open the edges of her gown, his thoughts on what his father might do in his guise as a highwayman or a pirate or whatever role he was playing to seduce his mother, but he didn't wish to frighten his wife-to-be. Although he had some skill with a fencing foil, there wasn't one handy to pluck the buttons from her back, nor was there a lady's maid available to sew them back on.

So he simply undid each button with his fingers and then slowly spread apart the edges of the gown. He slid a hand over her warm skin, pushing her sleeves from her shoulders. When he dropped a kiss at the nape of her neck, Rose inhaled softly.

"That tickles," she whispered.

"You're so warm and soft," he breathed as his hands pushed the sleeves from her arms and wrapped around to the front of her body. The gown was stopped from falling completely given the petticoats holding it aloft.

Rose placed a hand over his and guided it to the top of her corset where a bow held the laces in place. He plucked the end of one and felt with his fingertips to loosen the laces.

"Not all the way," she warned. "It will take forever to do up the laces again."

"All right," he whispered, glancing down to where the petticoats were tied. He undid three bows and felt about for another as yards of fabric slid down her legs.

He took the opportunity to undo the buttons of his top coat and toss it onto a nearby chair.

Still surrounded by her skirts and petticoats, her corset hanging open in the front, she turned around to face him. One of her hands covered his where he had begun to undo his waistcoat buttons. "Allow me," she whispered.

David's gaze dropped to the expanse of white creamy skin above the neckline of her chemise. He could see the silhouette of her nipples through the thin fabric, and for a moment he struggled to breathe. "Am I allowed to strip you bare?" he asked in a whisper.

Rose pushed the waistcoat from his shoulders and went to work on his cravat. "Not completely," she murmured. "My stockings stay on. Always."

His brows knit together, but he wasn't about to argue with her. Instead, he lifted the loosened corset over her head, which meant she had to pause in her attempt to free the cravat from around his neck.

He noted how her hands trembled as she moved them back to the silk knot, and he covered one of them with his own. "Please, don't be frightened of me," he whispered.

"I'm not," she insisted. "I'm... excited, is all. I've never done this before."

Grinning, he pulled the tie at the top of her chemise until the bow separated. "I should hope not." Pushing the fabric from off the top of her shoulder and down her arm until one of her breasts was exposed, he inhaled softly. "Neither have I," he breathed.

Rose was about to ask how that could be, but decided she didn't care at the moment. Her entire body was trembling with anticipation. Her body ignited with a desire she had felt long ago, before David's departure, one that sometimes haunted her late at night and was even more apparent the night of the ball, in the gardens.

She understood now why thoughts of him had frustrated her. Angered her, even. How could she allow one man to have such power over her?

Watching how he gazed at her naked breasts had her realizing she had that same power over him.

I lust for you, he had said in the gardens.

He had said he was falling in love with her, too, but at the moment, she wanted the lusting David. Needed him.

The one that could ease whatever it was that had her breasts swelling and the area at the top of her thighs throbbing with need.

"If you pin my arms, I won't be able to remove your cravat," she warned.

"Oh," he replied, about to lower his lips to her nipple. "Well, then." He gathered up the fabric of her chemise and lifted it over her head, which had her gasping in surprise before he tossed the garment onto the nearby chair.

Before he had a chance to take a good look at her, she had the cravat unwrapping from around his neck, the pleated silk passing before his face over and over until the last of it disappeared and the fine linen of his shirt blinded him as it was lifted over his head. A moment later, and he heard her soft gasp as her hands slid up from his waist through the dark, crisp curls covering his chest to rub over the nubbin of his nipples.

At the same time she leaned forward to kiss one of his nipples, he planted a kiss on her forehead. His sharp intake of breath had her pulling away, so he used the opportunity to capture her lips with his and kissed her thoroughly. Even before he ended the kiss, he felt her fingers fumbling at the top of his pantaloons. She had the two top buttons undone and was struggling to determine how to push down the garment when he reached down and stilled her hands. His erection pressed so hard against the fall, he feared the thread holding the buttons would break.

"I need to remove my boots first," he whispered, his breaths short.

Rose's look of frustration had him attempting to stifle a grin. Placing his hands at her waist, he lifted her until her legs were free of her skirts and then moved her to the edge of the bed. She let out a squeak of surprise, quickly gripping his shoulders in an attempt to keep herself upright. Well aware her breasts were at the level of his eyes, she knew there was nothing she could do to hide them. But then, she didn't wish to, not when she saw how they mesmerized him.

Power, indeed.

When her feet were back on the carpeting, she straightened. "I am not bending over this bed," she stated, her eyes narrowing as if she was daring him to try.

"I don't want you to," he replied, one of his hands smoothing up her side until his thumb could brush over her nipple. He lowered his lips to it and suckled gently before moving his lips to do the same to the other.

He lifted her onto the bed, but quickly turned so he could reach down and pull his boots from his feet. He knew once he saw her there, laid out on the dark green velvet counterpane, naked but for her stockings, he would be lost.

Hearing the rustling of fabric behind him, he was about to turn to see what she was doing, but one of her hands smoothed up his bare back. He inhaled sharply as he undid the last of the pantaloon's buttons and his manhood sprang free.

He couldn't help the sigh of relief, nor ignore how Rose had her breasts pressed into his back and her arms wrapped around his middle. When her head bent over his shoulder, he felt her inhalation of breath and knew she saw what he did when he glanced down.

"You're going to put that into me?" she whispered.

He turned his head as much as he could and nodded. "I have to if I'm to pleasure you completely. If not today, then..."

It was going to have to be today. He couldn't wait another day. He wanted her so badly. Wanted to claim her. Wanted to make her his.

"Well, what are you waiting for?" she asked on a huff. "I'm not getting any younger."

A guffaw escaped David just then, the pent up nervousness releasing all at once. He took one of her hands from his waist and lifted it to his lips. "Yes, my lady," he replied before he kissed it. He pushed down the pantaloons and kicked his feet out of them.

About to turn to crawl onto the bed, he realized Rose was leaning on one elbow, her gaze still on his groin. "Aren't you going to remove your stockings?" she asked in a whisper.

"Are you?"

Her eyes rounded. "No."

"Well, then," he said as he turned. His brows arched when he saw how she had pushed down the counterpane and bed linens and was now sliding into the middle of the bed. "Don't go too far," he whispered as he climbed onto the bed and moved his body over hers.

"What do I do?" she asked, one of her hands moving to his head, her fingers threading through his wavy hair.

He kissed her and chuckled softly. "I would tell you to relax, but—"

"Relax?" she repeated in a hoarse whisper.

"I doubt you will, so pretend you're the queen of the world and that I'm here to pleasure you until you beg me to stop." He didn't wait for a reply, but used a knee to spread her legs apart and then moved down her body until his mouth could cover one of her breasts.

"Oh, I can do that," she murmured with a grin, moving her legs farther apart until she could lift a knee.

The silk of her stocking-covered foot rubbed against his woolen encased calf. She wiggled her toes against him.

He flicked his tongue over an engorged nipple and raised his face to regard her with a curious expression.

"As your queen, I'm ordering you to remove your stockings," she stated.

David blinked. "Now?" His gaze raked her prone body as he moved to sit up.

She giggled when she saw his look of disbelief. "Must I do it for you?" she asked in a tease.

Allowing her to do it meant he would no longer have such a gorgeous view of her. "I'll be but a moment," he said as he rolled off of her and saw to stripping the offending garments from his feet. He was about to reposition himself atop her when she pressed her palms against his shoulders. "What's wrong, Your Highness?" he asked.

Despite his attempt at humor, David knew something had happened in that moment.

"Your queen demands to know how you learned to do this."

His eyes darting to her bare breasts, he scoffed. "Trust me when I tell you, any man's first thought when seeing such gorgeous breasts is to kiss them. We all learn to do so as babes."

Rose inhaled softly. "You think they're gorgeous?" she asked in whisper. "You don't think they're too flat, or... or too fleshy?"

His head lifted from her chest, and he aimed a look of disbelief at her. "They're perfect. Look." He moved a hand to the side of one of them and lifted it until it mounded in his palm. Not waiting for her to respond, he simply resumed what he'd been doing and flicked her nipple with his tongue.

"Oh!" she cried out.

He did the same with her other breast, glad when she inhaled sharply. He gave up his hold on her breasts and worked his way down the front of her body, kissing and suckling and using the tips of his fingers to incite frissons beneath her skin.

"Where are you going now?" she asked in a whisper.

"To the royal vault, Your Highness."

For a moment, she didn't move, and he took the opportunity to kiss the insides of her thighs. From her soft sighs and gasps, he sensed she was finally giving in as her slightly bent knees fell to the sides. He smoothed a hand from beneath one thigh to behind her knee and gently lifted it. "Open for me, my queen," he murmured, as he drew a finger along the folds protecting her womanhood. He felt her ambrosia coat the tip of his finger, and remembering what he had learned under the tutelage of the concubine, he placed his entire hand over her folds and began to gently rub her.

Of course her first reaction would be an attempt to draw her knees together. When he persisted, though, and his movements quickened, he was sure he felt her swollen womanhood beneath the pad of his middle finger.

On either side of his head, her thighs quivered, and before he replaced his hand with his tongue, he planted a kiss on one of them.

Rose cried out as his tongue flicked over her engorged nubbin. Cried out again when he repeated it from the other direction.

"What are you doing?" she whispered between gasps for air.

"I found the key to the vault," he said before he chuckled softly and then covered it with his lips. His tongue delved into her, which had her entire body reacting as her thighs closed around his head and her hips lifted.

Had his ears not been covered, he would have heard her say, "David," over and over again until he was sure her orgasm had begun. Her knees fell away as her keening increased.

When he felt her hand pushing on his head, he rose up over her body. "Breathe, my queen." He placed the tip of his manhood at her opening and pushed. Pushed again until he was buried in her, the last vestiges of her orgasm helping to draw him in completely. He groaned, sure he wouldn't last long.

If she felt any pain, she didn't show it. If she wanted him to stop, she didn't put voice to it.

When he moved to pull out of her, she had her hands lifted to his back. The pinch of her fingernails pressed into his flesh spurred him to continue, his thrusts at first slow and careful before increasing in speed and intensity. Knowing his release was imminent, he thrust hard into her one last time and was lost to the grip of ecstasy.

His last thought before passing out was how much he liked raiding the royal vault.

*R*ose watched in awe as David lowered his body to hers, watched as his eyes shuttered and his head landed on her shoulder and on a pillow she hadn't been aware was there.

At some point, she had lifted her knees to grip his thighs, the same moment she had felt his manhood fill her so completely, she thought she'd been about to burst. Now the discomfort settled into a sort of numbness occasionally broken by a dart of pleasure or a frisson that skittered beneath her skin.

The moment before he had taken her virtue had been pure bliss, though. The pleasure so all-consuming, she wished they hadn't waited so many years to admit their desire for one another.

If she had admitted she had feelings for him, would he have stayed in England? Or would he have still departed on his Grand Tour? Would he have returned sooner, knowing she waited for him?

In the end, did it matter?

She sighed and then realized he was stirring. His head lifted from her shoulder, and he regarded her with the oddest expression.

"What is it?" she asked.

He chuckled. "For a moment, I thought I'd dreamt it all," he whispered.

"That you were a thief after the queen's royal vault?" she teased.

Grimacing, David said, "I'd like to think I was invited to plunder the vault."

She giggled and then sobered. "If I invited you to visit me on occasion, at least until we're married and you're moved into the master suite, might you be willing to leave a deposit in the royal vault?"

He blinked before understanding she wished him to get a child on her as soon as possible. "I am at the queen's command," he replied.

When his brows suddenly furrowed, Rose asked, "What is it now?"

David lifted his body from hers. "I was to take my queen on a mission of utmost importance," he stated as he moved to sit on the edge of the bed. He pulled on his stockings, but when he noticed how she stared at him in disbelief, he added, "You're missing the most important royal jewel, my queen."

Rose blinked and sat up. "What might that be?"

He scoffed as he pulled on his pantaloons, a brief glance at her naked torso nearly convincing him to return to her side. "A betrothal ring, Your Highness."

Her eyes rounding in delight, Rose hurried off the bed, donned her chemise and corset, and stepped into the middle of her skirts and petticoats. In a few minutes, she was dressed and regarding her reflection in the cheval mirror.

Watching in wonder, David chuckled. "You do realize that now that I know how quickly you can dress, I'll expect you'll be able to do so when we're getting ready for an event," he warned as he pulled on his shirt and tucked it into his pantaloons.

"I'll be the one waiting on you," she replied as she made her way to the bed and pulled the linens and counterpane back into place. When she joined him on the other side of the bed, she had his cravat ready to wrap around his neck.

"Probably," David acknowledged as he lowered his head. When she had the cravat behind his neck, she pulled on the ends until his head was close enough she could kiss him. He returned the kiss in equal measure, and when he finally came up for air, he furrowed a brow. "We could just go back to bed for the rest of the day," he whispered.

Rose scoffed as she held up a hand and wiggled her bare fingers.

"Or we could go buy you a ring."

"This queen is rather liking her new knight in shining armor," she teased.

• • •

*I*n the billiards room at Bostwick House

"Have you set a wedding date?" George asked when David finished telling him about the townhouse and his plans for redecorating.

"Rose told the butler we'd be married by mid-May," David replied.

"That soon?"

David dipped his head. "She says she's not getting any younger. In fact... she's moving into the townhouse tomorrow."

"And you?"

He shrugged. "When we're wed. But... I've been invited for frequent visits," he admitted.

George grinned. "Did you find a ring?"

Chuckling, David nodded. "Alex had the perfect betrothal ring for us," he replied, referring to Alexander Tennison, heir to the Everly earldom and owner of the *Ewen and Ewen* jewelry shop in Ludgate Hill. "A sapphire with some diamonds set in gold filigree. Rose loves it."

Wincing at the thought of how much the bauble was going to set him back, George said, "And the announcement?"

"At the Ariley ball, of course," David replied. "Rose told her father yesterday, which is probably why he gave her the townhouse."

George nodded as he leaned against the billiards table and crossed his arms. "Something tells me yours won't be the only betrothal announcement at the Ariley ball."

"Oh?" David said as he placed his cue on the table and began retrieving balls from the pockets.

"Waverley has asked for Hope Batey's hand in marriage, at least according to your sister." He could just imagine Marcus Lancaster's reaction to learning his daughter would one day be a duchess.

David's grin widened. "I saw them dancing the other night. I never would have guessed they were betrothed." He drained his port and set aside the glass when he noticed his father's expression. "Anyone else?"

George dipped his head, his brows furrowed. "I'm beginning to think everyone in London is blind except for Ertuğrul."

Giving a start, David stared at his father. "Come again?"

His father huffed. "Nothing," he said before taking a sip of port. He glanced at the clock on the fireplace mantel and then at the billiards table. "Best two out of three?"

Shrugging, David's attention went to the clock. "Is there a reason you're delaying going to bed?" he asked as he retrieved his pool cue from the table. "This could take some time."

"I'm counting on it," his father responded.

Deciding not to ask—nothing had happened during dinner to suggest his parents were not speaking with one another—David said, "Challenge accepted."

CHAPTER 28
WHISPERS IN THE DARK

An hour later

Having won two out of three of the billiards games he had played with his heir, George made his way to the library. Elkins had obviously been there, for the main overhead light had been extinguished. The only remaining light in the room came from the fireplace, where the bright orange embers bathed the reading area in a golden glow.

At first glance, the room appeared empty. He had a thought to pour a glass of brandy and sit by the dying fire, a celebration of sorts for his son's betrothal.

His son and heir was going to marry a duke's daughter.

He had married a marquess' daughter.

The Bennett-Joneses were most definitely charmed in marrying above their station.

Chuckling softly, he filled a small glass from the salver on the library desk from the decanter of brandy and made his way toward the fireplace. About to sit in the single upholstered chair next to the couch, he gave a start when he realized he wasn't alone.

Opened books still on their laps, Ertuğrul and Adeline were sound asleep in each others' arms.

Almost embarrassed at seeing how his daughter's head rested against the şehzade's shoulder, one hand on his thigh, George was about to look away when he noted how Ertuğrul's head rested atop hers. How his arm had wrapped around her shoulders, his hand mere inches from the side of her breast.

Adeline would never have deliberately fallen asleep in the arms of the sultan's son, but she certainly looked comfortable. As for Ertuğrul... George could only imagine what must have gone through the young man's head when Adeline fell asleep against him.

Again.

He probably hadn't wished to embarrass her as she had been the night before in the coach when George had been forced to awaken her upon their arrival at Bostwick House. The moment she realized where she was—leaning against Ertuğrul—she covered her mouth with a silk-gloved hand as her eyes rounded and she apologized profusely.

Torn between waking her or allowing her to sleep, Ertuğrul had obviously chosen to allow her to sleep.

If he thought he was being chivalrous, he obviously didn't understand the rules of English society.

George had a thought to wake them. Had a thought that perhaps it would be best if he sent them off to bed with a gentle rebuke. Remind the sultan's son that in any other household, he would be expected to wed his daughter—marriages had been forced for far less.

Instead, he settled back in the chair and enjoyed his brandy.

What if Ertuğrul had already made his decision and had chosen Adeline to be his bride? His eventual sultana? Perhaps he was merely ensuring he'd be forced to wed her.

Charmed, indeed, George thought with a chuckle when he finally made his way to bed.

*O*nce he was sure his host had departed the library, Ertuğrul opened his eyes and breathed a sigh of relief. He was sure he'd been sound asleep when he heard nearby footfalls. He had thought to make his presence known. Rise from the couch and address the arrival to the library, but when he realized Adeline's soft body was snuggled against his own, providing a comfortable warmth the fireplace was no longer doing, he decided to remain right where he was.

Surely if he was quiet enough, the usurper wouldn't notice he was there. He didn't think the top of his head extended above the carved wooden frame of the leather-upholstered couch. He heard the sound of liquid pouring into a glass, felt the soft footfalls beneath his feet, and held his breath when he knew he'd been discovered.

If it was David, he would feel his friend nudge his shoulder and tell him to wake up.

Instead, the scent of George Bennett-Jones' cologne had wafted past his nose, and he nearly panicked. Inhaling softly, as if he were still sleeping, he had decided it best he stay right where he was. Pretend he was sleeping. Pretend he was merely trapped on the couch because Adeline had fallen asleep on him.

Again.

He had to fight the urge to grin. Fight the urge to kiss her once more. Did the young woman have any idea how much he adored holding her? How much he wished to take her to his bedchamber, place her beneath the covers, and hold her close for the rest of the night?

His cock certainly knew, for it had become uncomfortably large in the last few minutes. At least Adeline's body mostly hid the evidence of it from view of where the viscount had sat in a nearby chair, drinking something.

Ertuğrul had one time dared a peek from beneath his lashes, relieved to see George's gaze on the contents of his glass, an expression of amusement on his face.

A moment later, and Ertuğrul felt the viscount's departing footfalls.

He inhaled with relief, the movement of his chest bringing Adeline out of her slumber.

When she glanced up at him, she grinned. "I'm having the most amazing dream," she whispered.

"Are you?" He didn't know what else to say.

"Oh, yes. You're about to take me up to your room and make love to me," she murmured.

"Am I?"

"Hmmm."

Ertuğrul stiffened in more ways than one.

"Is this... after you marry me?" he asked in a whisper. "Or...?"

"Hmmm."

He stared down at her until her eyelids fluttered open. She didn't move her head, but her eyes darted about as if to determine where she was. "I fell asleep on you again, didn't I?"

Despite his disappointment at realizing she had awakened from a dream in which he had obviously played a starring role, he grinned. "You did, but I don't mind. Your father..." He stopped, his brows furrowing. George hadn't said a word. Hadn't attempted to wake him or scold him or threaten him with eviction. "Your father didn't seem to mind, either," he murmured in surprise.

Adeline sighed but didn't lift her head. "He likes you," she whispered. Her eyes suddenly widened and she moved to sit up. "Father saw us?" she asked in a hoarse whisper.

Ertuğrul nodded. "He was just here. Drinking something."

"Brandy, probably," she murmured before she pointed to the book that still rested in his lap. Apparently deciding they weren't in any imminent danger from an angry father, she asked, "Did you come up with a plan for your uncles' palaces?"

He glanced at the illustration that spanned two pages of the open book. "I was... distracted," he replied, as if he was trying to find the right word.

"Oh, dear. I'm so sorry," she said, straightening on the couch.

"You've nothing to be sorry for," he said. "But I might should your father find us like this again," he said as he struggled with what he wanted to do.

Had they been in one of his father's palaces, he would have asked her to join him in his bedchamber. Removed her gown. Pleasured her until she was ready for him. Made love to her until near dawn. Watched as the colored light from the stained-glass windows played over her features and her sleep-warmed skin. Kissed her nipples. Pulled her into his arms and held her close.

Perhaps she could read his mind, for her brows furrowed as her gaze fell to his lips. "What's the worst that could happen?" she whispered softly, although it wasn't apparent she was asking him the question.

"You would be forced to marry me," he said, wincing slightly.

Her eyes widened. "You'd be forced to marry *me*," she countered.

"There's nothing worst about that," he said, immediately realizing he had said the wrong word. "I mean... there's nothing wrong or... bad... quite the opposite," he stammered.

"I didn't mean to imply I didn't wish to," Adeline whispered, her gaze once again dropping to his lips.

Ertuğrul wasn't sure if she initiated the kiss or if he did, but when their lips touched, he experienced a moment of elation he hadn't felt in his entire life. He had never kissed a woman on the lips before. Never tasted the soft pillows of flesh that cradled his. Never felt the surge of desire the simple act of intimacy caused in his body. The twinge in his chest.

At the moment he thought the kiss was ending, he angled his head and placed a hand at the back of her neck to ensure he could continue the wondrous experience, sure there was more.

He had read about kissing, of course, but he had never understood the appeal of such an act. Lips and tongues engaged in some sort of dance? But when Adeline's mouth opened slightly, an invitation for him to deepen the kiss, his tongue darted to her teeth and then collided with hers, tangling and tasting, until he realized he had to breathe.

Ending the kiss slowly, Ertuğrul left his forehead pressed to hers as he inhaled and let the breath out in a *whoosh*. "If we don't stop now, I..." He swallowed as his brows furrowed with indecision.

Adeline lifted her eyes to meet his. "I understand."

"I'll speak with your father tomorrow."

"You will?"

He nodded. "Isn't that the way it's done? That I should let him know I intend to bed you?"

Blinking, Adeline attempted to suppress a grin and couldn't. "You may not wish to start with *that*, exactly," she said.

He considered her words and then winced. "I should let him know that I intend to *wed* you," he stated.

"It's probably best if you ask if you can do so," she suggested. "Although, you are a sultan's son, so maybe you don't have to?" she added with a shrug.

"I do not wish to offend your father," he countered. "He has been most gracious taking me, a stranger, into his home," he added. "And I sense he will not easily give you to me. He holds you in high regard. I shall have to devise a plan."

Adeline gave a start. "A plan?" she repeated.

"A proposal," he countered. "An offer."

Not quite sure what the şehzade had in mind, Adeline gave him a watery grin, deciding she wouldn't remind him that he really should include her in the proposal.

"I will see you to your room," he said as he closed the book and set it aside. He rose from the couch and turned around to help her up.

"Meet me at the statue of Aphrodite in the morning?" she whispered.

The dim light from the fireplace illuminated his brilliant smile. "Yes. It seems I may owe her my gratitude."

The two made their way out of the library and up the stairs, the hall clock chiming twice.

CHAPTER 29
A MORNING OF NEWS

*T*he next day

The first to arrive in the breakfast parlor the next morning, David filled a plate from the offerings on the sideboard and settled into his usual chair. He was sure his father would have shared what he had learned about David's afternoon with Rose, and he expected his mother would either congratulate him or thoroughly scold him.

She did neither, for when Elizabeth entered on the arm of George, she was reminding him of their schedule for that evening.

"We've already seen that opera," his father said, nodding to David before he helped himself to a plate.

"But Ertuğrul hasn't, and the Adelphi still has that magician—"

"The Great Wizard of the North," David interrupted, imitating the announcer who introduced John Henry Anderson to the Adelphi Theatre stage.

"—and *An Hour in Ireland*," his mother continued, ignoring her oldest son.

"So *The Bohemian Girl*, it is," George said with a shrug. "In less than a fortnight, they'll be starting a new one."

"*The Brides of Venice*, I think it's called," she said as George placed a plate of coddled eggs and toast points before her.

"Speaking of brides," George said as he returned to the sideboard to fill a plate for himself. "When can we expect Rose to marry you?" he asked of David.

"She wants to wed by mid-May," he replied with a grin.

"Well, I should hope so," Elizabeth said as a footman set a cup of tea before her. "She's not getting any younger."

David scoffed, wondering if Rose had said something to her. "Might I be allowed to bring her with us this evening?"

"Of course," his father replied as he took his seat. "There's plenty of room," he added as Elkins appeared with coffee. They usually sat in the Morganfield box. Given David Carlington's distaste for the theatre, the Marquess and Marchioness of Morganfield rarely attended.

David asked Elkins if a footman could be sent to Ariley Place with the invitation.

"Right away, sir," the butler said. Once he had poured coffee for George and David, he disappeared from the breakfast parlor only a moment before Ertuğrul and Adeline entered.

"Speaking of room, or *rooms* rather, we'll need to decide where you'd like yours," Elizabeth said, her attention on David.

His gaze darting to George—David had expected his father to have already shared the information with his mother—he said, "Actually, I will be moving out of Bost-wick House after the wedding."

"Good morning," Adeline said happily, immediately going to the sideboard.

"Good morning," Ertuğrul offered, his nervousness apparent when George glanced up from his newspaper.

"You're moving out?" Elizabeth repeated.

"Who's moving out?" Adeline asked, her happy expression faltering.

"To where?" Elizabeth asked in awe.

"An Ariley townhouse in Green Street. Rose is moving in today," David explained. "Her brother is to marry Hope Batey in June, and she'll be moving into Ariley Place."

"Green Street," Elizabeth murmured softly. "An excellent address. Well, you won't be so far away, I suppose," she said.

"Rose gave me a tour of it yesterday. Before I bought her a betrothal ring at *Ewen and Ewen*. There's some redecoration to do. I'll get started on the details right away," he explained.

"A betrothal ring?" Ertuğrul repeated as he held a chair for Adeline.

"She's a duke's daughter," David replied. "I thought it best I get her a ring with a bauble. Something that will work with the gold band I'll give her when we wed."

"Oh, what sort of bauble?" Adeline asked with excite-ment. "Sapphire, I hope. The blue will go perfect with her eye color."

David chuckled. "Sapphire with some diamonds set in gold filigree. Alexander Tennison made it," he stated proudly.

Adeline gave a start. "I can hardly wait to see it," she said. She turned her attention to Ertuğrul. "Alex is the heir to the Everly earldom, but he likes to make jewelry, so his father bought him a shop where he and his wife, who is some sort of expert in gemstones, can practice their avocations."

Ertuğrul nodded his understanding. "What will you be doing today?" he asked.

"Adeline will be joining me at the charity," Elizabeth said. "We have some new clients who need employment," she added. "Oh, and I have a final fitting for my gown for tomorrow night's ball at a modiste in Oxford Street, but we'll be home well before dinner and the time we need to leave for the theatre."

Adeline gave Ertuğrul an apologetic glance, well aware he was looking forward to touring another museum. "We can drop you somewhere if you'd like," she offered. "Since father will need the phaeton for Parliament."

"We can take a Hansom cab," David said. "I'll go with you. Haven't played tourist since we were in Sicily last year."

Ertuğrul shook his head. "I believe I should like to work on the designs for the palaces we spoke of last night," he said.

"Suit yourself," David said. "I'll go to the townhouse then. Get started on my own designs."

When George left the breakfast parlor and headed for his study, Ertuğrul followed.

"Might I have a word with you, sir?" he asked, his nervousness returning.

George waved him to a chair in front of his desk. "If it's about last night, I... I don't hold you responsible for my daughter's impropriety." When he took note of Ertuğrul's expression of guilt, he arched a brow. "Maybe I should—?"

"You should, sir," Ertuğrul stated. "That is, I didn't discourage her from sleeping on me when I could have done so. In fact, I am looking forward to her doing it again. Every night, should she wish."

Straightening in his chair, George was sure the şehzade had chosen the wrong words. "I think you… you might have mis-spoke."

Ertuğrul furrowed his brows as he replayed his comment in his mind. "I wish to marry your daughter, sir. If I understand correctly, I must seek your permission first and then offer what I must to complete the deal."

George blinked. "I understood the first part," he said, a combination of elation and dread making it hard for him to breathe. "But it is I who must offer you a dowry to wed my daughter. Seven-thousand pounds… to ensure she has a decent settlement for her and the children upon your death."

Frowning, Ertuğrul considered the viscount's words and shook his head. "I do not require money to wed your daughter, sir, since she will have much in the way of wealth upon my death, but I do think your viscountess will require recompense for losing her assistance at the charity."

Inhaling to respond, George let out the breath in a combination of surprise and frustration. "I suppose if you're inclined to provide a donation to the charity, Elizabeth would accept that as recompense," he said. "Adeline works there as a volunteer. She is not paid."

Ertuğrul seemed to think on this a moment before he held up a finger. "Very well. A donation then," he agreed. "Does that mean I have your permission to wed Miss Bennett-Jones?"

George swallowed. "You're going to take her to Constantinople, aren't you?" he asked in a quiet voice, tears brightening his eyes as the reality of Ertuğrul's words sunk in.

"I will. I plan to build her a palace where she can run her own charity, should she wish." Ertuğrul noted the viscount's demeanor, and he slumped in his chair. "Did I say something wrong?"

George shook his head. "No. Not at all. I'll miss her, though. More than I miss her older sister," he admitted as he sniffled. "You have my permission to propose, but... it will be up to her to decide," he warned gently. "I cannot force her to marry you."

"I understand, sir. I intend to make her an offer she cannot refuse."

Displaying a watery grin, George said, "It will have to be a very good offer, indeed." He glanced at the clock. "I apologize, but I must depart now, or I'll be late for Parliament."

Ertuğrul stood and bowed. "Thank you, sir."

George nodded as he rushed out of the study, barely acknowledging Elkins as he accepted his hat and great-coat and headed out the door.

When the Bennett-Joneses had all departed Bostwick House, Ertuğrul found Elkins and asked where he might find transportation. The butler explained how Hansom cabs operated and where he could locate one nearby.

Drawing architectural plans required large sheets of parchment, rulers, and pencils. A betrothal apparently required a ring. Armed with his list, Ertuğrul took his leave and hurried off to find a cab.

CHAPTER 30
A DAY OF DOING

*L*ater that day

By the time Elizabeth and Adeline had returned from *Finding Work for the Wounded,* George from Parliament, and David from the Green Street townhouse, it was too late for afternoon tea and already time to dress for dinner.

"When can I expect a tour of your townhouse?" Elizabeth asked of David as they made their way upstairs.

Her oldest son chuckled. "Do you wish to see it before the renovations are complete? Or after?"

"Both," she replied with a grin. "How is your betrothed? I haven't had a chance to spend one minute with her since you asked for her hand."

David paused at the top of the stairs. "Relieved, I think."

Elizabeth angled her head to one side. "Why do you say that?"

Dipping his head, David considered how to respond. "I think she was convinced no one was going to propose, and now that I have—and that her father seems to be happy about the matter—she wishes to get on with life. Having her own household has made her..." He winced.

"More agreeable?" his mother suggested.

He nodded, remembering how Rose had greeted him that morning at the townhouse, practically running into his arms and kissing him with abandon. Once her lady's maid and the footmen had left to retrieve more trunks and some small furnishings, she asked if he might make love to her in the master suite. Not about to argue, he did her bidding and helped her redress only moments before the servants returned to the townhouse.

When he'd left late that afternoon, he reminded her that he would be bringing her to the theatre that night and wondered where he might find her.

"Here, of course," she had said.

David shook off the brief reverie. "It's not that Rose wasn't agreeable before, but I did sense her... her annoyance with me, or perhaps it was merely her situation."

"Her annoyance wasn't because of you necessarily," Elizabeth claimed as she made her way down the corridor towards her apartments.

"I was gone three years, two months, and ten days," he reminded her.

"Yes, you were. You really should have taken that trip years ago."

"I did."

"I meant..." She sighed. "It was admirable of you to wait until Lord James was finished at Cambridge so he could join you on your Grand Tour, but you must admit, you should have taken it when you were one-and-twenty so you'd be home when you were three-and-twenty and then you two would be wed before she was on the shelf."

David scoffed. "She's not on the shelf, Mother.

Besides... I was not of a mind to marry when I was three-and twenty."

Elizabeth paused at the door to her apartments. "I suppose not." When she grimaced, David asked what was wrong.

"I'm quite sure there were expectations on Helen's part as to the rank of the people her children would marry—"

"Rose deserves a duke's son," David murmured.

"—However, her father is of a completely different mind. He simply didn't share that opinion with his children until a few days ago."

David furrowed his brows. "What's this?"

His mother placed a hand on his arm. "Ariley likes you. Always has. And Rose..." She sighed. "Rose has adored you your entire life. So it's all worked out, just a few years later than it might have, is all." She lowered her voice. "You are seeing to getting a child on her, I hope?"

Suspicious as to why his mother had brought up the issue in the first place, David's eyes suddenly rounded. "Is this about you having grandchildren?" he asked.

Elizabeth gave him a quelling glance. "And your heirs," she admitted.

Scoffing, David rolled his eyes and headed for his bedchamber. "I am my father's son," he called out, as if that was enough to answer her last question.

Grinning happily, Elizabeth entered the apartment she shared with George and a moment later was in his arms.

When he finished kissing her, he left his forehead pressed to hers. "You are a minx and a managing mother," he accused gently.

"When I need to be," she admitted. "Now we just have Addy and Daniel to marry off..." She stopped at seeing his expression of uncertainty, a look of alarm appearing on her own face when she noted how his eyes brightened. "What is it? What's wrong?"

"Ertuğrul spoke with me this morning. I've given him my permission to wed Addy if... if she agrees. Did she say anything to you today?"

Elizabeth's mouth formed an 'o' as a series of emotions played over her face. "No," she said. "Although she seemed happier than usual. Her color was rather high. But she didn't say a thing about it."

"Then he hasn't yet proposed," he reasoned. There wouldn't have been an opportunity.

"This is..."

"Unexpected, I know," George murmured.

"Not really. They're like two peas in a pod," she commented before her eyes rounded. "Our daughter could one day be a sultana," she added in an excited whisper.

"We Bennett-Joneses do seem to marry well beyond our stations," he commented. "Poor Daniel is going to have to find a European princess or a queen."

Elizabeth tittered. "I wouldn't put it past him," she said.

"We need to dress for dinner," George reminded her. "Act like we don't know anything."

"Agreed," she replied before she sighed, knowing it would be next to impossible to hide her excitement for her daughter.

An hour later
"Where do you suppose he is?" Elizabeth asked when Elkins appeared at the parlor door. She and George had been about to head down to the dining room

for a quick meal before they departed for the Royal Theatre, their son and daughter close behind. Ertuğrul hadn't yet made an appearance, though.

"His Eminence sends his apologies," the butler said. "He will join you at the theatre before the start of the opera."

George and Elizabeth exchanged curious glances before George turned to regard Adeline. "I thought he was going to spend the day designing a palace."

Adeline's eyes widened. "He did," she replied before turning her attention on her brother. "His drawings are in the library."

"Don't look at me," David said. "I've barely seen him since the Weatherstone ball."

When Elkins cleared his throat, all four turned to stare at him. "He wished to acquire clothing suitable for the theatre, but Mr. Garth was still performing alterations when a courier was sent with news of his delay and a wrapped bundle containing the clothes he was wearing when he left."

George chuckled. "A courier?" he repeated.

Elkins winced. "A street urchin, sir. Apparently overcompensated for the errand," he added as he arched a gray brow. "He was quite excited to have performed an errand for the emir."

"I hope Ertuğrul isn't being fleeced," Elizabeth murmured.

"I've warned him," David said as they descended the stairs. "And it isn't his first time in England."

"If he's at Garth's shop, he'll be fine," George said, referring to Jeffrey Garth, a tailor of some renown. "And end up better dressed than any of us." He turned to Adeline. "Have you seen him since breakfast?"

"I haven't, but he was obviously here for part of the

day because there are designs in the library. On the table," she repeated.

Adeline knew he'd left and returned to the townhouse at least once that day, for when she'd gone into the library to retrieve the book she had left there the night before, she found the library table covered with large sheets of parchment.

Studying the pairs of connected lines and curves, Adeline soon determined she was looking at an overhead view of a building with many rooms. She couldn't read the words written in the middle of the rooms, though, as they were in a language foreign to her.

Determined to leave the drawings the way she found them, Adeline had carefully lifted the top sheet and gasped at the sketch of an exterior view of the building. The Mogul architecture featured a dozen onion domes, ornate windows, and a huge door.

The sheet below was from another view, but unfinished.

"We must have missed him by only a few minutes," she reasoned when she considered how long it must have taken him to do the drawings. "He probably thought his dinner clothes wouldn't be formal enough for the theatre."

They took their seats at the table, the conversation mostly on David's upcoming wedding. From the number of times her father glanced in her direction, Adeline sensed something was amiss. When she remembered that he had paid witness to her sleeping in the library the night before, she wondered if he had plans to admonish her.

Surely he didn't know about the kiss she had shared with the sultan's son. About their talk of marriage. About a possible life in Constantinople.

If Ertuğrul hadn't pulled her into his arms that morning in front of the statue of Aphrodite and kissed her quite thoroughly, all before he said good morning and escorted her to breakfast, she might have spent the day thinking it had all been a dream.

Prepared for a scolding, she stayed silent for the coach ride to Rose's townhouse. When David stepped out to escort Rose to the coach, Adeline was sure her father was going to say something to her. Instead, he seemed especially quiet, murmuring something to her mother about that day's session of Parliament.

The mood inside the coach changed considerably once David assisted his betrothed into the coach, though. Rose took a seat next to Adeline, and the two spent the entire trip to Drury Lane talking about wedding plans and the townhouse.

Ertuğrul wasn't mentioned at all.

*D*ressed in new shoes and a formal suit of clothes appropriate for the theatre or a ball, Ertuğrul stepped down from a Hansom cab and thanked the driver.

He stood before the Royal Theatre and regarded the one-sheet that advertised that night's production: *The Bohemian Girl*, an opera by Michael William Balfe.

"Ticket, sir?"

Ertuğrul blinked. "Uh, I am to meet my party in the Morganfield box," he stated. "The Viscount and Viscountess Bostwick."

Annoyed he wouldn't be making a sale, the man waved him into the lobby. Ertuğrul surveyed the room, stunned to discover dozens of couples dressed in their finest clothes while others streamed in wearing garb they might have worn whilst doing their daily chores. The majority seemed dressed much like those he had seen on his shopping spree earlier that day.

His first stop had been at a shop featuring papers and parchments of all sizes, inks, pens, and fine charcoal pencils. The shopkeeper rolled up the parchment sheets and slid them into a pasteboard tube along with his other selections.

His second stop had been at *Ewen and Ewen*. A young woman with a withered arm had greeted him. When he asked to see betrothal rings made by Alexander Tennison, she brightened. "He's my husband," she had said proudly. "Might you have a gemstone in mind?" she asked as she led him to a display case with over twenty rings set in black velvet.

"All of them?"

Mrs. Tennison had blinked and then tittered as she removed the tray from the display case and set it before him. "Sapphires, diamonds, rubies…"

"Rubies," he said when his gaze stopped on a ring featuring a large round red stone surrounded by diamonds and gold filigree. The gold band featured tiny engraved leaves.

Pulling the ring from the tray, Mrs. Tennison held it out for him to examine. "The gem is the color of a red rose," she commented. "And it's flawless."

"How will I know if it fits?" he asked, examining the detailed workmanship.

"We can resize it if necessary," she replied. "Will you need a wedding band as well?" She pulled a thin gold band from the velvet and held it up. "This has the same leaves engraved in it, if you'd like something to match."

"I would," he had agreed. A few minutes later, he had left the jewelry shop and had the cab return him to Bostwick House, where he had drawn up the initial plans for a palace.

When Elkins had asked if he required help to dress for that evening, he had decided he wanted to wear more European style formal clothes. "If I don't return before seven o'clock, please tell her ladyship I will meet them at the theatre."

Elkins dared a glance at a nearby clock even as the şehzade was telling him of his plans. Ertuğrul realized now that he should have taken the butler's arched brows to mean his plan was optimistic at best.

The cab had delivered him to a shop in New Bond Street and then waited while he was fitted by a tailor. He hadn't expected the visit to the men's clothing shop to take so long.

Jeffrey Garth, his hair a distinguished gray and his manner rather serious, had held up a number of waistcoats, usually shaking his head before holding up another.

When Ertuğrul reminded the tailor he needed the clothes for that night's performance at the Royal Theatre, Garth had him dressed and last-minute alterations done within the hour. He arranged for his other clothes to be delivered to Bostwick House

Noting the late hour, Ertuğrul had the Hansom cab take him directly to the theatre.

CHAPTER 31
A NIGHT AT THE THEATRE

*R*oyal Theatre, Drury Lane

"What's become of your guest, the emir?" Rose asked as David helped her down from the coach.

"We're not sure," he replied, glancing about in the hopes of seeing his friend among the others who were departing all manner of equipage along Drury Lane. "He went off shopping this morning and then again this afternoon."

"Oh, dear," Rose said, her gaze darting to Adeline. "I do hope he attends the ball tomorrow night."

"He plans to," Adeline replied. "He certainly enjoyed the last one. I think he danced all but one dance."

"Well, he won't be dancing a waltz with me this time."

"You didn't like dancing with him?" Adeline asked in alarm.

"Oh, he's an excellent dancer," Rose claimed, "but I've already promised both waltzes to David."

Adeline giggled. "Does *he* know that?" she teased.

"I do, indeed," David said as he offered his arm to

Rose. With her mother on her father's arm, Adeline was left to walk behind the others as they made their way into the theatre. She nearly let out a yelp when a hand clasped one of hers and lifted it.

"May I escort you, my lady,?" Ertuğrul asked before he kissed the back of her gloved hand.

"Ertuğrul!" She stepped back to admire his suit of clothes. "Oh, my. You look positively European," she murmured in awe.

"Is that good?"

She grinned. "The best," she replied before she sobered. "We've been worried about you. Afraid you might have been fleeced by a street urchin."

Ertuğrul stared at her for a second. "What do sheep and sea urchins have to do with shopping?"

Giggling, Adeline explained the meaning of the words. They were halfway to the Morganfield box when her father suddenly stopped and glanced around. "There you are," he said when he caught sight of Ertuğrul.

"Yes, sir. I waited in the lobby for your arrival." Despite recognizing several people from the Weatherstone ball and from the *soirée*, no one had approached him. Dressed as he was, he didn't stand out from the crowd as he had at the ball, but the anonymity had allowed him to study the architecture of the theatre.

George led them all up several flights of red-carpeted stairs and then to a box that looked out over the stage. Even before David could help Rose with her chair, she was waving to the occupants of the box on the opposite side of the theatre. "I cannot believe my mother would attend the theatre the night before she's hosting a ball," Rose remarked. "She's always so nervous." She took a seat next to David, her gaze sweeping the rest of the boxes.

When Ertuğrul aimed a curious glance in her direction, Adeline said, "Much like Rotten Row, people go to the theatre to see and be seen," she murmured. She indicated the available seats. "So, would you like to see or be seen?"

He chuckled. "I should like to watch the opera, but I wish to do so next to you," he replied. "Is that allowed?"

"We'll find out," she said as she led them to seats in the front row closest to the stage. Her parents had settled into their usual seats near the back. Once the lights dimmed, they would be in the shadows.

"What language will they sing in?"

"English. It's an Irish romantic opera," Adeline explained. "With gypsies, royalty, and star-crossed lovers." When she saw his furrowed brow, she continued. "The main characters are Arline and Thaddeus. She's the daughter of a Hungarian count, and he's a Polish nobleman that's living in exile in Austria. When she is six years old, a wild stag attacks her, but Thaddeus saves her. During the attack, though, her arm is wounded and she's left with a scar."

"Go on," Ertuğrul encouraged.

"To show his gratitude, the count invites Thaddeus to a banquet, but when Thaddeus refuses to toast a statue of the Austrian Emperor and instead tosses his wine on it, he has to escape with the help of a gypsy friend who kidnaps Arline."

Ertuğrul furrowed his brows. "So Arline and Thaddeus eventually become lovers?" he guessed. "She's too young for him, though."

"Well, after twelve years, they are sweethearts," she explained. "But the gypsy queen is in love with him at the same time the count's nephew has fallen in love with Arline."

Ertuğrul' seemed to think on this point for a moment before he said, "He doesn't know she is his..." He paused as he considered the relationship. "His cousin?"

"Exactly. Because he doesn't recognize her. Out of jealousy, the queen steals a medallion from the nephew and plants it on Arline."

"This cannot be good," Ertuğrul remarked.

"When the nephew sees it, Arline is arrested for stealing and tried before her father."

"Does *he* recognize her?"

"Yes, but only because of the scar on her arm from the stag attack."

"That's good, right?."

"Yes, except she misses her gypsy friends and Thaddeus, of course, because she's in love with him. Thaddeus invades her father's castle during a ball, finds Arline, and proposes marriage."

Ertuğrul grimaced. "But the father—"

"He has forgiven Thaddeus and gives his blessing."

"But what of the gypsy queen?"

"She has followed Thaddeus into the castle," Adeline replied dramatically, although she was grinning.

"Rather persistent of her to pursue a man who does not love her," he said in a whisper.

Adeline sighed. "Indeed. So the queen tries to kill Arline with a musket and kidnap Thaddeus, but his gypsy friend finds out what she's about to do, and then struggles with her in an attempt to take the gun away."

"The gun goes off?" Ertuğrul guessed.

"And the gypsy queen dies," Adeline finished with a grin.

"So... Arline and Thaddeus are married?"

Adeline blinked. "I don't recall if they show that at the end or not," she replied. "But I assume so."

Ertuğrul straightened in his chair. He glanced around, stunned to see that in only the few minutes they'd been talking, the theatre was nearly filled. On the stage, the silhouette of a castle stood in the background. "Is that the count's palace?"

"Indeed," she said. "Speaking of palaces, I saw your drawings in the library this afternoon. I should think your uncles will be very pleased with the design."

"The palace in those drawings is not for them," he replied. "I was designing the palace I wish to build for you."

Adeline gave a start. "For me?"

He nodded. "A place from which you could run a charity like your mother's. Where we could both live. Where our children could live," he said in a quiet voice. "Where I might work on plans for new buildings. We would have servants, of course. Someone to assist you—someone who could act as a translator for you with your clients—and a nurse to help with the children."

Adeline stared at him in awe. "So... when you spoke of marriage last night... I wasn't dreaming?"

He shook his head. "I thought you were wide awake."

"Oh, I was," she assured him. "But a night of sleep can play tricks sometimes." She remembered the illustration of the palace. Although it was similar to Brighton Pavilion, there were subtle differences. The onion domes were more ornate, the windows a slightly different shape. "Where would you build it?"

He shrugged. "Near the waters of the Bosphorus, I suppose. In Constantinople."

"Oh," she replied, blinking several times. "When would we move there?"

He inhaled as if to respond and then furrowed his brows. "Well, it would take a year or more for construction to be completed, but we could live in the newest palace with my father and Sultana Charlotte until it is ready. Maybe go there after the Season is complete?"

Adeline dipped her head and then chuckled. "I hardly know what to say."

"Say yes. I'll be sure to ask you again after you're wide awake in the morning," he said before he swallowed.

She inhaled softly. "Does that mean you're going to make love to me tonight?" she asked in a whisper. She resisted the urge to glance back at her father, sure he was watching them. After last night in the library, she might find him standing guard at her door tonight.

"Nothing would make me happier. But... I fear if I did so tonight, you would wake up in the morning thinking it was just a dream." He reached into a waistcoat pocket. "So, to be sure you remember, I would be honored if you would wear this. At least until we are wed," he said as he held out the ruby ring.

Staring at the ring for a long moment, Adeline lifted a hand to the side of her face. "Ertuğrul," she breathed.

He slipped it on her finger and then kissed the back of her hand. "A rose for my rose," he said.

Adeline inhaled softly at hearing his words. "I'm wearing this for the rest of my life," she murmured. "Where ever did you—?"

"I met Mrs. Tennison today at *Ewen and Ewen*," he said. "I shall have to return there before we depart England to discover what else I might buy for you."

Her eyes rounded before she gasped. "Does this mean you spoke with Father?"

"This morning. Before he left for Parliament."

Adeline resisted to the urge to look back at her father. He hadn't said a word over dinner. No wonder he hadn't scolded her for what happened in the library the night before.

"I am not certain, but he seemed sad when he gave his permission," Ertuğrul said in a whisper.

"Well, that's because I am his favorite," she said with a watery grin. "Oh, and I suppose I need to say yes."

Ertuğrul grinned as the lights in the theatre dimmed and the stage lights brightened.

"Leave your door unlocked tonight," she whispered. When he turned to stare at her in shock, she added, "I want to wake up with you."

His gaze stayed on hers until the singing began, and he reluctantly turned to watch the opera.

Much to Ertuğrul's surprise, Adeline stayed awake for the entire production. She fell asleep on his shoulder in the coach on the way home, though.

CHAPTER 32
A BETROTHAL'S FIRST NIGHT

ater that night

Although she'd been about to burst with wanting to show off the ring Ertuğrul had given her before the opera started, Adeline instead climbed the stairs with everyone else and stayed quiet.

When they reached the second floor, they headed in different directions—George and Elizabeth to their apartments, David to his room, Ertuğrul to his and Adeline to hers—and Bostwick House grew quiet.

Removing the pins from her hair, Adeline watched as the locks fell about her shoulders. She would usually braid it for bed, but she had no intention of doing so on this night.

Instead, she wriggled out of her gown and underthings, pulled on a nightrail and a pair of bed slippers, and pulled down her bed covers. She crawled into bed and rolled around a few times before carefully placing her feet on the floor.

When she didn't detect any movement through the carpet—no servants or family members moving about—

she crept from her room, carefully holding down the door handle whilst pulling it shut so the latch didn't click.

Padding quietly down the side of the corridor to the other end, she reached Ertuğrul's room and stood before the door. Testing the handle, she was relieved when it easily lowered. A moment later, and she was in the dark room. She winced when she heard the *snick* of the latch and held her breath. When she didn't hear any other doors opening, she moved to the bed. Although the counterpane and linens had been pulled down, Ertuğrul wasn't in the bed. The sound of splashing came from the bathing chamber, though, and Adeline pondered what to do.

Her nervousness increasing, she climbed onto the bed to wait. After another moment, she slipped beneath the bed linens and inhaled the familiar scent of *him* when her head hit the pillow. She grinned at the thought that every night, for the rest of her life, she would fall asleep surrounded by it.

Ertuğrul appeared in silhouette when he emerged from the lit bathing chamber, a bath linen wrapped about his waist. Apparently he didn't notice her, for he doffed the towel and pulled a nightshirt over his head.

Adeline struggled to hold her breath. To resist the urge to gasp. For the briefest of moments, she had a view of his naked body, olive skin covered with dark hair stretched over a broad chest and taut torso, the hair narrowing down to the apex of his thighs where a nest of curls surrounded his manhood. His arms were thick from archery, his thighs muscled from horseback riding, and even after the nightshirt had settled over his shoulders, she could see he possessed strong calves.

He pulled something from the top of a trunk and unrolled it onto the floor. After that, he disappeared from her view, but she heard whispered words in a foreign language.

Prayers, she realized.

She prayed he wouldn't send her away when he discovered she was in his bed. They had agreed to spend the night together whilst watching the opera, right after it was assured Thaddeus and Arline would end up together, but the final terms of their clandestine arrangement had been interrupted when her parents asked Ertuğrul what he thought of the opera.

Every nerve ending of her body had been on high alert ever since. Now her body's reaction to seeing him naked sent the oddest sensations coursing through her. Her breasts felt as if they were larger than usual, her nipples pushing against the fabric of her nightrail. The space at the top of her thighs fairly throbbed with her arousal. Her desire to touch him—to press her palms to his chest and kiss him—was nearly overwhelming.

When the linens were suddenly pulled from atop her, she inhaled sharply.

Ertuğrul stared down at her. "I feared you were asleep," he whispered with a grin as he stripped the nightshirt from his body and climbed into the bed.

This time, Adeline did gasp, for his manhood was fully erect. "Asleep? I cannot sleep. I'm too excited."

His lips touched her forehead for a moment. "As am I," he admitted.

She moved her hands to his head, her fingers spearing his dark hair as his lips claimed hers and his tongue swept across her teeth. At the same time, he moved a hand to her breast, hefting and molding the mound in his palm.

Inhaling sharply at the sensation, Adeline broke from the kiss, which had him trailing kisses down her jaw, along her collarbone and down to the top edge of her nightrail. She managed to find the end of the bow that kept the garment closed at the top and pulled it loose.

With a sweep of his hand, he had one shoulder and a breast exposed. She arched her back when his mouth covered her breast. When his tongue laved over her nipple, she thought she had never felt anything so heavenly before.

Leaving one hand against his head, she slid her other along the side of his body as far as she could reach and then to the small of his back, stunned at the warmth of his skin. Her fingers followed the trail of the bumps of his spine until he caught her arms and spread them wide. Forced to give up her hold on him, she mewled her disappointment.

When one of his hands reached down and smoothed her nightrail up her thigh, lifting a knee in the process, she inhaled sharply. His hand was so hot, she was sure he was branding her skin. When he moved it to her mound and pressed his palm against her damp folds, she gasped.

She wasn't sure what he did next, but there was a moment when all she could do was grasp handfuls of the bed linens in an effort to stay on the bed. Her body felt as if it were being swept away on waves of pleasure that crested and crashed and were followed by more of the same.

Her attempt to remain mute lest she be discovered in his bed had her struggling against the urge to cry out. Instead she hummed and whispered 'yes' over and over again.

When he was suddenly over her, one of his hands reaching back to raise her other knee, she was practically boneless. A moment later, and his manhood, heavy and solid, slid along her damp folds and then the tip was at her entrance. She managed to lift her hips in invitation even as he lowered his mouth to her other breast. Wet and aching with need, she whispered, "Please."

He was inside her in a single thrust, a groan vibrating through his body when he was fully pressed into her.

Despite the sensation of a pinch followed by fullness —at first uncomfortable but not painful—she lifted her thighs to grip his. She stared up at him, not sure what to do or say as her body adjusted to the swift invasion. She lifted her hands to his sides and gripped in an effort to hold on.

For a moment, neither of them moved.

"Are you all right?" he whispered as his dark brows furrowed in the dim light. "I didn't wish to cause you pain, but—"

"I'm fine," she said, nodding in the pillow. "Really. I only wish I knew what to do."

Adeline remembered seeing his manhood as he climbed into the bed, and when she glanced down, she confirmed he had buried it inside her. All of it. She hardly knew where he ended and she began.

He kissed her forehead again. "We'll sort it," he whispered as he slowly pulled almost all the way out of her.

Her reaction was immediate as she lowered her hands until they smoothed over the mounds of his bottom and gripped them.

He chuckled softly as he pushed into her again.

Suddenly understanding what to do, she kept her hands where they were, allowing him the gentle thrusting movements. Her own hips met his with each thrust as her chest rose from the bed. She wished she had removed her nightrail, for the fabric seemed to abrade her nipples with every movement.

Perhaps Ertuğrul could read her thoughts, for he

paused his movements and helped her pull the offending garment up and over her head. He tossed it to the side and resumed his thrusting, this time with more force, his movements more quick. His tongue occasionally reached out to flick across a nipple, which had Adeline arching her back as frissons skittered through her entire body.

When he suddenly stilled, his back arching as his torso rose up, Adeline felt warmth wash over her and through her. A moment later, and he slowly lowered his upper body until his head rested on the pillow next to hers.

His labored breathing was loud in her ears, or that might have been hers. She didn't know. Didn't care as she hugged his body close.

"It will be better next time," Ertuğrul promised.

"How is that possible?" Adeline asked as she turned to regard him in wonder.

He chuckled softly and kissed her forehead again. "I should roll off of you before I fall asleep."

"Are you comfortable?"

"Very."

"Then please stay right where you are," she pleaded. Even as she said the words, she sensed his manhood lessening in size, the sense of fullness at her core dissipating.

"You were brave to come to my room," he whispered.

She regarded him with a questioning glance. "I cannot imagine how. I had no intention of not coming here."

"I was thinking I would go to your bedchamber, at least to kiss you goodnight," he claimed.

"I would have made you join me in my bed," she whispered.

"I would not have argued."

She mewled when she realized his manhood had escaped her body, and Ertuğrul slowly rolled off her body.

"Stay here," he whispered as he rose from the bed and disappeared into the bathing chamber.

Adeline immediately missed the warmth of his body and the closeness they had shared. About to leave the bed to discover what he was doing, he suddenly reappeared with a bath linen and a wet cloth.

"Lie down," he instructed, "and lift your knees."

Relaxing back onto the bed, she watched as he bent over the edge of the bed. The cloth was suddenly pressed to her quim, the warmth a welcome sensation even as it stung a bit.

"What—?"

"Shh," he interrupted, moving one of her hands to cover the cloth before lifting her body into his arms. Adeline immediately wrapped her free hand around the back of his neck. "Can you stand?" he asked. "You may wish to wash—"

"Of course," she whispered, curious as to what he was doing. Despite how her body trembled and how every nerve ending seemed to be on high alert, she was steady on her feet once he lowered her to the floor. She darted into the bathing chamber, wincing at the light but determined to finish cleaning herself without him paying witness.

*E*rtuğrul watched Adeline hurry into the bathing chamber, his breath hitching at the sight of her bare backside. The smooth, round globes of her bottom topped long thighs and shapely calves, and her skin appeared milky white under the gas light. Her mahogany hair fell in waves well past her shoulders blades, swaying across her back. When she disappeared from view, he turned and shook out the bath linen, covering the small blood stain that showed in sharp contrast to the white bed linen.

During the short time he'd been in the bathtub, he had thought only of her. Of what it would be like to join her in her bed. To hold her. To kiss her. To pleasure her. To claim her as his own and then hold her against his body for an entire night.

His desire warred with propriety, though, so when he heard the rustle of the bed linens when she had crawled into his bed, he felt immense relief.

From the moment he had stepped out of the warm water, his desire for her had nearly overwhelmed him. A semblance of sanity had him performing his nightly prayers. A sense of duty had him seeing to her comfort after he had taken his pleasure. How he treated her on this night would determine if she would be as willing to share a bed with him in the future, and now that he had discovered what it was like, he wanted her even more than he had before.

From the time they had shared the coach ride home from the museum, he had thought her a perfect match. Their shared interests were only part of it. He hadn't expected to feel such attraction to a young woman so quickly. To have his thoughts turn to her from early in the morning until late at night. To find any excuse to be in her company despite her insistence that he should consider courting Lady Rose.

Didn't Adeline realize she was a much better match for him?

Apparently she did now, for she emerged from the bathing chamber and immediately stepped into his hold, her bare breasts pressed into his chest and his manhood cradled against her belly as her lips found his.

"You will stay with me tonight?" he asked in a whisper.

"I don't want to be anywhere else."

"I'll join you in the bed in a moment." He kissed her again and then moved into the bathing chamber.

Adeline was about to protest, but given the sudden chill she felt upon the loss of his body heat, she quickly climbed onto the bed at the same moment the light was extinguished in the bathing chamber.

She gave a start at feeling the bath linen beneath her bottom when Ertuğrul joined her in the bed.

"It was rather considerate of you to cover the damp spot," she whispered.

"I want you to be comfortable," he countered.

She stretched out on the bed as Ertuğrul did the same, but after a moment, she was half atop him, her head resting in the small of his shoulder with a leg draped over one of his and an arm across his chest.

"I'm comfortable," she whispered.

He chuckled softly and kissed the top of her head.

CHAPTER 33
THE ARILEY BALL

The following morning, April 13, 1844

When Ertuğrul entered the breakfast parlor with Adeline on his arm, he paused and waited until George, Elizabeth, and David all looked up from their plates.

"Good morning," he said as he dipped his head.

"Good morning," Adeline said, her grin so wide she looked as if she was about to burst.

"I have an announcement to make," Ertuğrul stated. When the three occupants in the room turned their attentions to him, he said, "Adeline has agreed to marry me."

David's eyes rounded while neither of his parents seemed particularly surprised. "*What?* Am I the last to know?" he asked in shock.

"Best wishes, darling," Elizabeth said as she stood and kissed Adeline on the cheek. She regarded Ertuğrul with a wistful expression. "Your Eminence," she added as she angled her head and sighed.

"Thank you," Adeline whispered.

George stepped up and kissed her on the forehead. "I wish you all the happiness in the world," he murmured. He turned to Ertuğrul. "I was beginning to think you had changed your mind when she didn't say anything about it yesterday."

"I gave her the ring last night. Before the opera started," Ertuğrul explained.

"A ring?" Elizabeth repeated. "You didn't show *me*."

Adeline held up her hand and wiggled her fingers. "A rose for a rose, he said."

"Oh!" her mother said on a gasp as she took Adeline's hand with both of hers. "Alexander made this, didn't he?" she asked in awe.

Ertuğrul nodded. "His wife helped me choose it yesterday."

"Oh, George," Elizabeth breathed.

"All right. I can take a hint," he said with a chuckle.

"We'll have the Duke of Ariley make the announcement tonight. But after he announces your betrothal," she added as she turned to regard David.

"And after he announces Waverley's betrothal," her son reminded her.

"Yes, yes, of course," she said. "I need to pen a note to Helen right away," she said, hurrying from the breakfast parlor.

Ertuğrul and Adeline regarded one another with a grin before helping themselves to breakfast.

*L**ater that night*
The five-piece orchestra was still playing the prelude music for that night's ball when James, Duke of Ariley, hurried up to speak with George Bennett-Jones and Marcus Batey. "I'm not sure whether to thank

you or your son," he said jovially as he shook George's hand. His family had arrived only a few minutes earlier, the women already in conversation with others while David had moved on to find Rose.

"I only read him the list," George claimed as the duke shook Marcus' hand. "But something tells me I wouldn't have had to. He held a candle for your daughter long before he left on his Grand Tour."

"I must say, I rather wish I had ordered Rose and Waverley to marry far sooner than after the last ball," James remarked.

"What's this?" Marcus asked.

Chuckling, the duke took a sip of champagne and moved closer. "I'm old. I wanted to see them wed and to give me grandchildren before I die, so I ordered them to marry. Told them rank didn't matter these days. We all know fortunes are what pay the bills. Not titles."

"And yet, your son is marrying a viscount's daughter," George said. He turned to Marcus and added, "No offense."

"None taken. I was as shocked as anyone."

"That's another one off the list," George remarked.

"Only because Waverley thought he was expected to marry no lower than an earl's daughter. Can you imagine? He'd be waiting as long as I did for my duchess," James claimed.

"Thank you for providing a house for Lady Rose and David to live in," George said.

"It was the least I could do, especially since Waverley is staying at Ariley Place and Miss Hope will be moving in the day of the wedding. There's enough room, of course, and he can see to the dukedom from the study there."

"So you've put him to work on the dukedom?" Marcus asked.

"For several years now," James admitted. He surveyed the large salon, noting how guests were still filing in from the front entry. "So, which betrothal shall we announce first?"

"I should think your daughter's," George replied. "Isn't this ball in her honor?"

"Indeed, but your daughter is marrying an *emir*," he said as his brows arched. They'll live in Constantinople, will they not? Close to the Sultan Ziyaeddin and Sultana Charlotte?"

"Don't remind me," George said with a shake of his head. Emir Ertuğrul Effendi would do right by his daughter, that much George was sure. The reminder that he would take her far away from England had him wincing. "He's a good man, even if he's going to take her half a world away at the end of the Season."

"Well, then it's a good thing we have the entire Season in front of us," Marcus commented.

"It's a good thing we don't have anyone left on the list," George reminded him.

James chuckled and then suddenly sobered. "Are you forgetting you have another son?"

George blinked and dropped his head on his chest. "Ask me that again five years after he returns from his Grand Tour," he said on a long sigh.

"By then, there will be an entirely new list," Marcus said with a grin.

Armed with glasses of champagne, the three made their way to the dais to announce the betrothals.

EPILOGUE

*T*wo *years later, on the edge of the Aegean Sea*
 Adeline stood next to her godmother, Charlotte, as they leaned over the edge of a balcony and
watched their husbands play with their youngest children
in the garden below.

"He's really quite ridiculous," Charlotte murmured,
referring to her husband, Ziyaeddin. He was tossing his
grandson, Girgus, into the air as his daughter, Zehra,
giggled and his son, Ahmed ran in circles around his legs.

Sitting cross-legged on the short-clipped lawn,
Ertuğrul was chuckling at something his father had said
when he was suddenly bowled over by Ahmet. A chase
ensued before, breathless, the şehzade collapsed back to
the ground and the toddler went after a butterfly.

"I'm so glad we came," Adeline said. "Although I do
love the home Ertuğrul has built for us, it's good to
spend the first day of spring here. He's only twenty-four
years old today, but there are times I think he's far
older."

Charlotte winced. "Ziyaeddin usually mourns his first

wife's death on the first day of spring, but these past two years, he has not."

"That's because he loves you," Adeline stated.

"As much as Ertuğrul loves you," Charlotte commented.

Adeline gave her a brilliant smile. "I think he learned from watching my father."

Charlotte tittered. "When I first met Ertuğrul, he was so reserved. So timid. So quiet. Of course, back then, I didn't understand that he wasn't supposed to look at me."

"Perhaps that's why he liked staying in England for a time," Adeline remarked.

They had married and remained in the capital with her parents at Bostwick House until well past the end of the Season. Once they had helped welcome George Junior into the world—Adeline claimed she wanted practice caring for a newborn—they then opted to remain for Christmas of 1844. Her older sister, Christina, and her husband, Richard Hartwell, and their children had joined them for a fortnight. With Daniel home from university, the crowded house was a chaotic scene until all but Daniel departed in early January 1845.

He had left on his Grand Tour a month later, leaving Elizabeth and George with almost an entire house in which to engage in their playful antics.

"Any news from your older brother?" Charlotte asked. Although she usually heard from Elizabeth at least once a month, the latest mail hadn't been forwarded to the western palace.

"Rose wrote to me. She's expecting her second babe in a few months," Adeline said with a grin. "Georgie is walking and apparently babbling incoherently, and my father is probably behaving exactly like your husband is right now." Her gaze followed the sultan as he sat on a bench with her son mounted on his booted foot, his leg bobbing up and down while he imitated a horse.

Charlotte tittered. "Do you have any regrets?"

"About what?" Adeline asked in alarm.

A quelling glance was aimed in her direction. "Marrying a Muslim? Moving to Constantinople? Having to learn a new language and wear different clothes and eat different foods?"

Adeline shrugged. "Oh, not really. I do wish I was better at learning the language," she admitted. "I still have a translator to help at the charity."

"Is it going well?"

"It's better now. At first, I couldn't make the employers trust me, but I remember my mother saying she had the same problem when she started," she explained. "Once I was able to place a few men into positions, word began to spread. I do think having the sultan as my father-in-law helps a good deal."

"He is willing to help all he can," Charlotte commented, not adding that the first few wounded men had been placed in their positions of employment because Ziyaeddin had ordered it.

"Do you miss anything about England?" Adeline asked.

Charlotte sighed. "My oldest son, of course. Your mother and Hannah," she added, referring to her best friends. She shrugged. "I cannot imagine what my life would have been like if I had stayed, though. Once John married Arabella and I became a dowager duchess..." She rolled her eyes. "I might have ended up in Brighton or Bath pretending to enjoy the entertainments. I like this life much better." She tittered when Girgus ended up in her husband's arms, a huge yawn suggesting the boy was about to fall asleep. "What about you? Do you miss anything?"

Adeline angled her head to one side and said a drawn out "ahh" as Zehra hugged her younger brother and then an "oh!" when the young girl pushed him to the ground. "Although there are some things I miss about England—such as everyone speaks English—there are others I do not."

"For example?" Charlotte prompted.

"The clothes," Adeline stated. "I love these gowns. The fabrics are divine. And the food. So much better," she added. When she noticed the men appeared to be tiring, she asked, "Shall we rescue them?"

Charlotte glanced back over the balcony. "Oh, I suppose," she said. "If I have not said it before, I am very glad you agreed to be Ertuğrul's wife, as is Ziyaeddin."

"I think you have told me that at least a dozen times," Adeline said with a grin as they made their way through the wide corridors and down the steps to the palace's atrium. Had anyone told her she might one day be the sultana in charge of such a palace, she would have thought them a candidate for Bedlam.

"Ziyaeddin was so relieved when you two arrived. He was beginning to think Ertuğrul wouldn't return and that he'd have to choose a different heir."

"He had nothing to be concerned about," she insisted. "Ertuğrul is all about doing his duty," Adeline said, her hand going to her rounded middle. "In more ways than one," she added on a giggle.

AUTHOR'S NOTES

Where did these characters come from?

Ertuğrul first appeared in *The Lady of a Sultan*. George and Elizabeth's story can be found in *The Kiss of a Viscount*, and they make appearances in a number of other books, including *The Charity of a Viscount* and *The Conundrum of a Clerk*.

Billiards

The "Noble Game of Billiards," or in this case English billiards, has a long history going back to the 15th century. Based on croquet and played with three balls, the first version had players using a mace to shove a ball. The large head made it difficult to hit a ball when it was near the side rail or "bank" (named so because they were like the bank of a river). Men would turn around the handle or "queue" (which means "tail," from which we get the word "cue") and strike the ball with the other end.

These single shaft cues were replaced with a two-piece version made of hard maple and leather in 1829.

Chalk on the tip provided friction, which made it possible to add spin to a ball.

Although there were no set table sizes, the standard followed a two-to-one ratio of length to width, and early versions were twelve feet by six feet. The six pockets were located in the corners and halfway down the long sides.

Originally, the only reason a pool table had side rails was to keep the balls from falling off, but soon players discovered they could bounce the ball off them to make "bank shots."

Until 1835, the table beds were made of wood. Slate replaced wood since it didn't warp over time.

Although current billiard balls are made of resin, the originals were made of ivory from elephant tusks and dyed.

British Museum

The museum's collections were first housed in a 17th-century mansion, Montagu House, which was extensively refurbished before it opened to the public in 1759. As the collections grew, new galleries, like the Townley Gallery, were added to the original building.

The museum became Europe's largest building site when expansion commenced in 1823. Sir Robert Smirke's grand Greek Revival style building gradually arose. First to be built was the East Wing—now called the Enlightenment Gallery—to house King George III's library (ground floor). Handed over in 1827, it was described as one of the finest rooms in London. The rest of the East Wing was completed by 1831 while construction on the West Wing continued. In spite of dirt and disruption, the collections grew, outpacing the new building.

It wasn't until the 1840s that Montagu House was

demolished to make way for the colonnaded portico through which visitors still enter the museum. That building was completed in 1852. Sir Richard Westmacott designed the sculptures in the pediment above the entrance to reflect the progress of civilization as conceived by Victorians at a time when British confidence and global power through imperial expansion was growing.

Your Invitation!

Do you crave historical romance filled with passion and red hot chemistry?

Come join me and my author friends in the Facebook group, Historical Harlots, for exclusive giveaways, chats with amazing HistRom authors, raunchy shenanigans, and more!
https://www.facebook.com/groups/2102138599813601

ABOUT THE AUTHOR

A self-described nerd and student of history, Linda Rae spent many years as a published technical writer specializing in 3D graphics workstations, software and 3D animation (her movie credits include SHREK and SHREK 2). Getting lost in the rabbit holes of research has resulted in historical romances set in the Regency-era as well as Ancient Greece.

A fan of action-adventure movies, she can frequently be found at the local cinema. Although she no longer has any tropical fish, she follows the San Jose Sharks and makes her home in Cody, Wyoming.

For more information:
www.lindaraesande.com
Sign up for Linda Rae's newsletter:
Regency Romance with a Twist
Follow Linda Rae's blog:
Regency Romance with a Twist